FATALLY
INFERIOR

FATALLY INFERIOR

The Dunston Burnett Trilogy
Book Two

LYN SQUIRE

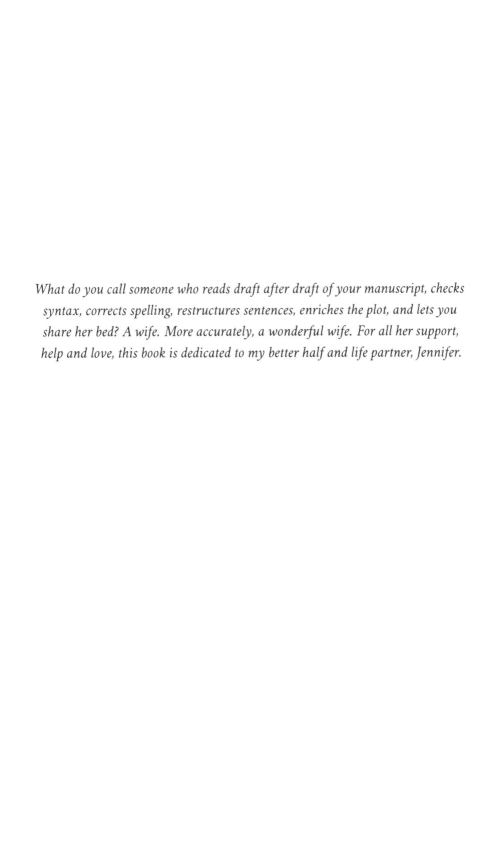

What do you call someone who reads draft after draft of your manuscript, checks syntax, corrects spelling, restructures sentences, enriches the plot, and lets you share her bed? A wife. More accurately, a wonderful wife. For all her support, help and love, this book is dedicated to my better half and life partner, Jennifer.

'The chief distinction in the intellectual powers of the two sexes is shewn by man's attaining to a higher eminence in whatever he takes up, than can woman.'

— Charles Darwin,
The Descent of Man, 1871

Contents

Characters

MAIN CHARACTERS

- Lucy Kinsley: A young woman fallen on hard times
- Archibald Line: A private inquiry agent
- Dunston Burnett: A retired bookkeeper and acquaintance of Archibald Line
- Jeremiah Fickett: Chief of Detectives, Metropolitan Police, Scotland Yard

CHARLES DARWIN'S HOUSEHOLD

- Emma Darwin: Charles's wife
- Richard Darwin: Charles and Emma's son, a doctor
- Henrietta Darwin: Richard's wife
- Jarke: Butler
- Parslow: Charles's valet
- Grace: Lady's maid

OTHERS

- Estelle Moxley: Henrietta's sister, a spinster
- George Mivart: A young biologist, recently converted to Catholicism
- Micus Loman: Owner-operator of a small London business
- Martha: Micus Loman's housekeeper

- Fingers: A London ruffian of the worst kind
- Gabby: Crusty old villager
- Nick: Dunston Burnett's manservant
- Eyesore Annie: Attendant in the women's ward, Shoreditch Workhouse
- Sir Edmond Henderson: Metropolitan Police Commissioner
- Matthew Cullingworth: A London doctor
- Betsy Smurkle: A former nanny
- Sir Winston Grissick: Lord Chief Justice

Chapter One: Vanished

Kent; Sunday morning, January 21, 1872

Archibald Line trudged along the lane in ankle-deep snow. The short walk from the village was taking longer than on his previous visit, but he'd allowed ample time and was soon approaching his destination, an eighteenth-century country house. Its ivy-clad central part, a three-storey, many-windowed, rectangular block, was the original structure. A new front entrance and hallway had been added to the right side, and a more recent extension, servants' quarters by the look of it, to the left.

The architecture, however, was not what slowed Line's step to a snail's-pace dawdle. It was the building's place in history. *This* was Down House, the home of Charles Darwin. *This* was where the great man developed his theory of survival of the fittest, where he researched and wrote *On The Origin of Species.* But, Line reminded himself, he was not there to admire. He was there to investigate.

He was greeted at the front door by the butler. His winter coat and hat were whisked away as if by magic and he was ushered into the drawing room. He settled himself in one of the two royal blue silk armchairs placed on each side of the fireplace and awaited the arrival of Mrs Emma Darwin. He'd received a message from her the previous evening asking for his assistance in finding her daughter-in-law, Henrietta. A missing-person case. A missing-*Darwin* case! This could be the biggest of his career, and totally different in scale and character from the other matter he was already investigating

1

on her behalf – a poison-pen letter lambasting her husband with what the sender claimed was the scientist's blasphemous assault on God's creation of man.

Line was not a man to concern himself unduly with his attire. Even as London's Chief of Detectives, he'd rarely worn his official uniform, preferring an everyday jacket, white shirt and navy-blue tie, the only one he owned, exactly what he was wearing today. Neither the police inspector he once was, nor the private inquiry agent he now was, ever had to rely on clothes to make his presence felt. With his square-shouldered frame, he cut a formidable figure, solid as the Rock of Gibraltar. And though his blondish hair, cropped short, military style, was greying at the sides, his ice-blue eyes were still as piercing as when they routinely loosened the tongues – and sometimes the bowels – of London's most hardened villains.

His left hand slipped inside his jacket's side pocket as he waited, coming to rest, as always, on a small, silver medallion. He traced the letters – *R* on one side, *M* on the other. They were almost worn away, but he knew them so well, he never had trouble identifying them. Nor the date etched into the rim – *July 17, 1850* – the day the sun left his world.

The butler had barely withdrawn when a young maid entered. Line squeezed the medallion between forefinger and thumb once, and then once more, his farewell signal, and turned his attention to the new arrival. Trim and neatly turned out in white apron and mob cap, she was scarcely into her twenties and clearly flustered, but still managed a half curtsey. 'Sir, madam sends her apologies, but she has to tend the master, one of his bouts of sickness. Said I was to answer any questions you might have about… about what happened.'

Line was not pleased with this development, but he acknowledged her with a quick nod and gestured to the remaining armchair. The maid perched herself on the very edge of it, eyes downcast, hands in lap, back straight, clearly apprehensive.

Archibald Line regarded her, deliberating how best to proceed. Need to calm her down first, he decided. 'I'm sure this is a very upsetting time for everyone,' he began, his voice steady, reassuring. 'But, as I always say, the facts will speak for themselves if we let them, so I'll just ask a few questions and you tell me what you can. Alright?'

'Y-yes, sir…' She sounded far from convinced.

'Very good. Let's begin with your name and position in the household,' he said, in hope of putting her at ease. He extracted notebook and pencil from his coat pocket and, as was his longstanding practice, readied himself to record her answers.

'Grace Trewin, sir,' she told him. 'I've been lady's maid to Mrs Henrietta Darwin, the one who's missing, for several years. She's really my mistress, but for the past six months I've also attended madam, Mrs Emma Darwin, after her regular maid, Lucy Kinsley, was dismissed from service.'

'Thank you, Grace.' Good, she's settling down. 'Now, tell me everything you can about your mistress's disappearance.'

'Yes, sir. Happened four nights ago.'

Four nights ago! She could be anywhere by now. Exasperated though he was, the maid would never have guessed it from his expression. He'd questioned countless suspects in his time, from the innocent-as-lambs to the guilty-as-sin and had long ago mastered the stone-face.

'Four nights ago, you say.' He kept his tone even. 'So that would be the night spanning Wednesday, January 17 and Thursday, January 18.'

'That's right, sir. Mistress had a terrible time every January 17, 'cos on that day three years ago, her eighteen-month-old son passed away. Mistress never got over it, which is why the family thought she'd slipped out in the night and gone to London to be with Mr Richard, her husband, who was there on medical business, but he'd neither seen nor heard from her. Obvious to a blind man she hadn't done that, sir,' Grace said. 'All of mistress's outdoor clothes were still in the wardrobe. The only clothes missing were those she was wearing that day.'

Young Grace was proving an excellent informant, eagle-eyed and quick witted, thought Line. May turn out to be a more than adequate replacement for the lady of the house.

'Very well. What next?'

'This inspector, name of Fickett, arrived Friday from Scotland Yard. Too full of himself by half, sir, but he seemed to know what he was doing. When he questioned me, I told him I'd seen tracks in the snow outside the back door just after I got up on Thursday.'

'You saw tracks on *Thursday* but didn't tell anyone until *Friday?*' Line said a little sharply.

'Tried to tell Jarke, sir, he's the butler, right after I saw them, but he just waved me off. Place was a madhouse, telegrams flying to and from Mr Richard, and nobody interested in what I had to say until Inspector Fickett arrived. Soon as he heard about the footprints, he organized a search party. Must've thought that my mistress, deep in her grief, had gone out into the winter night to... to end her life. Local constables, servants and neighbours combed the area all Friday and Saturday, but didn't find her body.'

Line rubbed his jaw, miffed that what he'd heard so far pointed to nothing more than a suicide, sad, to be sure, but otherwise straightforward. But it was still early days. Always inspect the evidence with your own eyes, that was one of his cardinal rules, this one straight from the Metropolitan Police Force Manual, most of which he'd written himself. He'd begin with the footprints.

'I'd like to take a look at those tracks,' he said, starting to rise.

'Oh, they're gone, sir. When Jarke wouldn't listen to me, I thought I'd better follow them myself and see if I could find my mistress, but by then, must've been mid-morning, the tracks were already covered by fresh snow.'

Yes, there was a heavy snowfall on Thursday, Line recalled. 'Well, you did your best.' He sat back down. 'Tell me what they looked like.'

'Just one set of footprints, sir,' she replied. 'Couldn't tell the direction from their shape, could've been coming or going they were so regular from front to back. Their size struck me as strange, though. Much too large for my mistress.'

This is more interesting. 'Anything else?'

'Not really, sir.' Then she added, almost as an afterthought: 'Just this odour. Sweet smell, noticed it soon as I entered mistress's bedroom Thursday morning.'

To Line, this was the kind of detail that turned a case on its head. He had a pretty good idea what the single, apparently directionless track of too-large footprints signified, and they, together with the sweet smell, were enough to convince him this was not suicide; nor a missing-person case; *Henrietta Darwin was taken.*

And if so, could there be a link to the other matter he was investigating? Could writing an abusive letter have escalated into kidnapping?

He was keen now to be on his way and get his findings to Inspector Fickett, already returned to London, as quickly as possible. He had just enough time, he gauged, to slip back to his cottage, write up his report on the morning's events, an absolute must in any Line investigation, and catch the afternoon train. He'd be at the Yard first thing Monday.

Grace, though, was just sitting there, looking more and more discomfited, biting her lower lip and twisting and twiddling the single strand of auburn hair that had slipped from her cap. She looked nervous, frightened almost, fidgeting like a skittish filly tip-tapping restless hooves.

As the interview progressed, Line had come to judge her as a sensible, level-headed young woman, smart too, but something, something that so far she'd been too afraid to mention, had clearly rattled her. Line didn't want to leave her in this state. He'd spare her a few more minutes.

'Grace, what has you so worried?' he asked.

'*Devil's handiwork,*' she blurted. 'No *Christian* way my mistress left this house. *She vanished into thin air.*'

Chapter Two: Lucy's Story

London; three days earlier

The makeshift mattress lay flat on January-cold flagstones, one hemp corner shredded by rodent scavengers desperate to reach the pallet's thin layer of mould-mottled straw. The coarse sheet covering the corpse was filthy, brownish smudges and yellow stains further besmirching the grey linen that the inmates of Shoreditch Workhouse called 'workhouse white'.

The curtained-off alcove was damp and dingy as befitted a holding cell for an unclaimed body destined for disposal in the nearest paupers' graveyard. It should already have been sent on its way except the carter, a ne'er-do-well who preferred the weight of a frothing tankard of porter in his hand to the tug of his horse's reins any day of the week, was nowhere to be found. Not that anyone cared; a day or two's delay couldn't possibly matter to the departed, nor indeed the living, as long as the carcass was out of sight. So there it lay, left to its own devices.

On the second day of death, the soiled sheet rose ever so slightly over the corpse's mouth and then sagged. The casual observer might dismiss the billow as inconsequential, attributing it to some verminous intruder – rat, cockroach, louse, or any number of other unwelcome visitors. Another rise-and-fall and even a third might also be overlooked but the sudden under-the-sheet commotion was impossible to ignore. A flailing right arm thrashed at the thin fabric until head and shoulders were clear of the suffocating shroud and the not-so-dead Lucy Kinsley was free to join every other living creature in the fight for one more gasp of precious air.

She might not have left this world, but Lucy soon returned to her former statue-still state, arm back at her side, slack as an empty sleeve. With the flow of oxygen restored, calmness settled her features, the anguish of only a moment ago conjured away much as a mother's kiss evaporates a child's tears. The strain of whatever calamity had befallen her still showed, but the strength and determination of a survivor were also evident in the set of her generously-lipped mouth and the firmness of her chin.

The stillness was finally broken by a slight fluttering beneath the bruised eyelids. A dream? Pleasant thoughts of life before the horrors of the workhouse? No, judging by the clenching fists, this was a vision filled with despair, an unwanted replaying perhaps of all that had dragged her down and landed her in this real-life nightmare.

She saw herself as she was that day, six months earlier, standing on the driveway leading from Down House. Jarke, the butler, on the doorstep. The kind face he'd shown her when she first arrived gone, replaced by a hateful scowl more in keeping with his true nature. Puffed up with his own self-importance, he pointed a white-gloved finger towards the gates. 'Be on your way, you whoring slut,' he yelled. 'Good riddance to bad rubbish.' He went back in the house and shut the door, putting an end to the only life she'd known since leaving Cornwall five years ago.

She straightened her bonnet, grasped her carpet bag and turned away from the house. She knew she should fight, stand up to him. After all, it wasn't her fault. She should tell Mrs Darwin; ma'am would understand. No, she couldn't do that. There was only one course left. With a heavy sigh, she let her free hand rest for a moment on the swell of her stomach, and then set out on her lonely journey.

The sorry image faded into nothingness for… for how long? Five minutes? Five hours? Five months? Dreamtime doesn't run according to any manmade clock. What eventually filtered into the void was not something *seen*, but something *felt*…

She was being pulled apart, her stomach and pelvis stretched to breaking point by that blood-red, larva-like creature inside her. Tiny at first, it grew bigger and bigger. She screamed for it to stop, but no force on earth could slow its progression.

Out of nowhere, a mournful mist settled upon her, swirling with the threat of even worse agony to come. And come it did. A witch-like harridan, dressed all in black, cleaved through the gloom, her grossly engorged throat pulsating as though alive with slithering, writhing creatures, ready to burst forth and do her hateful bidding. The cackling crone's hands circled slowly over Lucy's bloated belly, each rotation twisting her victim's entrails tighter and tighter, the hurting leaping to new, unimaginable heights. The pain couldn't get any worse, but it did. A final sweep of the hands and Lucy's swollen womb was turned inside out, her innards flushed out between spread legs.

'MY BABY!' shrieked the suddenly wide-awake Lucy, jerking upright.

'AAAAH!' screeched the open-mouthed hag peering into the cell. She yanked the curtain aside, and stepped into the alcove. Dressed in a shapeless, black shift, standard garb for an attendant in the women's ward, she looked oddly lopsided to Lucy, tilted, so it seemed, by the weight of the bulging goitre distorting the right side of her neck.

'Dead! You're dead, you are. Dead as me old man,' she said, pointing an accusing finger at the sole and obviously living occupant of the workhouse's make-do mortuary. 'An' dead'uns can't go bawlin' their soddin' head off like that,' the ugly shrew scolded.

'Dead? What d'you mean?' Lucy whispered, unsure whether she was looking at an apparition from her nightmare-memory or a real person in the here and now.

'Lor' bless us, you passed yesterday, at any rate that's what we thought,' the old fussock told her. 'Birthing was a bit tricky, little mite wouldn't come out, so Billy had to use the knife. Then, when it was all over, you stopped breathing, leastways that's what Billy said. According to him, you was a goner, and that's how you ended up here.'

'Billy?'

'Billy All-Trades. Lends a hand 'round here when he ain't got no better means of putting ready cash in his pocket. Him's the one what done the cutting, a tad too much, if you ask me, 'cos there was blood everywhere.'

'But the doctor. Where was the doctor… the real doctor?' A doctor, that was the only reason she'd ventured into this horrible place. A workhouse, for goodness sake! Lucy's mother would die from shame.

'What? That pickled old sot,' scoffed the drudge. 'Slewed more than he's sober, that one. Anyways, got his hands full with all them with the pox, and them with the fevers, and then there's the loonies with fits like you ain't never seen. Not much time left for midwifin'. To be fair, tho', he did come by to put his moniker on the death certificate.'

'Death certificate?'

'Aye, yer name's already been sent into the Parish. Be posted next week in the Registrar Gen'ral's death returns, dearie. Lucy Kinsley, if that's yer real name. Anyways, whether it is or it ain't, you can call yerself whatever you want now, 'cos Lucy Kinsley's dead.'

'And… m-my baby?' Her baby, nothing else mattered.

'Why you silly slummock, dead'uns can't look after babies, now can they? Babe's gone. Beadle Tonks, him what oversees the workhouse, took charge of the mite, skinny scrap of a boy, but how the little devil could scream, I can tell yer. Farmed him out quicker'n lightning. Much cheaper to send the little bugger to one of them biddies in the country than keep him here in London. So, there you are. You're dead, and the little'un's gone.

Chapter Three: Paired Brass Figures

Kent; the present

Archibald Line fixed Grace with those truth-winnowing eyes of his, pondering her strange outburst. *Devil's handiwork?* What is going on? he wondered, surprised at her outburst, so out of keeping with the opinion he'd formed of her.

'In all my years on the Metropolitan Police Force,' he said deliberately, 'nobody ever vanished into thin air. And, confounding as things may seem to you at present, I'm quite sure that if we go over the evidence, we'll get to the bottom of this in no time. Alright?'

'Yes, sir,' she said, and then belied her assurance by saying: 'There's no *earthly* way anyone could've left the house that night. The back door was locked and none of its keys could possibly have been used to open it,' she insisted. 'Unless... unless the Devil had a hand in it.'

'Let's not jump to any wild conclusions before we've gone over all the facts,' he said in a firm, father-to-daughter voice. 'Now, take a deep breath, and let's go through this step by step.'

'I-I'll try, sir.' She inhaled, held the breath for several seconds and then let it slowly escape, her anxiety leaving with the outgoing air. Once her breathing had settled into a steady rhythm, she began. 'It snowed late evening on Wednesday, and when I got up Thursday morning there was a blanket of pure white all around the house, not a mark on it anywhere *except* for the tracks outside the back door. That's the *only* door that could've been used.'

Line nodded, jotting down each point as she spoke.

'That door,' she continued, 'is locked every night. I saw Jarke lock it around nine on Wednesday, same as always, and I was with him when he did his rounds early Thursday morning.'

'And, I take it, your mistress was in the house that night?'

'Yes, sir. I popped into her bedchamber last thing, to see if she wanted anything. Then when I knocked on her door at seven the next morning, there was no answer. I went back half an hour later, knocked again and peeked in. The room was empty.'

'So you would have me believe that Henrietta Darwin, your mistress, disappeared from Down House through a locked door,' he said, eyebrows rising. 'Now, during my police days, we had many situations like this and always reasoned that someone must've used a key, stolen, borrowed or found, it didn't matter which. And we were always right.' He gave her a smile, to jolly her out of her silliness. 'But according to you, in this case, there was *no* key that could have been used...'

'That's right, sir. Every key for the back door was inside the house, exactly where it was supposed to be, *all night long.*'

'How many keys are there?' Line asked.

'Three, sir. Master has one. Keeps it locked in a drawer in his desk in the study. It's never used, just there as a back-up. When he checked Thursday morning, the key was exactly where he'd left it, nothing in the drawer had been touched, or he'd have known. Then, Jarke has one, stays with him all the time. That night, I saw him, key still in hand, going into his bedroom right after locking up. His door has a squeaky hinge, screeches like a barn owl every time it's opened or closed, makes enough noise to wake the dead. No one could've gone into or out of that room in the night, without the servants hearing it. There wasn't a peep 'til he got up.'

'Clearly rules out those two keys,' Line muttered. 'Must be the third.'

'That's what I thought until... until I saw what I saw on Saturday.' Grace tensed, as though bracing herself for a fast-approaching blast of ice-cold, Arctic air.

'Calm yourself, Grace,' Line said quickly. 'Let's not get ahead of ourselves.

We'll come to Saturday in a moment. First, tell me about the third key,' he said mildly enough, and then much more sharply: 'Whose is it?' The change in tone was one of his favourite techniques for throwing suspects off balance and dragging confessions from even the most tight-lipped. This time, it was intended to pull the girl back from whatever memory was unsettling her and re-root her in the present. And it did.

'It belongs to Mr Richard and my mistress,' Grace said, back in control of herself. 'Master gave it to them when they married and came to live in Down House. It's kept in the mistress's dressing table in their bedroom.'

'So, with Mr Richard in London, it would have been child's play for someone to remove it during the night.'

'But that's *impossible*,' the maid protested. 'That key did not leave that room for one second. It couldn't have. That's what's so scary,' she said. 'Makes my blood run cold. If you take a look at mistress's dressing table, you'll see what I mean. I can show you if you like.'

He followed Grace upstairs. Her mistress's bed was neatly positioned below a small, porthole-style window on the far wall. A wardrobe stood to its right, and to the left was the object of interest, an ornately decorated Oriental vanity in a dark wood, cherry perhaps. It stood on four elegantly curved legs, with a pair of drawers each side of a shallow, central panel. A framed, oval mirror and a fabric-covered stool completed the stylish piece of bedroom furniture.

'See this,' she tapped the panel, 'it's false, hides a secret cubbyhole. It's where the mistress keeps her jewellery, the master's gold cufflinks, *and* the back door key. It can only be opened by using these... well, not sure what to call them. Here, sir.' She picked up a small object from the vanity and showed it to him.

Line saw a brass cast of a lady in a summer gown and a domed sunhat, perhaps three inches long, an inch wide and an eighth deep, its front and back surfaces lined lengthwise with grooves of various shapes and sizes.

'There's two of them. This one belongs to the mistress. Mr Richard has the other, though his is shaped like a gentleman in a top hat. When they're placed head first into these two slots,' she pointed to two horizontal slits, one each side of the panel, 'and pushed in, there's a click, and the panel drops down. Then, when they're pulled out, the panel goes back up.'

'Quite extraordinary. Has to be some sort of mechanical device inside the dressing table that operates the panel's hinge. An intricate system of cogwheels, springs, weights, levers and goodness knows what else, I expect. Took a highly skilled craftsman to put this together in such a tiny space. Ingenious, too. The slot openings, which look like plain oblongs from the outside, must be configured on the inside to match exactly the grooves of their respective inserts. Nothing except those specially carved, brass figures, each placed in its own slot, could possibly release the switch and set the mechanism in motion. Truly remarkable.'

'Suppose so, sir. Anyway, I saw Mr Richard put his in his waistcoat pocket right before he set off for London on Wednesday morning. Without it, the cubbyhole *can't* be opened. When the police inspected it on Friday, it was closed, the false panel in its upright position. That's why they couldn't check if the key was inside until Saturday, when Mr Richard returned. And *it was*. So, the whole time he was away, and that includes the night my mistress disappeared, *that* key *never* left its hidey-hole.'

Line stroked his chin, searching for explanations; only one came to mind. 'Perhaps someone took the key *before* Mr Richard left, when both inserts, the lady-shaped figure *and* the gentleman-shaped figure, were still here.'

'Doesn't make a ha'porth of difference, sir. Even if the key was taken out of the vanity before Mr Richard's departure, it couldn't have been replaced and the panel closed *after* my mistress's disappearance *without* both figures. And Mr Richard's top-hatted one was in London all the time, as he confirmed when the police questioned him. So, before or after makes no odds.'

Line stared at her. A missing woman, a locked door, the key sealed inside a hidden cubbyhole; none of it made any sense. This was more than just a kidnapping; this was a *real mystery*. Line had to admit he was thoroughly flummoxed, but, he reassured himself, the facts would throw up an explanation in due course, and when they did, it would have nothing to do with devilry.

'Sir,' said Grace, as though reading his thoughts, 'no matter what anyone else believes, I *know* what I saw. I was *there*…I saw Mr Richard insert the two brass figures…I saw the false panel drop…I saw the key, clear as day…and that's when I *knew* my mistress's disappearance was the Devil's doing.'

Chapter Four: A Friend in Need

Lucy stared at the cracks and damp patches patterning the ceiling until they slipped out of focus, blurring and blending into starry constellations, mythical creatures half-remembered from some childhood fantasy and, peeking out here, there and everywhere, the scrunched face of a newborn. She shook her head to clear her vision.

She'd been drifting in and out of consciousness in the three days since escaping the Grim Reaper, mostly blacked out but with enough clear-minded interludes to formulate the plan she intended to put into action that night. First, though, she had to find out what she might have revealed to Lumpy Lubber, as she'd named the workhouse attendant on account of the ugly bulge of flesh on her neck. Twice she'd woken to find the hideous creature standing by her bedside, staring down at her.

The girl had taken an instant dislike to the old harpy, far too shifty for Lucy's taste. To be fair, though, she was feeding Lucy, even if it was only stale bread and watery gruel, and letting her stay in the workhouse mortuary 'leastways, 'til it's needed for the nex' customer'.

It was Sunday afternoon when the woman next came in and Lucy was ready. 'Been wanting to thank you for helping me with, well, everything, bed, food, shelter,' she began. 'After all you've done for me, I'm 'shamed to say I don't even know your name.'

'Wants to know me name, is it? First time anyone's asked me that. You c'n call me Annie, if you like. That's what everyone calls me or, often as not, Eyesore Annie,' she said with no sign of rancour. Her hand, though, strayed unconsciously to the goitre disfiguring her neck.

15

'Annie it is then, and now that I know your name, I can say thank you very, *very* much, Annie.' Lucy paused to gauge the woman's reaction, but the sly creature's face remained as blank as a schoolboy's freshly wiped slate.

'S'alright, lovey. Weren't no trouble. Anyways, ain't never seen nothin' like you. Like that Lazarus feller in the Holy Book, you are. Never believed any of that fiddle-faddle but ain't so sure now. Won't forget you any time soon, missy, I can tell yer.'

Drat! Not what Lucy wanted to hear. 'I'm sure you'll forget me the minute I leave this place,' she said, wishing it to be true. 'Most like, you'll be glad to see the back of me and all my gabbling and babbling when I was blacked out.' She checked Annie's reaction to this feeler. Still difficult to read the woman's wooden-plank face. Was that a trace of guile in the eyes? Or just a reflection of Lucy's own apprehension?

'Everyone carries on in this place, dearie. Some worse than others. You weren't so bad.'

'Well, I hope I didn't give offence or say anything untoward. Goodness knows what rubbish I might've come out with while I was passed out. You know how sleep-talkers twist things and mix up truth and fancy 'till you can't tell one from the other...' She let her sentence hang, hoping that Lumpy Lubber would jump right in.

'Don't worry yer pretty little head 'bout yer ramblings. Carried on a lot 'bout some butler, funny name... Jarde, no, Jarke, an' other stuff, but as I always says, what Annie hears in the ward is kep' locked up tight in the old noggin.' She tapped her head and winked. 'Safe an' sound as anything 'fessed to the Good Lord Hisself.'

Again, not what Lucy wanted to hear. But she'd pressed as hard as she could, any harder would only create suspicion.

After her afternoon talk with Annie and what passed for dinner, Lucy lay awake on her pallet until the bells of nearby St Leonard's told her it was three o'clock in the morning. She pulled back the curtain of her cell and stepped barefooted into the main ward, feeling her way carefully, testing her legs, and checking the lie of the land. The nurse on duty was asleep in a chair, totally oblivious to the ugly sounds issuing from the forty or so beds crammed into the ward. If the moaning, sobbing and occasional scream were not enough to wake her, then quiet-as a-mouse Lucy was not likely to disturb her.

Her plan was simple – grab clothes, take whatever cash she could lay her hands on, and, most important of all, find the address where her son had been sent. Then get as far away as possible. Clothes proved easy. She reclaimed her floral cotton dress from a peg where it had hung ever since her arrival, and slipped it on over her worn-thin workhouse shift. After that, it was a simple matter to pick up a shawl from the end of one bed, bonnet from the next, and a pair of old leather shoes from a third – a little from each so that none of her victims would suffer unduly from her thieving. Cash was a different kettle of fish. The office used by the governor of the workhouse was the most likely place to come by any loose pounds, shillings or pence, but she spent a good half hour searching drawers and shelves without finding even a farthing.

The search, though, turned out well in another respect – she found a ledger listing all those unfortunate enough to end up in Shoreditch Workhouse. And there he was, the only baby born in the last two weeks:

> *Boy, January 17 in the year of our Lord, 1872.*
> *Father, unknown; Mother, dead.*
> *Discharged to the care of Mrs Moranda Sayter, Rose Petal Cottage,*
> *Titchfield, county of Hampshire.*

She fixed name and address firmly in her mind, and slipped out of the workhouse as quickly and quietly as possible.

Two hours later, Lucy was sitting in the pre-dawn darkness on the icy steps of St Clement Danes Church, several miles from Shoreditch Workhouse, eating what remained of her bread from last night's supper. Stiff and chilled, yet thrilled to be free, she wrestled with her challenge – how was she to get to Titchfield, almost one hundred miles away, with only the sixpenny piece sewn into the hem of her dress by her mother?

'Is there anything the matter, my dear?' asked a kindly voice out of the gloom. Lucy turned. The speaker, a placid, pale-faced man dressed for the winter weather in muffler, heavy coat, and felt hat, had the look of an indoors worker about him, probably a clerk or shopkeeper, she thought, something modest and respectable but otherwise unremarkable. His gentle manner and honest face were so unexpected after all her horrible experiences, that Lucy took to him in a heartbeat and before she realised it, she was pouring out her sad tale, ending up with her intention to go to Titchfield and find her baby.

'There, there, my dear,' said the newcomer. 'Essentials first, I always say. What we need to do is get you some proper food and a place to rest. Allow me to introduce myself. Micus Loman at your service.'

Lucy mumbled her name in response.

'Lucy, is it? Very well,' continued her new friend. 'I live nearby, and you're welcome to join me for breakfast and then you can take your time to sort yourself out. How's that sound? Come, it's not far.'

Acting on his word, Mr Micus Loman escorted Lucy to his small but presentable house in Brew Crescent, no more than a stone's throw from Piccadilly Circus. He joined her for breakfast and then left her in the care of his housekeeper, Martha, a long-faced, dour woman in her mid-fifties.

Lucy had every intention of using the remainder of the day to work out how best to make her way to Titchfield, but it was not to be. The larger-than-usual breakfast, the fire burning brightly in the grate, the comfortable armchair, and, above all, the knowledge that she had one friend in the city, one person other than herself, concerned about her and her son, were more than enough to send her into a peaceful slumber.

Chapter Five: Dunston Burnett

The roly-poly, garmented figure struggling out of the carriage that had just pulled up in front of Meadowlark Cottage, Archibald Line's two-storey, straw-thatched house on the outskirts of Down village, was Mr Dunston Burnett, a middle-aged bachelor. He looked around for his host, but saw no one except a scruffy old man huddled in the cottage's small porch.

The hunched sentinel, well wrapped in a shabby winter coat, baggy corduroy britches and mismatched cap and muffler, nodded and offered a rather odd word of welcome. 'London,' he said, running his eyes over the newcomer.

'N-no, not from London. Strood,' Dunston replied, his five feet and two inches similarly bundled in a heavy overcoat, plaid travelling blanket around his shoulders and a tweed deerstalker covering his head, its side flaps pulled down tight over the ears. His round cheeks, beady brown eyes, bulbous nose and small mouth could hardly be described as handsome but they nonetheless conveyed a pleasing impression and hinted at a kindly nature.

Dunston usually wore a bemused expression, but this uncivil greeting, more like a busybody's quizzing than the genial reception he'd been expecting, had him totally perplexed. Line had invited him to visit on this very day, Monday, January 22, and stay as long as he liked, yet here he was left in the hands of an unpleasantly surly codger he'd never set eyes on before.

'Inspector,' said the word-miser.

'Ah, you mean former Inspector Archibald Line?'

The curmudgeon nodded, and then said, 'LON...DON.' His over-articulation intended to make sure the dim-witted city gent grasped where Line had gone.

'But he invite—'

'Sir,' cut in Dunston's manservant, dismounting from the carriage's lead horse. 'Best sort this out inside.' Nick, a wiry man in his twenties, buttoned up to the chin in a travel-worn Ulster coat, was taking matters into his own hands as usual whenever the situation called for action rather than words.

Dunston had 'acquired' Nick two years earlier when his great aunt had died and left him a modest legacy and a country house outside Strood. Happily quitting the tedium of bookkeeping, a job circumstances had obliged him to take as a young man, he'd become master of Woods View House and everything therein, including Nick. Although rocky at first, their relationship had quickly sorted itself out, with Nick a staunch Sam Weller to Dunston's pudgy Mr Pickwick.

'Bit cold out 'ere,' Nick added unnecessarily.

The New Year had indeed brought with it a bitterly cold spell and the entire journey from Strood had been on highways and byways rutted with the iced-over tracks of their predecessors. No more than twenty miles, it had taken a good five hours, and riding postilion had left Nick's face whipped red-raw by the wind, and his fingers, poking out of woollen mittens, chilled to a winter-blue. With darkness closing in, returning that night was not an enticing option.

'Nice cuppa tea would be just the ticket,' pressed the manservant.

The old fellow was obviously of like mind. He dug in his pocket, withdrew a key, evidently left with him by the absent Archibald Line, and let them in.

'Gabby,' was how he introduced himself once they were inside. Gabby? Hardly. All he'd produced so far by way of conversation was four standalone nouns; adjectives, adverbs, prepositions, verbs, all apparently missing from his vocabulary. Still, noun-only communication did have the distinct advantage of eliminating all those bizarre rules of English grammar, a linguistic simplification that friend Gabby might find most convenient, thought Dunston.

Quite at home in the cottage, Gabby discarded his outerwear, grabbed the kettle and set to work. The kitchen was on the chilly side despite a small fire burning in the grate. Gabby, though, seemed quite comfortable thanks to a grimy, cable-patterned jumper. Not so the other two. Having also removed their greatcoats and hats, Dunston in an ill-fitting, dark grey, three-piece suit, high-collared, white shirt, and slate-grey bowtie, and Nick in his usual, rough spun, brown jacket and work-worn trousers, were left rubbing their hands for warmth until the arrival of tea brought welcome relief.

Half an hour later, all three men were sitting around a wooden table in Line's modest kitchen, finishing their mugs of Gabby's body-warming, spirit-reviving brew. Gabby, reclining in what was surely the owner's personal chair, a fine, hoop-back Windsor, broke wind with a grimace and scratched his privates. Immediate needs attended to, he turned his wrinkled face to Dunston and, pointing to the dresser, announced, 'Letter.'

Nick handed the folded note to his master who quickly opened it and started to read.

Sunday, Jan 21
Meadowlark Cottage

My Dear Burnett:

My sincere apologies for not being here to greet you. I'm involved in a baffling case and must dash off to London. Have to get my findings to Inspector Fickett at Scotland Yard.

I'm leaving my reports on the investigation with you for safekeeping. Feel free to take a look. Think you'll find them interesting. They're in two manila folders on the dresser, the first dated December 28, the second January 21.

Looking forward to welcoming you properly to Meadowlark Cottage on my return in a day or two.

Apologies once again,

Archibald Line

What? How could this be? He scanned the letter again, but the gist remained the same: *sincere apologies… baffling case… dash off to London… Scotland Yard… leaving my reports… two manila folders.*

How odd, mused Dunston, most unlike the man, always so organized and well prepared, never rushed or in a hurry. Must be something extraordinary to send him scurrying off to London in this weather, especially when he knew I was scheduled to arrive today. He checked the letter again – dated yesterday. My goodness, must've caught the afternoon train, wanted to be at police headquarters first thing today by the look of it.

The pair were opposites in many respects – the former policeman decisive, clear thinking, action-oriented; the retired bookkeeper hesitant, muddled, wavering; the one carrying himself with a military bearing, broad in the shoulders, upright; the other with the girth and stoop of a sedentary office worker. Different though they were, happenstance had brought them together a year and a half ago when Dunston found himself involved in Line's investigation of the murder of Ellen Ternan, a London actress rumoured to be Charles Dickens's mistress.

Sadly, the case did not end well for Line. Dunston was with him when the policeman, revolver in hand, entered the novelist's study to apprehend the murderer, a mere lad, no more than twenty. The ten seconds of chaos and tragedy that followed were a nightmare Dunston would never forget: the killer lunged at a young housemaid, convinced she'd betrayed him; 'Stop! Or I'll shoot!' shouted Line; the young man didn't even hear him, his hands already around the girl's throat; Line aimed; the pair struggled; Line fired. His bullet, meant for the lad, struck the maid, killing her instantly.

A week later, Line informed Dunston that he was resigning from the force. When Dunston protested, Line said, 'The maid, a mere child, shot in the back by my own hand… As man and police officer, I have no choice but to step down.'

That might have been the end of their acquaintance had it not been for one circumstance – both men were fascinated by Darwin's theory of evolution. *On The Origin of Species* had caused an uproar throughout England the instant it was published on November 24, 1859. Battle lines were quickly drawn between the new breed of fact-based researchers who readily embraced Darwin's ground-breaking thesis, and the old guard of religious traditionalists with their unshakeable belief in the Bible's account of God's creation of man.

Dunston still recalled the Great Debate in Oxford held barely six months after the book's appearance – an ugly clash between firm-in-their-belief theologians and Darwin's band of truth-seeking scientists. Both factions behaved in a most unbecoming manner with tasteless taunts and simian slurs from one side answered by childish name-calling and anti-church abuse from the other. The city of dreaming spires was rocked to the core, buzzing with increasingly far-fetched accounts of the opening salvos in what was from then on all-out war.

It didn't take Dunston or Line long to decide into which camp they fell. Having devoured every word of Darwin's treatise, they were fully persuaded converts. But even here there were differences between them, not regarding the concept itself, but in their appreciation of how the scientist reached his simple yet profound conclusion.

Line admired Darwin's thoroughness in assembling as much evidence as possible *before* releasing his revolutionary idea. Darwin, he liked to point out, spent five years aboard HMS Beagle collecting specimens throughout the Galapagos archipelago, and then another twenty-three years conducting experiments and compiling observations before he felt his life's work was ready for public scrutiny. Line approached his investigations in like manner, gathering all the facts necessary to lead him step by step from crime to culprit, never once jumping ahead of what the evidence proved.

Dunston, on the other hand, stood in awe of the scientist's monumental intellectual leap from the cluttered confusion of a myriad seemingly unrelated observations to the structured sense of a single, unifying theory. Survival of the fittest! One general law governing the evolution of all organic beings – *multiply; vary; let the strongest live; let the weakest die.* That *flash* of genius was what enthralled and enthused Dunston, for he too had moments of insight which if right, could open up entirely fresh avenues of inquiry, but if wrong, as often happened, could send an investigation chasing its tail down a blind alley.

A few months after Line's resignation, both Darwinian devotees happened to be in London to attend the presentation to the scientist of the Copley Medal, the Royal Society's highest scientific honour. Dunston was caught in the crowd pouring out of the auditorium after the ceremony and knocked to the ground. The strong arm that pulled him to his feet belonged to none other than Inspector Line, or 'just Mr Line these days,' as the former police officer reminded him.

The pair's budding friendship progressed over the next eighteen months, mostly by post but occasionally in person at various Darwin events, so it was not surprising that the ex-policeman had invited the retired bookkeeper to spend a few days at Meadowlark Cottage. And Dunston, in his turn, had been pleased to accept the invitation, keen to see how the man he regarded as the finest detective in England was faring in his new career.

Dunston was naturally disappointed by his host's absence, but the promise of a baffling case was more than adequate compensation. He was anxious to take a look at the folders, knowing that Line's reports would provide a record of the investigation so thorough that reading them would be as good as being there. Probably best though to wait until he had the place to himself and could explore – and possibly solve – Line's latest mystery in peace and quiet.

'Fancy a pint or two, Gabby?' Nick asked, as though reading his master's thoughts.

'Aye,' was the one-word reply, and the pair immediately began readying themselves for the short walk to The Queen's Head in Down village. As they were heading for the door, Gabby turned to Dunston, pointed to the oven and by way of farewell, said, 'Dinner.'

For once, Dunston was not in the least bit interested in food. He picked up the top folder and saw that it was dated December 28, three weeks ago. He would start with this one in order to follow the progress of the investigation from its beginning. Leaving the other, the one dated yesterday, on the dresser, he settled himself at the kitchen table and opened the folder.

Case No. 9-1871, he read. Hmm, only nine in the whole of last year. Not much business coming his way. But his eyes widened when he noted the subject: *Meeting with Mrs Emma Darwin.* Emma Darwin! Charles Darwin's wife! My goodness! Dunston could not believe his eyes. Line's 'baffling case' involved the *Darwins*.

Chapter Six: A Disappointment

At the time of these events, Dunston Burnett was in his forty-second year. He'd lost both parents before his sixth birthday, his mother dying giving birth to him, and his loutish father drinking himself into an early grave. The lonely, insecure boy was placed with his great aunt. Though kindly enough, she was set in her spinster's ways and with no idea what to do with a young child, packed him off to boarding school, where, as the shortest, fattest boy in his class, he was routinely bullied and mocked for twelve long years. Then, since all young men in Auntie's view were expected to earn their keep, Dunston was shunted from the cruelty of school to the monotony of keeping the books for a small, Southampton-based shipping company, and there he remained out of sight and out of mind.

Perhaps the being that emerged from the womb would have grown into a diffident, socially awkward man of its own accord. Or perhaps the unhappy experiences on life's journey led to that particular outcome. Whatever the explanation, Dunston was exactly that man, firmly entrenched in a lonely, unobtrusive existence that, it seemed, was to be his lot for the rest of his days.

As indeed it was until the unexpected companionship of Archibald Line, a man who, like Dunston, trod a solitary path, blazed a dazzlingly white light through the greyness of his dull life. Middle-aged Dunston experienced friendship for the first time, and equally important, felt that he'd finally earned the respect of another human being.

Line, a keen observer of people, spotted qualities in Dunston that others missed. During the case that first brought them together, he saw how

Dunston, trusting his own remarkable instinct, persisted until he found the one man who could identify the killer of Ellen Ternan, the London actress. 'Would that my fellow detectives were as astute and persevering as you, Mr Burnett,' Line had said.

Praise indeed, but Dunston was even more pleased by what he'd read in the letter that Line had left for him at Meadowlark Cottage. The man whom Dunston had come to admire as both detective and human being had entrusted him, Dunston Burnett, with his personal reports, no doubt much fuller accounts of his investigation than the weekly summaries inquiry agents typically submitted to their clients. And that wasn't all. He'd invited Dunston 'to take a look.' And look he did. He let his eyes linger for a few moments on those enticing words – *Meeting with Mrs Darwin* – and then worked his way steadily through Line's first report.

An hour later, he snapped the folder shut in dismay. Alert and upright when he'd started, he'd slumped further and further into the kitchen chair as his excitement drained away like specks of silvery sand trickling through the narrow neck of an hourglass. What a disappointment! Nothing like the 'baffling case' he'd been expecting. Just a petty squabble between two academics.

He wandered over to the oven to see what it might hold by way of dinner. Shepherd's pie, still warm. He served himself a portion fit for a man of his girth, and returned to the table. As he ate, he frowned at the folder. Could he have missed something? He had nothing better to do, so he might as well take another look. But not in the kitchen, thus far a singularly unrewarding hunting ground.

I'll be better off in bed, thought Dunston, then, if the second reading proves as uninteresting as the first, I'll be able to drop straight off to sleep. He rose with the folder in hand, picked up its unread mate from the dresser, and headed upstairs.

Five minutes later, clad in night shirt and cap, sitting up in bed, a candle flickering beside him, he reached for Line's report once more. This was what he read:

Case No. 9-1871

Meeting with Mrs Emma Darwin, Down House, December 28

Mrs D was concerned about her husband's feud with Mr George
Mivart, a biologist and, at least initially, a committed supporter of
Mr D's theory of survival of the fittest. All went well to begin with.
The first inkling of trouble occurred when Mivart converted to
Catholicism and began to nuance his support for natural selection
with a strong overlay of religious dogma.

As on his first reading, Dunston could see exactly where this was heading.
Mivart, it appeared, was switching from the Science camp to the Bible camp.

Mivart continued to accept that survival of the fittest was the
natural rule governing the evolution of animals and plants but
now believed that man was created by a divine being exactly as set
out in the Bible. Matters came to a head with the recent publication
of Darwin's *The Descent of Man.*

Ah, yes, *The Descent of Man.* What a book, marvelled Dunston. Focused
exclusively on the evolution of mankind, it must have seemed to Mivart like
a personal affront, a slap in the face of his newly found religious beliefs.

He thoroughly savaged the book in the prestigious *Quarterly
Review.* Darwin and his followers were furious. A 'stab in the back'
was Mr D's reaction according to Mrs D, and he and his inner
circle immediately began planning their revenge. As it happened,
Mivart was seeking membership of the famous Athenaeum Club
and Darwin and his supporters, all prominent members, decided
to scuttle his election. Although unsuccessful, they disparaged the
man's scientific work so unmercifully, they effectively made him
a lifelong enemy.

This wasn't helping, thought Dunston. Still nothing but a petty dispute between academics with egos that bruised as easily as overripe plums. How could these supposedly educated men behave like this? Worse than little boys squabbling in the schoolyard. Nothing so far for Line to investigate. He resumed his reading.

Mrs D handed me an envelope. It had arrived four days ago, she said, and was postmarked London. I took out the enclosed letter and saw immediately that it was unsigned, composed of words cut out of a newspaper – *The Times* by the look of it – and pasted on notepaper bearing the crest of the Athenaeum Club. I read the note and returned it and the envelope to Mrs D but not before copying the contents:

It is for good reason the Almighty is called the Creator.
  When you, Mr Darwin, stand before your MAKER,
  you will learn this TRUTH.
  And your FATE!
  I swear by Aesculapius that the Hounds of Hell
  will feast on your flesh for all eternity!

This is what Mrs D wanted me to deal with. Darwin had been disparaged mercilessly in reviews in the serious newspapers and cartoons in the penny broadsheets, but this, a poison-pen letter sent to his home, was taking it too far. I didn't understand the reference to Aesculapius, a Greek god perhaps, but otherwise the invective was typical of the many published attacks on the scientist.

Mrs D then made a very astute observation. 'It seems to me,' she said, 'that a man whose efforts to join the Athenaeum Club were nearly thwarted by my beloved husband, might be tempted to write an offensive message to him on notepaper from that very institution.'

The same thought had occurred to me, but there was no proof. If I was certain Mivart was the guilty party, I could easily pay a few of my old Whitechapel 'acquaintances' to 'persuade' him that sending such letters was not a healthy enterprise. But I wasn't certain.

Instead, I suggested that I ask my former superior in the force, Sir Edmund Henderson, Commissioner for the Metropolitan Police, to have a quiet word with Mivart which, without accusing the man of any wrongdoing, would make clear the serious consequences of sending threatening letters to prominent members of society. Then, if no more letters showed up, we could consider the problem resolved.

Mrs D was pleased with this suggestion. She thanked me profusely and our meeting drew to a close.

Dunston applauded the detective's sensible way of dealing with the perpetrator, but he could still see no reason whatsoever to describe this as a 'baffling case'. Line, and Mrs Darwin, had it right on the nose – Mivart was behind the letter, end of mystery.

Placing the report on the bedside table, his eye fell upon the second folder, the one bearing yesterday's date. For a brief moment he debated whether to take a look, but a long yawn and a warm bed decided him otherwise, and he settled down for an early night.

Chapter Seven: Flower-selling

I t was late evening before Mr Micus Loman, Lucy's new-found benefactor, returned. 'Ah, I see you're looking much better, young lady. I trust Martha,' he nodded towards the morose housekeeper, 'has been looking after you. Good, good. Now, my dear, am I to take it you're alone in this big city of ours?'

'Yes, sir. My family's all in Cornwall.'

'Cornwall, you say. And is your family aware of your little boy?'

'Oh no, sir. I daren't tell them.'

'I understand. Well, it seems to me, then, you're in need of support from elsewhere, and in that regard I may be able to provide a small service. You see, I have a little flower-selling business. That's how I came to run into you this morning. I'd been to Covent Garden market to pick up a few violets from the hothouses of Kent and Surrey and some dried lavender. What I do is pass them on to the girls with a modest margin for my trouble, and they sell them at whatever price they can get. See?'

Lucy nodded.

'Only have two girls working for me through the winter season, but I could set you up and in no time at all you could earn enough to get yourself down to Titchfield. Now tell me, my dear, what do you think of that?'

'Oh, that would be wonderful, sir.'

'Excellent. Now, down to business.' He smiled. 'Do you have any money to put into this venture?'

'Not really,' she replied. 'All I have is sixpence.'

'A tanner? Hmm, that's not much help.' He paused in thought and then to

Lucy's great astonishment, said, 'My dear, I have an idea. I'll give you half a crown's worth of flowers on account, an advance if you like, to go with what your six pennies buy you. Then, when you can, you pay back my loan and, that done, the rest is yours. There, that would get you off to a good start, don't you think?'

Lucy was overjoyed, and she thanked him over and over again.

'That's enough, my dear. You'll need a good night's rest if you're to begin your new trade tomorrow, so you'd better sleep in my daughter's bedroom tonight. And we'll need to smarten you up a bit. One of her wool dresses should fit you just fine, and be a sight warmer than your cotton one. You remind me a lot of her, you know. She passed away giving birth to my grandson who, sadly, only survived a few days. There was nothing I could do to help either of them, but I can help you and your little one and, as God's my witness, I'll do everything in my power to see you and him reunited.'

Lucy spent that night in a real bed, the first since being dismissed from service by the hateful Jarke six months ago. The next morning, wearing one of Mr Loman's daughter's dresses – a heavy wool, dark green, day dress – and the shawl and bonnet she'd taken from the workhouse, she set out after an early breakfast, eager to start her new adventure. She stationed herself at the Strand end of Waterloo Bridge, exactly as Mr Loman had advised. Lots of passers-by, he'd said, and he was right. By three o'clock, she'd sold all the lavender and all the violets except for two posies.

She'd done the sums in her head and knew she'd already covered Mr Loman's half a crown and pocketed two shillings for herself. Not bad, but if she could only sell these last two posies… One went quickly to an elderly gentleman with a walking stick for a whole shilling. She couldn't believe her good fortune. One more to go.

It was getting dark and she was about to give up when a young man sauntered over. Her hopes rose but then quickly fell when she saw he was nothing but a common layabout, his scruffy bowler, coarse jacket, and shoddy boots only partially offset by a bright red kerchief around his neck, a feeble attempt to give his appearance the swagger much admired by louts like him. Not someone likely to hand over his money for anything but ale, grub, and cheap whores.

Still, he inspected the remaining posy, paused and then, much to her surprise, reached into his pocket. Had her prayers been answered? He pulled out something shiny, silver… another shilling? That's what it looked like, but as he held it out, it slipped from his fingers. Lucy bent to pick it up for him, but before she could do so, gorilla-strong arms grabbed her from behind. Terror flooded through her, then anger, but she could neither flee nor fight. All she could do was watch.

The young man doffed his bowler with one hand and with the other snatched her tie-up purse from her belt, snapping the strings with ease. He replaced his hat, picked up the coin he'd 'dropped' and nodded to his partner who shoved Lucy to the ground. Grinning, her customer-turned-thief kicked her hard in the ribs. 'Fingers! Leave 'er be,' growled his mate. 'Let's get out of 'ere.'

Curled up on the cold pavement, her left side a cauldron of pain, Lucy saw the man called Fingers stamp on her last posy, crushing it to a purple and green mess before he strolled off with her hard-earned cash.

Chapter Eight: The Family Curse

Dunston spent the first part of Tuesday morning working his way through a substantial breakfast of sausage and eggs with all the trimmings, compensation for Line's lacklustre report. Full to bursting, he decided a short walk was in order. The weather had changed and although still cold, the dull, snow-threatening clouds had been nudged aside by a weak but determined winter sun. He put on his great coat and deerstalker, exited Meadowlark Cottage and set off towards the village.

He soon spied the steeple of St Mary the Virgin, the parish's flint-stone church. And there, sitting on a bench in the churchyard, bent over, sobbing, was an elderly woman – but not any elderly woman, no, unless he was mistaken, he was looking at Emma Darwin, Mrs Charles Darwin, in the flesh.

He'd seen her only once when she and her husband were leaving Burlington House in London after the scientist had delivered a lecture to The Royal Society. Dunston remembered the occasion only too well, and the incident popped unbidden into his mind...

As the great man paused to shake someone's hand mere inches from Dunston, the crowd pushed forward thrusting him into the unsuspecting naturalist's back. Darwin, totally unruffled, turned, looked down, and said in a quiet, friendly voice:

'Beg your pardon.' He held out his hand in affable apology and introduced himself, 'Charles Darwin, sir.'

This was the admirer's chance to say something truly memorable, a stylish salutation or clever quip, but all that trickled out was a single stuttered

syllable:

'D-D-Duns—'

'Dunce? Really, sir!' exclaimed the intellectual giant.

'Dunston,' clarified the silver-tongued enthusiast. 'B-Burn—'

'Burn! Burn what?' demanded Mrs Darwin. Hearing what sounded like yet another threat to torch her husband's writings, she stepped forward smartly and moved him out of harm's way.

Mrs Darwin's words faded away, and the episode drew to a close. Not his finest moment, perhaps, but still one he cherished.

Approaching her, he saw that she still looked decidedly more sprightly than her sixty-odd years, a sick husband, and ten childbirths would have suggested. She was bare-headed, grey hair parted in the middle and drawn tight on each side, but her roundish body was well protected from the cold by a dark grey winter coat edged with lamb's wool.

Dunston was hopelessly at a loss when dealing with members of the fairer sex, and the best he could do was to stand before her, stiff as a board, and silently proffer his handkerchief. A gloved hand reached out for the folded square of linen which was quickly put to use wiping tears from reddened eyes.

'Thank you, sir, most kind.'

'N-not at all. Glad to be of help. Um… Mrs Darwin, isn't it?' he ventured. She nodded without looking at him.

'Dunston Burnett at your service, ma'am,' he said a little more boldly. She glanced up and stared at him, blankly.

'We met several years ago. In London,' he prompted.

'Ah, yes, I remember,' she fibbed. Then, making an effort to be polite, she inquired, 'Are you visiting?'

'Indeed I am. Staying at Meadowlark Cottage as the guest of Archibald Line.'

'Mr Line? What a coincidence.' She examined him more closely. 'He's helping me with… oh, dear… f-forgive me.' She dabbed at fresh tears. 'It's… the problem is… she's m-missing… Hen… Hen…'

'Your hen's missing?'

'No, no. My daughter-in-law. Henrietta... She's missing.'

'Oh dear. How distressing for you.'

'Yes, I'm afraid something terrible has happened. It was the anniversary of her baby boy's passing, you see, and she so mourned that child. We feared that overwhelmed by grief, she'd left, intent on... on doing herself harm. The police searched everywhere for her but to no avail, and... and now they suspect Henrietta's been... k-kidnapped.'

'Kidnapped?' Dunston exclaimed. 'Surely not!'

'I pray not, but I was so worried I called in Mr Line. He was already helping me with... with another matter.'

Dunston nodded, having spent yesterday evening being less than enthralled by the other 'matter'.

'He kindly came to Down House first thing Sunday,' she continued. 'I was attending Charles, Mr Darwin that is, and had to leave Mr Line with Grace, my maid. He talked to her for a full hour, asking about footprints in the snow, a sweet smell in Henrietta's bedroom, and goodness knows what.'

Mrs Darwin, blinking away more tears, stole a quick look at Dunston, debating, he sensed, how much to tell him.

'Then... it got really strange,' she said. 'Ridiculous though it sounds, the kidnappers are supposed to have taken Henrietta out through a locked door *without* the benefit of a key. I do *not* believe for a moment that my daughter-in-law just vanished into thin air as Grace insists, but with no key, how was such a thing achieved?'

Ah, a body disappearing from a locked-house! This sounds more like a mystery befitting Line than that inconsequential squabble, thought Dunston. *This* is the 'baffling case' that sent him scurrying off to London. He scolded himself for having left the second folder unopened.

'After talking to Grace,' Mrs Darwin continued, 'Mr Line rushed off without a word to me, and I've been at my wits' end ever since.' More tears and much dabbing. 'I hope he shows up soon.'

'He's in London, I believe, but I'm sure he'll be back in a day or two,' he reassured her.

'Oh, I do hope so, and with good news, I pray,' she said, but her voice lacked conviction and the tears returned.

'Mrs Darwin, is there anything…?'

'No, no… nothing, thank you. I must get back. I just need a few minutes to myself if you don't mind.' She made good use of Dunston's already damp handkerchief once more before returning it to him.

'Of course, I quite understand.' Dunston was keen to get back to Meadowlark Cottage and take a look at the unread report. 'Let me, then, bid you good day.'

He'd only taken a few steps when Mrs Darwin started speaking again. Not to him, though. No, her words were not meant for his or any other mortal's ears. He knew he should leave, knew he shouldn't listen in on her soul-baring, but despite the tug of the unopened folder, his feet were rooted in the sod as firmly as the headstones in the graveyard.

'My fault… Dear Lord, all my fault,' she whimpered, staring out over the church wall to the snow-and-grass patchwork of the fields beyond, oblivious to his continued presence behind her.

Her fault? wondered Dunston. Whatever can she mean? Not the kidnapping. It's something else, something *she's* done, something she now deeply regrets.

'My children… how they've suffered… my family… weakened and blighted… cursed for all time… and all generations. My darling babies… Anne, Mary, little Charles…all taken from me. The others… so sickly. *And I'm to blame.*'

Like many other families, death had been an all-too-frequent visitor to the Darwin houschold, Dunston granted, but whatever made Mrs Darwin think she was responsible?

'I – should – never – have – married – Charles,' she said, her words sounding like some pagan chant. 'The laws of nature… so unforgiving. One *selfish* action… and my family is cursed *forever.*'

Of course! Inbreeding! Marriage between close relatives, a sin in the eyes of many, widely believed to cause ill health, loss of vigour, reduced fertility in offspring, frailties then passed on to future generations, the yet-to-be-born progeny already burdened by their inheritance. Dunston knew why Mrs Darwin felt the weight of her family's health-misfortunes like an ever-present millstone around her neck. Emma and Charles Darwin were *first cousins*; Josiah Wedgwood was grandfather to both her *and* her husband.

Little wonder Darwin devoted so much time and effort to researching the effects of marriage between closely related people. Far from being just an intriguing line of scientific inquiry, this was frighteningly personal. Its singular application to him and his marriage must have been a permanent worry, the poor man never knowing whether or not his and Emma's union *caused* his children's many sicknesses.

Dunston put his troubling thoughts aside as soon as he realised Mrs Darwin was still talking. '...Richard's little angel... my only grandchild... snatched away only eighteen months after coming into the world.'

Ah, yes. Dunston recalled the newspaper accounts of the child's tragic death three years ago – left in his grandmother's care while his father visited a sick patient, dead before the father returned. Death stealing into the next generation, confirming Darwin's worst fears, thought Dunston.

'Dear Lord, you know how much my husband and I have longed for a grandchild, but... our innocent babe is gone and we'll never have another unless... unless You see fit in Your Great Compassion to grant our wish. I beseech You, as I've done every week for the last three years, for Your divine intervention.'

Every week for the last three years... Dunston was astounded. He'd assumed he was witnessing a once-only event occasioned by Henrietta's disappearance but no, this was only the *latest* in an endless series of pilgrimages in search of God's beneficence.

He watched in awe as she raised clasped hands to the sky. 'Our Father, which art in heaven,' she began softly. 'Hallowed be thy Name. Thy Kingdom come. Thy will be done on earth, as it is in heaven...'

Dunston, not a religious man, nonetheless recognised the opening words to the Lord's Prayer. He really should leave, let her speak to her god in solitude. He took one last look at the small, life-scarred form of the praying woman, turned, and started back to the cottage.

Chapter Nine: A Chance Encounter

Perfectly positioned above the entrance to the Athenaeum Club, the statue of the Greek goddess of wisdom who had granted the establishment her name, gazed down on the likes of Benjamin Disraeli, Alfred Lord Tennyson, John Stuart Mill and the many other great men gracing the reign of Queen Victoria. Inside, a magnificent staircase drew the eye up towards the face of the club's clock, which for no reason known to God or man, bore two figure sevens and no figure eight, with the inevitable consequence that anyone with an appointment for seven was doubly anxious to be on time, while those scheduled for eight never feared being late.

Sir Edmund Henderson, Commissioner of the Metropolitan Police, didn't have an appointment for either time, but he still kept a close eye on the clock's minute hand as it ticked its way towards two on the Tuesday afternoon after Henrietta's disappearance. He was standing at the foot of the stairs in hopes of 'bumping' into George Mivart as he came down from lunching in The Picture Room, the smaller of the club's two dining rooms.

His former chief of detectives, Archibald Line, had informed him almost three weeks ago that Mivart might be responsible for the anonymous letter sent to Charles Darwin, and Sir Edmund had been looking out for the man ever since, albeit quite casually. Having heard yesterday morning from his current chief, Inspector Fickett, about the disappearance of Darwin's daughter-in-law in odd circumstances, he'd decided a more determined effort was called for.

Henderson had not fully made up his mind about Fickett. Probably unfair to expect him to step straight into Line's shoes and perform at his level. Without a doubt, Line had been the best detective on the force, and the commissioner had tried desperately to persuade him to stay on. Best give Fickett some time, he'd concluded, see how he manages this business with the Darwins, good test of his investigatory skills, not to mention his political savvy.

Not expecting his wait to be long, Henderson still had his greatcoat on and was beginning to feel uncomfortably warm. He ran his hand through his hair, pushing it back from a broad, intelligent brow, and shifted his weight from one leg to the other. He was a heavy-set man and standing on one spot was not his favourite pastime, having stood at attention many a long hour when still a lowly subaltern in the army, good discipline for sure, but unforgiving on the feet.

The minute hand crept around to ten past the hour. Where was the man? Henderson knew Mivart, but not well. He was more familiar with the man's father and brothers, all of whom held important positions in the judiciary. George Mivart had also studied law for a while, but had chosen to pursue a career in biology, eventually taking the Chair in Zoology at Imperial College London.

Ah, here he came at last, a short man with the stooped posture and rounded shoulders that seemed to be a hallmark of his family. As he came closer, the commissioner was struck by the pallid face and pink, baby-smooth cheeks. Fellow must be in his early forties, but it looked as though he'd barely started to shave. Dark-suited and dark-tied, he made his way down the stairs into the waiting arms, as it were, of London's most powerful policeman.

'I say, Mivart. A word if you don't mind.'

'Commissioner, how nice to see you. What can I do for you?'

'Nothing really. Saw you coming down and wanted to offer my congratulations on your election to the club.'

'Jolly decent of you.' Mivart nodded, already beginning to move towards the cloakroom. 'Much appreciated.'

'I'd heard,' continued the other quickly, 'about the disagreement with Darwin and... well, the attempt to blackball you. In my position, it's vital I don't take sides in these matters, but I'm glad to see you join our ranks.'

'Good of you to say so.' Mivart stopped, evidently more than ready to explain the rights and wrongs of his election to anyone willing to listen. 'Matter was in doubt, I have to admit. Darwin organised quite a powerful opposition. Of course, every single member of the club who believed in the Almighty's creation of man was in my corner as was the club's entire legal contingent given my family's connections. Darwin and his crowd were never going to overcome the combined forces of church and law.' A none too pleasant smirk creased his face.

'Well, all that's behind you now. Time perhaps to bury the hatchet.'

'Yes, capital idea,' Mivart said, his expression making it clear precisely where he believed the hatchet should be buried.

Henderson, a practised reader of faces, added both Mivart's voiced and countenanced response to his mental file on the biologist.

'Well, must be getting along. I'll bid—'

'Hold on,' Henderson cut in. 'You might be interested in a little news about your adversary. This isn't general knowledge, so please keep it to yourself, but well, Mr Darwin received an anonymous letter, rather abusive, words cut out of The Times and pasted on club notepaper.'

'What? Good Lord. A poison pen letter. On club notepaper, you say?' Mivart allowed what looked to the commissioner like a moment of triumph to flicker in his eye. 'How strange. You don't think it was from a club member, do you?'

'Possibly. Obviously someone with access to club stationery. But whoever it was, I have my top man on the job, so we'll soon put a stop to this despicable behaviour. My promise to you, sir,' he declared forcefully, accompanying his words with a sharp, forward thrust of his head and a smack of fist into palm, 'is that there will be no more anonymous letters on my watch.'

Mivart was left in no doubt that the offender, should he dare to put pen to paper again, would be crushed beneath the full weight of the law. 'V-very commendable,' he stammered, backing up slightly, a watchful eye on the clenched fist. 'Can't believe anyone calling himself a gentleman would do such a disgraceful thing. Take me, for instance. I have a serious disagreement with Charles Darwin, but my argument with him will be conducted in the pages of the academic journals. That's the honourable way to demonstrate that he and his cronies are barking up the wrong tree.'

Henderson nodded, though he was far from convinced. The man was quite capable of addressing the scientific community through his professional writings *and* causing Darwin serious distress anonymously.

The commissioner had come across men like Mivart in his army days – sly as weasels, perfectly capable of stooping to something as underhanded as a poison pen letter; but also, he believed, cowardly enough to be open to a little robust persuasion. Time to finish this fellow off, he decided, and make damned sure his venomous quill is never again aimed at Charles Darwin.

'Unfortunately, it gets worse for Darwin,' he said. 'You see, his daughter-in-law, Henrietta, is missing.'

'*Missing?* That's shocking,' Mivart exclaimed, but again with that glint of delight in the eye. 'I had no idea. You'd think the newspapers would be full of it, but I haven't seen a thing.'

'Only happened last Thursday and for now Darwin has been able to keep it quiet, so please, not a word to anyone. As you can imagine, this is an extremely distressing time for the Darwins. One more upsetting letter and by God I'll make the fellow who sends it pay with his blood!' Fist and palm met forcibly once more, this time with a solid, bone-crushing thump.

Mivart flinched and quickly stepped back out of range, barely hanging on to the man-about-town composure he'd shown when he'd sauntered down the staircase only minutes earlier.

'G-glad to hear it,' he managed at last. 'I truly believe Darwin is a blaspheming sinner,' he said more stoutly, 'but as a devout Catholic, I would never wish any harm to him or his family. I bid you good day, commissioner.'

'And I you, Mivart.'

Excellent. Message sent and received. Henderson smiled as he watched the unpleasant little man slouch off.

Chapter Ten: Competing Suspects

Case No. 1-1872

Meeting with Inspector Fickett, the Yard, Monday, January 22

I arrived at police headquarters as early as I could, keen to share my findings with Fickett. He apparently had other ideas. Obviously wanting to show his predecessor that he was now the boss, he kept me kicking my heels for a good two hours. I was being put firmly in my place.

L ine had written up an account of yesterday's meeting with Fickett, his replacement as chief of detectives, immediately after he'd returned to his hotel from Scotland Yard. Today, as he re-read his first paragraph, he fretted that he may have let his annoyance with his successor's inconsiderate behaviour affect his usual dispassionate prose. Unlikely, but worth checking. Best read through it again, he decided, while the events were still fresh in his mind. Their encounter had not started well...

When Line eventually entered what had previously been his own office, Fickett's head was buried in a report. The police officer studiously ignored him for a long minute, then glanced up and said: 'Ah, Insp—, I mean, *Mr* Line.' He openly ran his eye over Line's civilian dress, and then took a moment to underline his official status by straightening his police uniform's perfectly straight jacket. 'Good of you to come. Understand you have some information for me. Please, take a seat.'

Mr Line, indeed... Line eyed his replacement. The man had dark hair slicked to either side of a razor-sharp centre parting, and a sallow complexion, the perfect background for his black pinprick eyes. He was lean of build, with sloping shoulders and long arms, and had, Line recalled, a Spartan way of moving that spelled doom for any felon thinking to escape.

'Thank you, Fickett.' Line softened his usual tone slightly, not wanting the familiar way of addressing his successor to sound too demeaning. 'And yes, I do. It's about the Henrietta Darwin disappearance. As you know, Grace, the maid, saw a single set of footprints in the snow outside the backdoor. She couldn't tell whether the tracks were coming or going, but she thought they were too large to be her mistress's. In my many years of experience, I've seen all the tricks of the trade...' He paused to let the other man know the gap was meant to be filled by *unlike you.* 'And I believe we're looking at the old single-track trick.

'It works like this. The villain with the bigger feet walks through the snow first. His smaller-footed mate follows, stepping only in the prints of the leader. On the way back, same business, except now, the broader part of the leader's foot comes down on the heel-end of the incoming print, obscuring the direction of the marks. So, the tracks seen by Grace, unclear as to direction and too large to have been made by Henrietta Darwin, belonged, I suspect, to *two men, coming and going.*'

Line watched Fickett closely during his explanation but couldn't tell whether this was news to him or something he'd already figured out. All right, young feller, let's see what you make of this.

'Now,' Line said, 'the sweet smell Grace noticed in her mistress's bedroom the morning after the lady's disappearance is a sure sign of... *chloroform.*'

Fickett blinked.

Ha! He didn't know about the chloroform. 'So,' Line continued, 'the evidence shows that Henrietta was drugged, and then carried away by two men. Far from it being suicide, the lady was most definitely... *kidnapped.*'

Fickett took his time before answering. 'I appreciate your efforts greatly,

Mr Line, but I ruled out suicide long ago. The lady couldn't have gone far on such a bitterly cold night wearing only a day dress, and our thorough search around the house didn't turn up a body. The only reasonable conclusion, as you've now realised yourself, and as I told the Darwins, is that she was abducted. Of course, we didn't let the matter rest there...' It was his turn to pause, and leave a gap for the unspoken words *as you seem to have.* 'We have a suspect.'

Line was floored. His chiselled expression gave nothing away, but he'd not imagined for a moment that the police would have got this far. Nothing could have surprised him more, except the young inspector's next words.

'Yes, Richard Darwin, the missing woman's husband. Didn't commit the crime himself, of course. Plenty of cracksmen around to do the dirty work for him. But he's our man. Should always look at the spouse in these sorts of situations,' Fickett advised, as if lecturing a raw recruit.

Richard Darwin? What nonsense, Line thought. What about Mivart? His ugly dispute with Darwin gives him an obvious motive. He should be top of the suspect list. Or, if not him, one of those other crazy religious zealots out for Charles Darwin's blood. But Richard Darwin? Makes no sense. Have to find out what's behind this absurd allegation. 'And what, may I ask, leads you to this conclusion?'

'It's a matter of assembling the pieces in the correct order,' Fickett replied in the same condescending tone. 'Had a feeling about him from the moment I first saw him, policeman's instinct, you could call it. Richard, at his father's insistence, stayed in London for two nights after Henrietta's disappearance in case his wife tried to reach him there. So I didn't meet him until Saturday, at which time he had no idea I suspected kidnapping. I alerted him to this possibility and the blood drained from his face.'

As it would for any man on hearing his wife had been kidnapped, Line noted silently.

'Could've been a natural reaction, of course,' Fickett continued, unwittingly addressing Line's unspoken comment. 'But what I saw was *guilt* written across his face in capital letters. Hardly said a word after that, but I sensed his brain was working at a hundred miles an hour. You see, I believe his plan was to make his wife's disappearance *look* like suicide – don't forget that it happened on the anniversary of her much-loved son's passing – but, with that plan crumbling before his eyes, he was panicking.'

This isn't *evidence,* Line barely resisted pointing out.

'This may not seem like much but it put me on alert. And that is perhaps why, when I reviewed the anonymous letter sent to Darwin that the commissioner shared with me this morning, one word jumped right out at me – just one, but enough to lend weight to my suspicion.'

Word? What word? wondered Line. And how could any word in that poison pen letter implicate Richard Darwin? If anything, it connected *Mivart* to the kidnapping.

'You see,' resumed the inspector, eyeing Line with an increasingly self-satisfied smile, 'the casual reader is likely to conclude it was written by Mivart, the fellow Darwin's having a dispute with, because it has all the right Christian-sounding words: Creator, the Almighty, Hounds of Hell and so on.' He paused, theatrically. 'Except for one. *Aesculapius.*'

Line was momentarily discomfited. The name had struck him as odd, but he'd not had time to follow up. Fickett obviously had.

'Now, as I'm sure you know, Aesculapius is the Greek god of medicine. He's usually depicted with a serpent-entwined staff, the symbol used by the medical profession to this day. Including *that* name in the letter was the writer's mistake. He wanted us to believe Mivart had penned the note, but that word tells us it was a *doctor.* A doctor, Mr Line, like Richard Darwin.'

Line digested Fickett's reasoning. 'Interesting, very interesting,' he eventually said. 'But Mivart has a clear motive to harm Charles Darwin, whereas I don't see any reason why Richard Darwin would want to hurt his father. Do you?'

'Not to harm Charles Darwin, no, but this case is about the kidnapping of Richard's wife, so that's where we must seek motive. We don't have it yet, but my men are looking into the younger Darwin's background and I'll wager we'll find something soon enough.'

'But,' said Line, 'if Richard's plan was to create the impression that Henrietta had wandered off and taken her own life, why send the anonymous letter in the first place?'

'Should've thought that was obvious.' Fickett's tone was that of someone explaining the same point for the umpteenth time to a slow-witted child. 'It's a back-up plan, in case the suicide story didn't fly. The letter was sent to throw suspicion on Mivart in the event that we began to investigate Henrietta's disappearance as a kidnapping. If, as he hoped, the suicide story was accepted, then the letter would be dismissed as the ravings of one of the anti-Darwin clique, and that would be that. Unfortunately for him, the suicide version was quickly discarded, so the back-up plan suddenly seemed like a marvellous piece of foresight... and it was, except for that one crucial mistake, the reference to Aesculapius. There, that sews it up rather neatly, don't you agree?'

'Well, it would *if* you've also figured out how Henrietta's body was actually removed from Down House,' countered Line, moving into uncharted waters. Even though he was essentially confessing to this whelp that he had no idea how this trickery was managed, he was keen to see if Fickett did.

'Ah, I wondered when you'd come to that. Quite a puzzler, a body disappearing out of a locked house without the aid of a key. All I can say is that this is still being investigated.'

Ha! Line knew from years on the force that 'still being investigated' meant 'absolutely clueless'. He felt a little better on hearing they were both in the same boat, but the feeling didn't last long.

'And we're making progress.' A sly smile flitted across the inspector's face. 'But it's too early for me to say more.'

Blast, the arrogant buck's onto something, seethed Line, and he's going to keep it to himself. Thoroughly irritated, but still granite-faced, Line stood and bade Fickett good day.

An hour after he'd started his review of his account of Monday's meeting with Fickett, Line was satisfied. He'd scrutinised every single sentence and each was fully up to his usual professional standards. That done, he penned a short covering note to Dunston saying that he planned to return to Meadowlark Cottage on Wednesday and asking him to keep this report and the preceding two safe since they were the most detailed records of his investigation. He then prepared the first of what would be weekly summaries of his doings for Mrs Darwin whom, he imagined, was anxious to hear from him. He put both reports in envelopes, addressed them and gave them to the hotel porter for posting.

Chapter Eleven: Storytime

It was almost ten o'clock before Lucy found the strength to raise herself from the pavement. Her ribs, where that brute had favoured her with the weight of his boot, pained with every breath, but it was despair that had kept her face pressed to the cold stone. Her assailant had walked off dangling her little purse from his hand – to him, just a few coins, no more than beer money; to her, the only hope of reaching her son.

Numbed by that split-second plunge from the swell of an ocean full of promise into the miserable hopelessness of its icy depths, the girl was still vaguely aware of another worry worming its way into her wretchedness – Mr Loman… his loan… half a crown. How could she ever repay him? She knew she couldn't. She'd have to tell him. But how? How could she face the man after accepting his kindness, so freely given, only to ruin everything in her eagerness to sell that one last posy?

It was a ten-minute walk from Waterloo Bridge to Mr Loman's lodgings but Lucy, dreading her arrival there, dragged her feet. Like a clockwork doll winding down, her pace slowed with each step, but no matter how much she delayed, she couldn't avoid the moment of truth and long before she was ready, she found herself turning into her benefactor's street.

Brew Crescent had seemed pleasant enough yesterday morning when her new friend had brought her to his house, but in the winter darkness, the neighbourhood filled her with dread, as though Evil's treacherous tentacles were slithering down the cobbles towards her. Thank goodness for the likes of Mr Loman.

She finally willed herself to knock on the flower-seller's door but her rat-a-tat-tat was barely audible, even to her. She tried again a little more forcefully, and after a short pause the door flew open.

'About time you showed up. Where the shittin' 'ell you bin?' Dour Martha, the housekeeper, her coarse, grey work dress a perfect match for her pasty, pinched face, glared at her. 'Best get yerself in. You've missed supper but you still have to settle up yer accounts. Then you can get yerself off to bed. 'Nother day tomorrer.'

Lucy did her best to explain what had happened as Martha strode down the hall, but before the sorry tale was finished, the woman turned and said: 'So, you've lost Mr. Loman's half crown, have you? How you going to pay him back, then?'

'I don't know,' the girl whimpered. 'I'll do everything I can to set matters straight.'

'Well, that's only proper, ain't it? Now, get yerself off to bed. You'll sleep with the rest of the girls tonight and then tomorrer Micus'll see what's to be done.'

Lucy hesitated for a moment and then ventured that last night she'd slept in his daughter's room. 'Perhaps I could sleep there tonight?'

'Daughter's room, eh? Ha, he's got a different tale for each of the wenches what comes across his path. He don't have a daughter, you silly mot. Follow me.' Martha set off up the stairs to the landing and then clumped her way up a wooden ladder to the attic, beckoning Lucy to follow.

As Lucy's head rose above the top rung, she saw a surprisingly large room filled with a dozen pallets spread out on the floor, not unlike the women's ward in Shoreditch Workhouse, except here she saw hats, perfume bottles, scarves, even underclothes. She struggled to understand. Mr Loman had said he only had two flower-sellers working for him but she could see that at least ten of the beds had been used recently. And where were the girls? Surely he didn't allow them out at this time of night.

'I don't know why you've brought me up here,' Lucy said, clambering into the loft. 'Please fetch Mr Loman and he'll explain. He's my protector.'

'Protector, is it?' Martha said. 'Well, he's out protecting his girls right now, so get along with you. You can have the bed over there in the corner where you won't be a bother.' She gave Lucy a push to help her on her way.

'The other girls, where are they?' Lucy asked. 'How can they be selling flowers this late at night in the middle of winter?'

'Stupid sapscull, you know less about the ways of the world than a newborn. These girls ain't selling flowers, child. They're selling whatever the gentl'men want.' Noting Lucy's blank look, Martha sighed. 'They're strumpets, you simpleton, night-jobbers, Covent Garden nuns, wag-tails, out doing their business. And that's what you'll be doing.'

'You… you mean whoring? Never! Let me out of here!' Lucy tried to force her way back to the ladder but Martha shoved her to the floor.

'Well, you're a little hellcat an' no mistake. Listen to me. You owe the man two an' sixpence, right? How you going to pay yer debt, eh? I'll tell you how, flat on yer back, that's how.'

'You beast!' Lucy charged at Martha and the two struggled perilously close to the open hatch. Lucy was younger and stronger even with bruised ribs, but the woman had dealt with girls like Lucy for most of her life, and she quickly dragged her by the hair to the corner pallet, threw her down with enough force to knock the wind out of her and then plopped herself down on the neighbouring mattress, puffing and blowing from her exertions.

'Listen, missy, I ain't got no grudge 'gainst you. Jus' business 'sfar as I'm concerned. And to show there's no hard feelings, let me give you a piece of advice. Listen well, 'cos it may save yer life. You're a gutsy one, and next time you may get the better of me, but if you do, it'll be the worse for you. See this…' Martha opened the bodice of her dress, to reveal a deep purple scarring, the skin puckered from throat to breast.

'That, dearie,' she continued in a flat, matter-of-fact tone, 'is the price I paid for trying to run off when Micus first got his hooks into me. Acid. Burned like the devil. Feller what done it said it'd be my face next time. Wasn't Micus. He don't do the dirty stuff. Too clever by half is Micus. Always got some bloke 'round the place ready an' willing to give any girl stepping out of line a proper larruping. The one what done me is long gone, thank the Lord, but the new one's even worse, according to the girls. Just listen to this.'

Like mother and child readying for a bedtime story, the women had settled down, the older breathing easily again, in command, the younger, spittle still on her chin from her outburst, subdued in defeat.

'There was this lad, growing up in Seven Dials,' Martha began, 'living day-in, day-out midst nothin' but whores an' thugs. One day, he saw his ma slumped 'cross the kitchen table, slewed as usual, and under her paw he spotted a tanner. Now sixpence may not sound like much, but to him it was more than he saw in a month of Sundays. So he lifted her mitt and filched the piece of silver. Gin-soaked the fishfag might be, but sixpence is sixpence, and before the lad knew it, the sodden old hag grabbed a heavy-bladed butcher's knife, pressed his hand flat on the kitchen table, chopped off his little finger and took back her coin.'

Lucy, already caught up in the story, winced. 'Oh dear, what did the poor child do?'

'Poor child, ha, that's a good'un. Well, the *poor child* didn't do nothin'. In Seven Dials you takes yer punishment and gets on with it. And that's what he did, leastways, so it seemed. He let the stump of his pinky scab over, and then, when it was more or less healed, he snaffled a bottle of gin – his ma's favourite – and left it in the kitchen. When the old fussock returned, she couldn't believe her eyes. She took a swig, settled herself at the table, and drank 'til her head sank to the table. And there she stayed, arms splayed, all alone,'cept for the watcher peeking through the window.'

'The boy?'

'Aye, the boy.'

Lucy was transfixed, Martha's story so vivid, she could picture every detail, every action as though she was right there…

The boy slips into the kitchen, sees the bottle is three-quarters empty, and picks up the same knife his mother had used on him.

'Hey, Ma. Wake up.'

The drunken slut lifts her head from the table, sees her son and smiles woozily. 'That you, lad?' she croaks hoarsely.

The youngster remains silent, edging a little closer to his mother. Sensing through the liquor-induced fog that something's wrong, the woman struggles to rouse herself, doing her best to sit upright and unclog her head. And then she sees it. The knife.

'My darlin' boy, what're yer doin' with that shiv?'

'This!' A quick flash of the blade and his mother's little finger falls away from her right hand.

'Arrrgh! Me finger!' the woman cries, shock more than pain, shaking loose the gin-pickled cobwebs dulling her senses.

'Not just yer pinky, Ma.' He presses her hand down on the table and lops off the next finger.

'NO!' She struggles to pull her hand free, but her booze-weakened efforts are no match for the boy's lust for revenge.

'Hold still, Ma. Yer makin' a real mess on the table.' So saying, he systematically works his way across the spreadeagled hand severing each remaining finger with a single clean cut until he reaches the thumb. Thumbs, it turns out, are a bit tougher and the boy has to hack at it several times before it comes away. Still not done, he moves on to the other hand. Same thing – four sharp strikes, one hefty chop, and it's fingerless.

Ten bloodied digits litter the kitchen table. Ten red rivulets trickle on to the floor. Ten bleeding stumps pulse with stinging ferocity. The terrified sot screams, 'My hands! My hands! What've you done?'

'Don't worry. Yer don't 'ave to look at 'em if yer don't want to, yer stupid slammock.' The boy jerks her head back by the hair and with a gleeful smile lighting his face gouges out one eye, then the other. The shrieks build to an agonized wail and then suddenly stop. The woman is dead.

Martha, her tale told, fell silent.

'That's such a horrible story. Whyever did you tell me?' Lucy reproached her.

'Thought you should know about the lad. Ten he was at the time. Twenty or so now, and going by the name of Fingers.'

'Fingers?' Lucy gasped. 'But that's the name of the beast who stole my takings and kicked me in the ribs.'

'Aye, same fellow. Ask me, you got off lightly. When Micus sends Fingers to do a job for him, there's usually a sight more damage than just a kick in the side.'

'You mean Mr Loman *sent* this Fingers?'

'Course he did. How d'you think Fingers found you? Waterloo Bridge, Strand end, that's what Micus told you, right? Same as he told Fingers. And that's why I told you a bit about him, 'cos if you ever cross Micus Loman, you'll have Fingers to deal with.'

Chapter Twelve: What the Post Brought

Grace, Emma Darwin's maid, picked up Wednesday's afternoon post. All for the master, as usual, and from people with the strangest names in the world – Monsieur Saint-Hillaire, Count Keyserling, Dr Schaaffhausen, Compte de Buffon. Why the master had to be involved with so many foreigners when England was full of the brightest and best was beyond her, but if it helped with his books, then she supposed it was alright.

Anyway, names didn't matter for present purposes. All she was interested in was any envelope addressed in words cut out of a newspaper like the one that came several weeks ago. That was what her mistress had told her to look out for. Nothing like that had come through the letter-box since Grace had been on watch… until today.

The envelope in her hand was much the same as any other, except for the address, each word of which had obviously been clipped from one of the dailies. The words were an odd mix of sizes, some capitals, others lowercase. Made no sense to her. Couldn't imagine anyone going to all this trouble. The vigilant correspondence-lookout stuffed the letter in her apron pocket and hurried off to find Mrs Darwin.

'Richard, where have you been?' Mrs Darwin asked an hour later. 'I've been looking for you.'

'Sorry, Mother,' he replied. 'Needed a moment to myself. Not so cold today, so I went for a walk along Father's thinking path.'

'Ah, the Sandwalk. Yes of course, I should've thought of that.' Emma

Darwin regarded her son anxiously. Outwardly, he seemed to be bearing up well, but she saw straight through his composed exterior to his inner suffering. Of all her children, she'd always had a special fondness for Richard, a mother's boy, true whether viewed from her side or his.

He almost matched his father's six feet, and his square shoulders and solid chest were only slightly less imposing. Both had beards, Charles's mostly white and intentionally unkempt, Richard's brown and neatly trimmed, as befitted a younger man.

She saw the many physical similarities and yet, even though she did her best to quash this thought, couldn't help but think of her favourite child as a rather pale image of her husband. The son's dull grey eyes lacked the father's sparkle, and his expression never matched the vivaciousness that so enlivened Charles's, especially when one of the scientist's little in-house experiments brought to light a previously unknown fact, a trivial advance in knowledge perhaps, but a genuine delight to him.

'How are you holding up?' she asked.

'It's… difficult… not knowing where she is.'

'I know, my dear. But there's been a… a development. Please prepare yourself, the news is not—'

'Mother, tell me!' Richard was transformed, the sad-eyed pup suddenly a restless watchdog.

'Of course, my dear. You see, we've received another… another anonymous letter.'

'What? Where is it?' Richard looked around wildly, eyes darting left and right, until he spotted the sheet of notepaper held tight to his mother's skirt. 'Is that it? Let me see!'

'My son, be warned,' pleaded Mrs Darwin, 'it's so… so shocking.'

Richard was not to be stopped no matter what she said or did. He snatched it from her, skimmed the newspaper words, and sank to the floor, blood draining from his cheeks. Mrs Darwin hurried to him, knelt beside him and gently rocked him in her arms.

'Richard,' she murmured, 'don't despair. Think what this means. Don't you see? She's *alive*.'

'Alive, yes, but in such danger. I… I don't see how we can hope to save her. It's father's work, his lifetime's labour. I cannot ask him to throw it a—'

'Hush, my son, it's done. Or almost. Your father is in his study drafting a letter for The Times this very minute. There was never any hesitation, not even for a second. He'd do anything for you and Henrietta. He says you're to take it to London first thing tomorrow, and also take this… this atrocity…' she stabbed a finger at the note still in Richard's hand, 'to Inspector Fickett. And, for my peace of mind, please share this development with Mr Line, the private inquiry agent I hired, whom I believe is also in London. Are you up to travelling?'

'Of course, it's the least I can do, trifling compared to Papa's… sacrifice, all his achievements since the Beagle voyage, thirty years of work. I must go to him at once and thank him with all my heart, though words can never fully express a gratitude as profound as mine.'

'Yes, go to him. It will mean so much to him.'

Mother and son helped each other up. Richard, with a look on his face that was more hopeful than she'd seen since his wife's disappearance, returned the note to her and hurried off to his father's study. Mrs Darwin placed the obscenity on a side table, picked up two other sheets of paper and rang the bell for Grace.

'Yes, ma'am. What can I—' Seeing her mistress's distress, the maid stopped in mid-sentence. 'Ma'am, what's the matter?'

'Nothing to worry about,' replied Mrs Darwin, her eyes brimming with tears. 'I need you to send these telegrams for me.' She struggled to keep her voice steady. 'This… this one is to go straight to Inspector Fickett at Scotland Yard. And this one to Mr Line. He's in London, staying, I believe at The Golden Cross Inn.'

'Yes, ma'am.' She took the telegrams from Mrs Darwin. 'Anything else, ma'am?'

'No, no, thank you, Grace,' said Mrs Darwin, feeling the tears well up again. 'That will be all. I just… need to lie down for a few moments.' She hurried out of the drawing room, desperate for the sanctuary of her bedroom, knocking the foul letter to the carpet as she brushed past the side table. Grace swooped on the fallen correspondence like a kingfisher plucking its breakfast from the river, but fast though she was, her mistress had already left the room.

Grace was totally committed to the Darwin family. She never pried into their private affairs but at the same time she always strove to help them in whatever way she could. Note in hand, she stood there, frowning, the needle of her moral compass seemingly stuck midway between the two competing dictates. Several moments passed before the indecision that had clouded her face suddenly vanished.

One quick glance was enough to reveal what had so upset her mistress – six lines of ugly, cut-out words pasted on the innocent white of a single piece of Athenaeum Club stationery. This was what she read:

> *You HAVE been warned*
> *now you MUST act!*
> *Retract your blasphemous THEORY*
> *in a LETTER to The Times*
> *BEFORE January's end.*
> *Or YOUR daughter-in-law will PERISH!*

Chapter Thirteen: Lucy in Titchfield

arly evening on the day after Martha's bedtime story, Loman cornered Lucy and informed her she'd be out on the street that night. 'Graduated from flowers to favours, you have,' he snarled.

'NEVER!' screamed Lucy, charging the whoremaster and ripping at his face until blood spurted from both cheeks. A victory for her, for sure, but short-lived. In seconds, Fingers appeared and had Lucy pinned to the floor.

'Shove the soddin' hellcat back in the attic,' ordered an enraged Loman. 'Let's see how the little slut feels about servicing some of London's young stallions after a few days with no food.'

A terrified Lucy spent the next hour curled up on her pallet, incapable of fashioning any plan of action, her wild imagining of a whore's life quashing all rational thought. Her mind was bombarded with visions of naked limbs, frantically thrusting and bucking; freakishly engorged members with massive, purple heads; and, worst of all, her own face, twisted and flushed by her efforts to resist her loathsome abusers and their urgent writhing.

Deliverance finally came in the form of her son, the only one who could rescue her from her despair, as she must rescue him. His plight snapped her to her senses. Lucy knew what she had to do.

Later that night, she carefully made her way down the ladder, and sat at the top of the stairs, listening for the whores to return. It was past midnight when she heard Martha greeting the first with a callous *How much d'you make, then?* Callous, but exactly what Lucy had hoped for. She caught the clink, clink of coins dropping into a tin canister, and then the sound of tin on wood as it was placed on a shelf. She had all she needed. She made her way back up to the loft, crossed to her mattress and slid beneath sheet and blanket, face to the wall.

The girls straggled in and went straight to bed, barely stopping to remove their outerwear, thankful to crawl under the flimsy covers, close their eyes and seek the oblivion of sleep, free from the brutality of the streets and the stench of men. Lucy waited a full hour after the last arrival had drifted off, and then, still wearing the dark green dress borrowed from Loman's 'daughter' and the shawl from the workhouse, she tiptoed to the ladder, barely breathing lest she wake one of the sleeping whores. No one stirred.

She climbed down the ladder quiet as a mouse, and then took the stairs, stopping on each one to listen anxiously for any sound. The last thing she wanted was to bump into any night owls and especially not Loman, or worse yet Fingers. She moved cautiously into the kitchen and immediately spotted the canister on the shelf. She took out the handkerchief she'd found in the pocket of the green dress, laid it on the table, and then carefully removed the coins, one by one, from the tin and placed them noiselessly on the square of linen.

She didn't stop to count the money but it looked to be at least two and possibly three pounds in silver. She tied the four corners of the handkerchief together, replaced the canister on the shelf, and was about to leave when she spun around. A footfall! Was that a footfall? Lucy was not going to wait to find out. She grabbed her spoils and rushed to the front door, not caring now if anyone heard her. She wrenched back the bolt, heaved the heavy door open, and stepped out into the cold but safe night air of Brew Crescent.

By seven o'clock, Lucy was sitting in a third class, open-topped carriage on the early morning train to Southampton, the nearest stop to Titchfield. Pleased with the tidy sum found in the tin canister, tummy full of hot Cornish pasty, and lulled by the pulsing monotony of iron wheels clunking over the track's joints, she slipped into a half-doze. She couldn't believe how easy it had been to walk off with the night's profits. Sweet revenge for all of Loman's lies and mistreatment. Friend indeed! She'd been an utter fool. But she'd got the better of him and was well on her way to her baby.

Tired though she was, her worries wouldn't let her rest. It should be straightforward to walk to Titchfield and find Mrs Moranda Sayter of Rose Petal Cottage, but then what? Bribe the woman to hand over her son? Perhaps, but how much would that cost? And wouldn't Lucy need all her money to feed and shelter the two of them until they found some permanent arrangement? There had to be some other way. Maybe there was… maybe Martha's story about Fingers and how he exacted revenge on his mother… yes, that might work for her.

Lucy exited Southampton Docks Railway Station and set off on her eight-mile walk. It was approaching one o'clock when she spied a small country inn, The Badger's Sett, no more than a mile or so from her destination. Time to put her plan into action, and time also for food and drink, unsure as she was when the next opportunity to recharge might arrive.

Not much sign of life, but the door opened easily enough and she went in to the ringing of a bell. The dark room was totally deserted and sparsely furnished – a pair of tables with mismatched chairs; a bench along one wall; a narrow serving hatch, top half open; and a fireplace, its logs unlit despite the cold. Was the establishment closed? Out of business? Both suppositions were quickly proven wrong when the lower half of the hatch swung open and the innkeeper stepped in.

A burly man with a mop of shaggy hair and ruddy complexion, he looked as though he'd spent his life working in the fields rather than pulling pints. He regarded Lucy with interest. 'Durn't 'ave 'ardly a customer this time o' day,' he began. 'Nor 'ardly a one of the fair sex, neither,' he added, continuing his inspection of this unexpected arrival.

'No, I suppose not,' volunteered Lucy, not sure how to conduct herself in what was evidently a night-time watering hole for locals of the non-fair variety. 'If it's not too much trouble,' she finally said, 'I was hoping I could have something to eat and drink. Whatever you—'

'Durn't 'ave much by way of food,' interrupted the proprietor. 'Could see what the missus has if you like. Pork chop, maybe. And a glass of porter. Or a shandy-gaff may suit you better.' Before she could answer, the man disappeared back through the hatch, only to reappear a moment later. 'Pork chop, 'taters an' carrots, how does that sound?'

'Just right, and a shandy-gaff, please.' The last thing she wanted was a heavy porter that would dull her senses for the rest of the day. She sat down at one of the tables, running her fingers through her hair, straightening her dress, doing everything she could to make herself as presentable as possible before her encounter with Mrs Sayter.

Chop and shandy-gaff were soon served and Lucy began her meal, only slightly put off when the landlord joined her at her table. 'Durn't 'ave many visitors in this part of the world,' he said with an inquiring look.

Lucy pondered how much to reveal, quickly deciding that he probably knew everyone in the area and might be of use to her. 'Well, I'm looking for Mrs Moranda Sayter.'

'Moranda Sayter, you say. That'ud be Rose Petal Cottage. Keep going on this road 'bout two hundred yards. Turn right and you'll find the cottage no more than half mile 'long Badger's Lane.'

'Oh, thank you so much. Do you know Mrs Sayter well?'

'Durn't 'ave much to do with the lady, but her old man's in 'ere most nights. Pub's only place he can get a bit of peace an' quiet. Can't stand the wailing an' howling of all them foundlings his missus got stuffed in the back room, the Pig Pen as he calls it. Little buggers are half-starved and sick with the fevers most of the time. Scores of 'em, not just one or two but *scores* of 'em, met their Maker in Moranda's Pig Pen, and glad to do so.'

The Pig Pen! Lucy listened with a stony face. It was over a week since Beadle Tonks, as Eyesore Annie had called the overseer of Shoreditch Workhouse, had sent the newborn to Titchfield. If Mrs Satan, her name for Mrs Sayter, had breathed even one foul breath on her child, then the woman, Lucifer's wife or not, would have more than the Devil to deal with, vowed Lucy.

The conversation drifted on for a while but she learned nothing more of interest and, her meal finished and bill settled, she told the innkeeper she'd like to make a purchase. Fearful that the man would begin with one of his *Durn't 'ave* pronouncements and put an end to her scheming before it had even begun, she sighed with relief when he readily handed over what she'd asked for. The payment made, she got back on the road.

Her purposeful stride soon brought her to the turning and, half a mile later, she found herself in front of a delightful, straw-thatched, single-storey dwelling. Several rose bushes stood in narrow strips of garden each side of the porch, their branches bare now, but in full bloom their blossoms would be a magnificent sight and ample justification for the cottage's name.

As she approached, she heard angry shouting from within. When she knocked on the door, it was thrown open. A blowsy, grey-haired woman stood at the threshold, rolling pin in hand, ready to deliver a wits-scrambling clout to any annoyance in her path, including Lucy.

'Wot d'you want, then?' she demanded.

Lucy took a step back before beginning her well-rehearsed fabrication. 'Mrs Sayter? I'm here on behalf of Beadle Tonks, superintendent of Shoreditch Workhouse.'

Sometimes, one word can transform a person's demeanour. On this occasion, Tonks was that word.

'Oh my dear Lord, whatever is the matter? Dear lady, tell me at once.'

'Calm yourself, Mrs Sayter, I'm just here to inspect your recent arrivals. Nothing amiss, purely routine, I assure you. In fact, the beadle thinks so highly of you and your fine establishment that he asked me to bring you a small gift in recognition of all you do for the less fortunate amongst us.' Lucy produced the bottle of gin she'd bought at the inn.

'Well, 'pon my word,' replied Mrs Sayter, 'this is most unexpected. I'd ask you in, my dear, but 'fraid it ain't very tidy at the moment, ain't had a second all day to get to me reg'lar chores, and the little dears haven't had their mornin' meal neither, so perhaps you'd like to come back—'

'Quite unnecessary,' Lucy interrupted. 'Been in this business long enough to understand these matters. No cause to worry about me.' And with that she headed straight for the back room.

It was the foulest place she'd ever seen. Seven young children dressed in the meanest rags lay in their own filth, so emaciated she could see every bone through their wafer-thin skin. The stench was overpowering, but worse was the blank expression on the orphans' wasted faces, removing them from this world as surely as if they were already in the next.

She spotted a wooden crate on the floor, and there, wrapped in a gunny sack on a mess of sodden straw, face scrunched, eyes shut tight, breathing laboured, was a tiny baby.

'Thank you so much, Mrs Sayter,' she said, fighting to control herself. 'I believe I've seen everything I need to see and can promise you that I will deliver a very satisfactory report to Beadle Tonks. Please enjoy the gift he sent you. Good day to you.'

Lucy quickly left the cottage, sickened by the sight of the seven cadavers-in-waiting, and her little one in their midst. She sank to her knees, heaving and retching, meat, potatoes and carrots somersaulting and cart-wheeling their way out of her stomach and onto the verge.

Her belly emptied, the intestinal violence subsided, leaving her shaking and sobbing. Gathering her strength, she struggled back to her feet, only to be struck rigid with fear. There, standing right in front of her, was Fingers.

Chapter Fourteen: Mivart's Other Motive

Line observed Richard Darwin closely as the man entered the foyer of The Golden Cross Inn on Cecil Street on Thursday morning and introduced himself. Mrs Darwin had sent a telegram yesterday informing him that her son would be in London today and requesting his indulgence to meet with him. Line had willingly agreed, and Richard had arrived promptly at eleven o'clock.

In his late thirties, Richard's most distinctive facial feature was a well-kept brown beard. His eyes, often downcast or directed sideways, were a lacklustre grey; his nose, set between flat cheekbones, was medium-sized and the colour of putty, and his mouth narrow and weak, a poor copy of his mother's warm and caring version. But then again, he was hardly likely to be looking his best in the present circumstances.

Once the cloakroom attendant had taken Richard's overcoat and hat, they settled themselves at a small table in the hotel's parlour, and, coffee served, Richard explained the reason for his visit – the arrival at Down House of a ransom demand. He'd left the note with Inspector Fickett earlier that morning, but from his description – Athenaeum notepaper, words cut out of The Times, posted in London, unsigned – it sounded suspiciously similar to the anonymous letter the Darwins had received in late December.

'Can you tell me what it said?' asked Line.

Richard proceeded to recite its contents as though he knew them by heart: 'You have been warned. Now you must act. Retract your blasphemous theory in a letter to The Times before January's end or your daughter-in-law will perish.'

Line noted no reference to Aesculapius, the 'clue' leading Fickett to the ridiculous conclusion that Richard Darwin was the writer. No, this demand pointed directly to George Mivart, the holier-than-thou convert, who expected everyone to adhere to the strictest interpretation of his freshly acquired faith.

Richard, it turned out, was of like mind. 'As Mother told you, he's in a nasty dispute with Father, but that's not all. You see, Mivart was also romantically involved with my wife's sister, Estelle Moxley.'

Line would've welcomed a minute or two to digest this news but Richard continued speaking.

'According to Henrietta, and she's very close to her sister, the relationship was serious, although not to the point where talk of engagement was in the air. But then, in December, when Father and his colleagues were doing their utmost to blackball Mivart from the Athenaeum, poor Estelle, feeling she had no option but to side with her sister's in-laws, severed all links with him. Apparently, he was furious, saw it as an unwarranted rebuff of his honourable intentions towards her and hasn't spoken to her since.'

'Thank you for sharing this sad history with me,' Line said. 'It's not my place to comment on Miss Moxley's action, but it does provide Mivart with a second reason for harming your family, one possibly more powerful than the academic dispute. Did you convey all this to Inspector Fickett?'

'No,' he replied. 'The inspector ended our meeting before I had a chance to do so.'

'Well, he needs to know. I'll try to see him this afternoon.'

'That would be most kind of you,' Richard said. 'I'm staying in London for a day or two if you need to follow up with me. But now, sir, if you'll excuse me, I have an appointment with the editor of The Times. I want to make sure that Father's retraction appears in Monday's edition, well before the end-January deadline.'

Line arrived at Scotland Yard at two o'clock, and this time was ushered straight into Fickett's office. Not bothering to remove his greatcoat, he took the chair in front of the desk, dispensed with the usual pleasantries and immediately laid out the case against Mivart beginning with the ransom demand, exactly what someone in a heated dispute with Darwin over evolution would send, and then moving on to Mivart's additional motive – the estrangement between him and Henrietta's sister.

Fickett, looking as officious as ever in full uniform, couldn't have had any inkling of the second but he showed no sign of surprise. The annoying fellow remained silent for a moment, probably turning over in his mind what he'd just heard, searching for some way of acknowledging with as little embarrassment as possible that he was wrong about Richard, and his predecessor right about Mivart.

'Well, thank you for bringing these snippets of… gossip… to my attention. Let me see if I have it right. According to you, a petty academic dispute about some fanciful theory of evolution that will be forgotten in a few years, has led one of the participants, a well-respected biologist, to resort to kidnapping. I'm not a scholarly man myself, but squabbles like this pop up all the time in the scientific community, without resulting in the mayhem you suspect.'

Line couldn't believe his ears. Time to put the little twerp in his place. 'That's n—'

'Then,' continued the little twerp, 'there's the unfortunate breakup. Let me stress that relationships with the fair sex are not an area where I claim special expertise, but tiffs between those in the throes of love happen every day of the week, and are often made up in no time at all.'

'Tiff? It's much more than—'

'In sum, *Mr* Line,' carried on the policeman, 'a minor disagreement between men of science, and a courting couple's falling-out, lead in your mind to kidnapping and ransom demands. Forgive me if I say this sounds rather melodramatic, not what I would call the result of sound detective work. Frankly, when you analyse it carefully, it all seems quite flimsy, but, and this is the most important point, it's *exactly* what the *real* perpetrator wants you to believe.'

'Real perpetrator? Who d'you mean?'

'Why, Richard Darwin of course.'

'Richard Darwin? How—'

'Yes, a very clever fellow. Let me explain.' Fickett was almost drooling. 'As I told you, I saw a guilty look on young Darwin's face when he learned I'd not fallen for the obviously manufactured suicide story, and was instead treating his wife's disappearance as an abduction. Of course, he'd hoped this would not happen, but just in case, he'd written that first anonymous letter, the one that arrived at Down House on December 24, to cast suspicion on Mivart. I explained this to you at our last meeting… yes?'

Line remembered perfectly, but was not going to admit it to this maddening pest.

'That,' lectured Fickett, 'was just a back-up, to be brought into play if the fake suicide didn't stand scrutiny. Well, it didn't, and the contingency plan became his only chance of saving his skin. Hence the second anonymous letter with its explicit ransom demand, intended to convince the gullible that Mivart was the perpetrator.'

Gullible! Line was nettled by Fickett's disparaging insinuation, but worse was to come.

'Mistakes, Mr Line, like shooting innocent young girls in the back, must be avoided at all costs. Don't you agree?'

Fickett had chosen his point of attack well. The maid's death by Line's hand was unquestionably accidental, but from that day forward Line's soul was scarred, scored by a wrong he could never right. Slipping his hand into his jacket pocket, Line sought the silver medallion. He squeezed his talismanic keepsake, but didn't feel the strength that normally flowed through the coin from those whose initials – R and M – were engraved in its metal. Fickett's poisonous dart had pierced his inner armour and found its mark.

But Line was Line, and he was not about to give the son of a whore the satisfaction of seeing the pain he'd caused, even though it took all his willpower to maintain his give-nothing-away, dead-eyed expression, his Death Mask as a former colleague once called it. He couldn't hold back, though, from firing off a quick riposte, aimed at the first weakness he saw in his opponent's argument. In a measured tone that belied his burning desire to rip out the inspector's tongue, he said, 'But Richard Darwin was at Down House when the ransom note was posted in London.'

Fickett took his time before responding, regarding over steepled hands the man he was about to squash.

'Indeed, Mr Line, you're correct, but Richard Darwin could have prepared the ransom note at Down House, sent it by messenger to his henchmen in London and have them post it back to Down House. Diverts suspicion from him.'

Line cursed silently. He'd blundered, broken one of his cardinal rules – look before you leap. Goaded by the pipsqueak's cruel barb, he'd leapt without even a glance and landed in a pile of shit.

'That, I believe you will agree,' Fickett continued, 'is a much more plausible explanation. Jumping to the obvious conclusion – that Mivart sent the ransom note – is something even our novices are trained to be wary of, a lesson of special importance in this particular case because the obvious conclusion is exactly what Richard wants everyone to believe.' The inspector smiled, apparently considering it unnecessary to add, *and you, sir, fell for it*.

Damn his eyes, Line swore to himself. Obvious conclusion? Of course it's the obvious conclusion, because that's what most likely happened. Mivart, you silly ass, has an *obvious* motive, two in fact, whereas Richard Darwin has nothing remotely like one. Line stood, bid the inspector good day and left.

Exiting the Yard, he strode briskly along White Hall towards the Strand and The Golden Cross Inn. Fickett's cutting remark would rankle for a long while, but he pushed it aside and turned his mind to the interview's substance. Fickett was obviously set on nabbing Richard, gunning for him, Line suspected, because convicting the son of Charles Darwin would garner much bigger headlines than collaring a second-tier biologist like Mivart. Nothing but a convincing explanation of how Mivart conjured Henrietta Darwin out of a locked-tight Down House, if in fact he did, was going to change that donkey's mind, and Line still had no idea how that stunt was pulled off.

He knew that eventually he'd find out what lay behind the trickery, but where to begin? Perhaps Dunston will have one of his *pre*-ductions as Line jokingly called them. He smiled at the thought, but didn't dismiss it out of hand. They were not what Line considered proper deductions since they jumped well beyond the known facts, but he'd seen first hand how Dunston's mind could join the dots in new ways, and even conjure up as yet *unseen* dots to create a picture invisible to everyone else.

One of Dunston's out-of-nowhere insights in the Ellen Ternan case had in fact revealed the motive behind the London actress's murder, the key to solving the case. At first, Line had attributed Dunston's revelation to a sixth sense, but after two more of his pre-ductions had proven embarrassingly wrong, on both occasions accusing perfectly innocent men of the crime, he'd demoted it to no more than an extra *half* sense. He smiled again.

His musings brought him to his hotel. He settled himself in the parlour and wrote up his report of the day's meetings. Satisfied with his account, he placed it in a manila folder; put that in a large brown envelope; and addressed it to Dunston at Meadowlark Cottage. If he posted it now, Dunston would have it tomorrow morning, and, who knows, perhaps it would spark something in that strange brain of his.

Chapter Fifteen: The Pig Pen

For the second time in four days, Lucy found herself face down on the cold ground after an encounter with Fingers. This time, though, she was seriously bruised and battered... and cut. Fingers had held her while his mate punched her face and torso with powerful, full-swing blows. When Fingers felt her slump, he threw her to the ground, added a kick to the stomach for good measure, and slipped his knife out of his pocket.

Lucy watched through one eye, the other already closing, as he spread her right hand on the path, and with one stroke sliced off her index finger close to the knuckle. 'Fingers by name, fingers by trade,' he said, tossing the severed piece of flesh and bone into the woods. He wiped his knife on her dress and tipped his bowler hat, his customary salute to those short of a digit or two thanks to his efforts. Then, with a nod to his bruiser crony and a warning to Lucy never to let him catch her in London, he sauntered off.

A full hour passed before Lucy, cold and numb, struggled to a sitting position, trying to gather her wits. She checked gingerly with her left hand for broken bones, none as far as she could tell, but the pain in her chest and stomach felt as though iron-hard fingertips were digging deep into her flesh. Her right hand, blood still oozing from the stub of her index finger, the knuckle already badly swollen, wouldn't be of much use for several days. She wrapped a piece of linen torn from her dress over the wound and around her palm, closing her hand over it to hold it in place. That would have to do for now.

How could they have tracked her down so quickly? Loman! The only one to know about Titchfield. He must have sent them after her as soon as Martha discovered she, and the night's earnings, were missing. Martha had warned her. Loman, she'd said, always makes sure that any girl stepping out of line gets *a proper larruping*. She should've listened. Too late now, his message – never mess with Micus Loman – had been viciously delivered and painfully received.

She reached out, searching for her purse. It was gone, and with it the takings she'd stolen from the brothel. She'd intended to spend the night, at least the first part of it, at The Badger's Sett, before carrying out the rest of her plan but that was no longer possible. What could she do? She was within a stone's throw of her precious son, but, penniless, pummelled and one-handed, how could she possibly save him?

All she could think of was her baby in that foul crate, barely breathing, barely alive, but slowly despair gave way to anger, and anger turned into a mother's determination to rescue her offspring no matter what the cost. The first part of the ploy borrowed from Fingers – giving the gin to Mrs Sayter – was already done; the next called for her to break in through the Pig Pen's backdoor, collect her son and walk straight back out before the drunken sot knew what was happening. But how could she force entry with only one working hand? There *had* to be a way.

She pictured the room again, this time searching every detail until she remembered what had struck her as odd. Bolts were placed on the inside of doors to keep intruders out and protect the householder's belongings within, but she'd not seen any sign of one on the Pig Pen's backdoor. Then it hit her... the bolt was on the *outside*. That was it! Occupants of Mrs Sayter's personal Hades would take the first chance to scarper if they weren't locked in. And no fear of anyone breaking in to steal them. Or so thought Mrs Sayter. But she hadn't bargained on Lucy Kinsley.

If she was right, she didn't have to break through a door; all she had to do was pull back a bolt. Even one-handed, she could do that. But first she had to find somewhere to keep warm and conserve her strength until it was time to move. The temperature had fallen ten degrees with the arrival of darkness and would only fall further. Where could she go?

The shack! She'd seen it just past the turning into Badger's Lane, a flimsy construction, not likely to provide much shelter, but better than staying in the open with only a shawl to protect her from the winter cold. She struggled to her feet and hobbled towards the hut. It was more dilapidated than she'd thought, obviously no longer used, but she pushed open the wooden door and collapsed onto a bundle of sacks on the floor. Now she must wait.

When she reckoned it was almost midnight, she summoned all her strength, stepped stiffly out into the frigid night air, and made her way back to the cottage. She peeped in the front window and saw Mrs Sayter in her chair in the front parlour, passed out, just like Fingers' mother, the now-empty gin bottle lying at her feet. The Beadle's 'gift' had done its work. She looked in the next window, the bedroom, and saw Mr Sayter, fully dressed, flat out on the bed, noisily sleeping off another long evening in The Badger's Sett.

She stole around to the back of the house. And there was the bolt, as she'd suspected. Rust and a shaking hand conspired against her for several minutes, but finally she slid it back, opened the door and stepped inside. None of the seven coffin-candidates even moved. She would leave the door open for them, though she doubted it would do them much good. She grabbed her son, pressed him to her bosom, and hurried back to the shack. There, she examined her sweet child, kissed his filthy, beautiful face for the very first time, and loved him like no mother had ever loved her child.

Chapter Sixteen: A Scream in the Night

Thursday's late-night prayer meeting at the People's Mission Hall in Whitechapel Road didn't end until after midnight. Mrs Geraldine Hawksby, the charity's meals lady, had not meant to stay so late but, having done so, she was anxious to get home to her family as quickly as possible. She'd kept to the main roads, fairly safe even at this late hour, but prompted by the bite of winter cold, she'd opted for a shortcut that took her along Upper East Smithfield and dangerously close to the Thames waterfront, a risky choice, given the frequent robberies and murders bedevilling that neighbourhood.

Mrs Hawksby's scream began its journey from lungs to throat as she was passing Nightingale Lane, a squalid little passage running down to the Thames, desolate and forbidding at any time of day but especially so in the small hours. She took a quick, nervous glance down towards the river-end of the alley and there, caught in a shaft of pale, wintry moonlight, she saw what looked like a pair of drunken revellers brawling on the ground, the one in a dress, flat on her back, the other, a man, bent over her, but that notion was rapidly dispelled by the vicious blows raining down upon the woman's spreadeagled body. No, this was a beating, with deadly intent.

The scream stalled in Mrs Hawksby's windpipe, her vocal cords fright-frozen into temporary paralysis. Mouth agape, she watched as the assailant hammered the undefended head with a stout club, each blow landing with a sickening thud. The attacker shifted focus to the torso and Mrs Hawksby heard a cracking sound, collar bone perhaps, or rib, and then he moved down to the poor wretch's stomach, splitting open the woman's gut, blood and bile spattering clubber and clubbed alike.

Mrs Hawksby's scream finally entered the world of sound midway through the wooden cudgel's bone-crunching assault on the victim's hips, the left joint already crushed, the right about to receive similar treatment. Her piercing screech burst jarringly into the otherwise silent January night but apart from a slight upward tilt of the thug's head to detect its source, his attention remained focused on his prey.

The shrill, unmistakable blast of a police whistle, though, was a different matter. He dropped the bloodied bludgeon, grabbed the woman's left hand, tugged something free, and shoved it in his jacket pocket. Collecting his club, he set off along the river, ducked down a side street and disappeared.

Chapter Seventeen: Dunston's Investigation

T he postman was brushing snow off his boots outside The Queen's Head when he saw Gabby walking in his direction along High Street.

'M-m-morning, G-gabby,' he stammered.

'Arse,' replied Gabby with a friendly nod.

Arse might not sound like a very polite salutation, but it was considered a perfectly acceptable way of addressing the postman. Burdened with a severe stutter, he'd never been able to pronounce his given name – Robert – without the prefix R-R-R, leading the villagers to call him 'Rs'. Robert accepted his fate, thankful his surname wasn't Hole.

'G-going near Meadowlark Cottage, Gabby? C-could deliver this one for me if you was.' The postman was holding up a large brown envelope.

Seeing a chance to earn an easy sixpence from Line's roly-poly guest, Gabby wordlessly took the packet and set off in the direction of Meadowlark Cottage.

'Yours,' he said on arriving at Line's cottage ten minutes later.

'Thank you.' Dunston handed over the requisite fee. 'Most kind.'

It was early Friday morning and Dunston was still in his white nightshirt and paisley dressing gown, having only just finished breakfast. He'd read Line's account of the interview with Grace on Tuesday, immediately after his encounter with Mrs Darwin in the churchyard. And ditto the third report detailing the testy meeting between the former Chief of Detectives and his successor on Wednesday. This would be a further update. He shut the door after Gabby's departure, sat back down at the kitchen table and quickly opened the envelope. The enclosed fourth report briefly documented Line's meeting with Richard Darwin and then, more fully, his second encounter with his nemesis, Inspector Fickett.

An hour later Dunston closed the folder, grumbling to himself that Fickett had turned all of Line's evidence upside down while persisting with his own inverted view of events. The ransom demand and the break-up with Estelle Moxley made a compelling case that Mivart was the kidnapper, yet Fickett still had his sights set on Richard Darwin.

Which of them – Richard Darwin or George Mivart – is the guilty party will not be known, Dunston feared, until someone figures out how Henrietta Darwin was conjured out of Down House. Time perhaps for an amateur to step in and show the professionals how to solve this apparently insoluble mystery.

Dunston was rational enough to know that it was not some English Ali Baba with a fairy-tale 'Open-Sesame' password who magicked his way in and out of Down House. No, there had to be some way of accounting for what happened without resorting to fantasy, and Dunston intended to find it. And when he did, he'd impress his stumped detective-friend not with the forty thieves' treasure trove, but with something even more priceless – a wonderfully simple explanation for the otherwise inexplicable.

In Dunston's mind, there were only two possibilities: either Down House was entered and exited by some means other than the backdoor; or the backdoor key was removed from the vanity and then later replaced without using the two brass figures. Time to take a leaf out of Line's book and find the hard evidence – Line's gold standard – in favour of one explanation or the other. Yes, Dunston thought, should have this all wrapped up and ready to present to him on his return.

Dunston completed his daily ablutions, dressed, donned his overcoat and tweed deerstalker, and exited Meadowlark Cottage. A short stroll into the village and Dunston found his first 'source' in The Queen's Head exactly as expected.

'Good morning, Gabby.'

'G'day,' replied the village layabout. He was seated at a corner table in the dimly lit pub, a half empty tankard of ale in his hand, Dunston's sixpence evidently having been put to good use.

Gabby may not have any useful purpose in life, but he knew everything about the village, and about Down House. Hence, Dunston's interest in him. Dunston explained what he wanted to know. Gabby eyed him sourly and, true to form, held out his hand and said, 'Sixpence.'

The payment made, Gabby replied in his usual one-word style, 'Bed—'

'Bed?' queried the keyed-up fact-finder. 'Whatever to you mean?'

'...rock.'

'Rock? Ahhh... bedrock.'

'Aye.'

'Mmmm, I think I understand,' said Dunston glumly. And indeed he did. Since the snow around the house was undisturbed except for that single set of footprints outside the backdoor, none of the other doors or windows could have been used to enter and exit Down House. Dunston had, therefore, been banking on a secret underground tunnel, but a layer of bedrock beneath the house effectively ruled that out. No, the only way in and out for the kidnappers was through the backdoor.

'Yes, well, thank you anyway.' Dunston visibly drooped as he spoke, folding in on himself like a collapsing soufflé.

Gabby nodded, and, tankard in hand, made for the bar and a refill.

Dunston took his leave, disappointed that his sixpenny investment had yielded nothing by way of return. But then he took heart. Gabby's information may have eliminated one hypothesis, but that only meant the explanation must lie in the other. Dunston set off for Down House to confirm that the backdoor key could be accessed without using the his and her brass figures.

His knock at the front door was answered by a maid who, on inquiry, turned out to be Grace, the young girl mentioned in Line's second report. This bodes well, thought Dunston, sure now that he'd soon have everything tied up to his satisfaction, and to Line's.

'Sorry, sir, but madam's out and the master's not receiving, one of his poorly days,' she informed him.

'That's alright. This is not a social call,' Dunston replied and quickly explained the purpose of his visit, adding that he was acting on behalf of Mrs Darwin's private inquiry agent, Mr Line. A bending of the truth, perhaps, but in Dunston's view no more than a slight, well-intentioned deviation from the straight and narrow.

'Sorry, sir,' she said for the second time, 'but peelers had the same idea, and they had no luck.'

'Yes, well, that's the police for you. Perhaps if I could have a look...'

With a quick curtsey, Grace turned and led him upstairs to her mistress's bedroom. Dunston entered and immediately saw the ornately decorated vanity to the left of the bed.

Dunston smiled confidently and stepped up to the dressing table, con-vinced he'd find that the cubbyhole had been jimmied open. He began with the front panel, scrutinising it inch by inch. Not a mark or scratch anywhere. Next, he inspected the underside of the vanity; no sign of it being forced open. Then he pulled out the drawers and examined the panelling adjoining the cubbyhole; the wood on both sides was unmarked, not a nick or dent to be seen. Finally, he studied each of the slots. Neither had been tampered with.

'Police did all that, sir. They didn't find anything either.'

'Must be a secret catch then.'

Grace smiled. Dunston set to.

He checked everywhere: pressed every knot in the wood; fiddled with each of the handles on the drawers; probed the frame of the mirror; poked any odd bits of pattern in the Oriental designs carved into the wood. No matter what he did, the panel refused to drop.

'Police did that, too. Didn't find a sausage, same as you,' said Grace primly.

'Yes, well, thank you anyway,' Dunson said for the second time that morning, and, noticeably red-faced, look his leave.

Detection is a bit trickier than I thought, Dunston conceded, as he walked back to Meadowlark Cottage. All I've done is make Henrietta's mysterious exit from Down House all the more mysterious. Still, searching for evidence is Line's cup of tea, not mine. Should leave that to him, and give my mind free rein, let it wander around this seeming impossibility unencumbered by bothersome facts. Something is sure to pop up.

Chapter Eighteen: The Locket

You wanted to see me, Fickett?' asked Metropolitan Police Commissioner Sir Edmund Henderson. In a double-breasted, dark frock coat and high-collared white shirt, he was seated at his desk in his office at Scotland Yard.

'Yes, sir,' replied Inspector Fickett, dressed, as usual, in his navy-blue uniform. 'Two developments in the Darwin business.'

'Very well. Better sit down and tell me what's going on. But be sharp about it. Important dinner engagement this evening.'

Perfect, thought Fickett. He'd intentionally left it until late on Friday afternoon, hoping the commissioner would pay only cursory attention to what he had to say. Henderson, or Lamb Chops as he was called on account of the bushy whiskers decorating each cheek, had always struck the inspector as crusty and stilted, still stuck in his army ways and lacking any understanding of modern policing methods. But the man was his superior, at least for now.

Fickett sat down on the single wooden chair in front of the no-frills desk and wondered again why the most senior man in London's constabulary was content with such barracks-austere furnishings. When I'm Her Majesty's top officer, I'll have the most imposing desk in all of England, Fickett vowed.

'First item's a body, sir, female,' he began. 'Found down by the waterfront.'

'Dead bodies by the river, female or not, turn up every day. Hardly a matter you need bother me with.' The commissioner gave him a practiced arch of an eyebrow.

Fickett tensed. Need to tread carefully here. Must keep the old boy on my side. Don't want him closing down my investigation of Richard Darwin. What a coup if I can nail that fellow for murder, not just a feather in my cap, but a whole Cherokee chief's headdress gracing my brow.

The inspector intended to bring Henderson up to date while leaving him totally in the dark regarding his suspicions of Richard Darwin. No need to share his thoughts with the commissioner just yet; better to wait until he had all his ducks in a row and the guilty party gift-wrapped ready for the noose, only way to keep Lamb Chops from stealing the glory.

'Of course, sir,' he replied quickly. 'But this body may be of some interest. Killing happened in the early hours of this morning in Nightingale Lane according to the constable on patrol. When the doctor – sharp-eyed fellow – examined the corpse, he found this locket in the pocket of the woman's dress. Judging by the mark on her neck, he reckons it must've been yanked off during the struggle and then probably dropped, giving her a chance to recover it and hide it away.'

Henderson was not one for jewellery – cheapened ladies and impoverished gentlemen in his view – and showed little interest in the heart-shaped trinket Fickett handed him. He opened it nonetheless, and saw a man's portrait on one side and a woman's on the other, typical of the silly mementos society wasted its money on. 'What exactly am I supposed to make of this?' There was more than a hint of impatience in his voice.

'Thought you might recognise them. The gentleman is Richard Darwin—'

'Good Lord! Charles Darwin's son?'

'The same, sir. I've met him twice now, once at Down House and then yesterday at the Yard. And the lady is almost certainly—'

'The missing wife.'

'Yes, sir, Henrietta. I've only seen a likeness of her but the dark hair, parted in the middle with ringlets either side is the exact style she favoured, and the way her lips tilt up slightly on the right side is quite distinctive. Saw it in the photograph Mrs Darwin showed me and it's exactly the same in this portrait. So, the interest, sir, is that we have a woman missing from Down House in Kent, and we have her locket on a dead body in London.'

'Hmm. Think the dead woman is Henrietta Darwin, is that it? Locket doesn't prove it, could've been stolen,' he said. 'But you've seen the corpse, so, is it her?'

'Can't say for sure, sir. The woman's been badly beaten from head to hips. A family member *might* be able to identify her but it wouldn't be easy, and of course, incredibly painful for anyone close to the deceased.' Fickett smiled to himself, pleased with the way he'd neatly laid the groundwork for his planned manipulation of his superior.

'Yes, tricky waters here,' said the older man, taking the bait like a mouse nibbling at the poisoned cheese dangled in front of its nose. 'Don't want to upset the Darwins by asking them to view a mangled piece of flesh and bone that might not even be their daughter-in-law.'

'Had the same thought myself, sir, and if I may, I have a suggestion that might help.' Fickett held his breath, praying Lamb Chops would give him the nod to proceed with the next morsel of toxin-laced cheddar.

'Well, let's have it, man.'

'Right, sir. If the deceased *is* Henrietta Darwin, the best person to identify her is her spouse, and Richard Darwin happens to be in London so I could ask him to view the body. If it's not his wife, then we don't need to bother Mr and Mrs Charles Darwin, and if it is his wife, then at least they'll be spared the nightmares that will surely plague the husband for the rest of his days. Not ideal, but it may make the whole business less stressful for the elder Darwins.'

A thoughtful suggestion it might seem, but in reality, the next step in Fickett's manoeuvre. From what Fickett's seen, it's unlikely Richard, or anyone else for that matter, will be able to identify the woman's remains, but Lamb Chops didn't know that. More importantly, nor did Richard, and therein lay Fickett's plan for trapping his man.

Richard, Fickett reasoned, would have made damn sure he wasn't anywhere near Nightingale Lane when the murder was committed, so he couldn't be certain that what was left of his wife was beyond recognition. And that was all the inspector needed. He intended to inform Richard, or at least imply as strongly as he could, that the corpse was Henrietta's and see how the man reacted. He was banking on Richard being so staggered, he'd admit his guilt before he knew what he was doing.

And staggered he would be since *he never expected to see his wife again*. In Richard's plan, if Fickett had fathomed it correctly, the unclaimed corpse would be dismissed as another sixpenny draggle-tail who'd met a violent end and then dumped in the nearest paupers' graveyard. Without any evidence that Richard's wife was dead, the investigation into Henrietta's disappearance would never expand into a full-blown murder inquiry. A perfect crime, except for one tiny giveaway – the locket in Henrietta's skirt pocket.

'The husband, yes, good idea,' agreed the commissioner, swallowing the second serving of baited cheese. 'Best we can do in the circumstances, I suppose. Where's the body now?'

'Laid out in a shed behind The Six Jolly Porters, closest pub to where the body was found.'

'Alright. Let's move on. You said two developments.'

'Yes, sir.' Now, fretted Fickett, comes the dicey part – the ransom demand. If Lamb Chops determines Mivart sent it, he'll want me to focus on him, and I'll have to set aside my investigation of Richard. 'The Darwins received another anonymous letter, sir,' he began cautiously. 'This one demands that Charles Darwin publicly take back all his nonsense about creation and about apes being our ancestors and suchlike if he wants to see his daughter-in-law again.'

'Good Lord! Let me see it.'

The note was quickly produced and the few lines read just as quickly, the key phrases – *retract your blasphemous theory, before January's end, daughter-in-law will perish* – ploughing deep furrows into Henderson's brow.

'Damn. When did the Darwins get this?'

'Delivered to Down House on Wednesday.'

'Wednesday!' The commissioner glared at his Chief of Detectives, eyes flashing venomous darts, causing the inspector's on-tenterhooks expression to give way to a worried frown.

Fickett saw suspicion darkening Lamb Chop's face, and guessed immediately the questions running though the commissioner's mind, exactly the ones he'd ask if positions were reversed – Why didn't my inspector report this at once? Is he stupid? Or up to something? Something to further his career? At my expense?

Henderson had been famous for his temper in his military days but, thanks to age and a determined effort on his part, he'd learned to hold his tongue for a full minute. The sixty-second, self-imposed rule respected, the commissioner resumed firmly but calmly. 'Should've brought this to my attention immediately, Fickett. What were you doing? Pomading your hair? Still, not to worry,' he lied. 'No real harm done.'

Fickett breathed a sigh of relief.

'From some religious crank, I expect, same as the other one,' the commissioner continued. 'Definitely not from Mivart, though. When I spoke to him on Monday, I made damned certain he understood the consequences of any more of this anonymous letter business. Put the fear of God into him.' Right fist smacked into left palm, exactly as it had when he'd warned off Mivart. 'My guess is he didn't write the first letter, but after my chat with him, trust me, he didn't write this one.'

The conceit of the man, marvelled the inspector. Still, shouldn't complain, got exactly what I wanted. Lamb Chops has ruled out Mivart, leaving me free to pursue my target.

'But that doesn't tell us who did send it, or who abducted Henrietta. Any ideas, Fickett?' Henderson arched his eyebrow once more.

'Not at this point,' Fickett lied in his turn. Richard Darwin, you clown, he said to himself. He arranged Henrietta's disappearance and then sent the ransom note once he realised I'd not swallowed the suicide fiction. Wanted to make us suspect Mivart. Then, aloud, 'Perhaps you have an insight, sir?'

'Let's proceed as follows,' the commissioner responded coolly, ignoring the inspector's impudent question. 'Get Richard Darwin in to view the body, as you suggest. And give him the locket while you're at it. Then make sure Charles Darwin's retraction is in The Times as soon as possible.'

'Should be in Monday's paper, sir.'

'Good. Pound to a penny, Fickett, the corpse is not Henrietta Darwin's. She's the bait to make Darwin renounce his theory and for that the kidnappers need her alive. If I'm right, and she's still being held captive, our best chance of rescuing her and collaring her abductors is to nab them as they're handing her over after their demand's been met. And, Fickett, when that happens, be sure I'm there to make the arrest. That's all, inspector.'

'Thank you, sir.'

Fickett quickly took his leave, breathing a little more easily. A highly successful meeting, he congratulated himself. The old fool's up to date; I still have a free hand to pursue Richard Darwin; and, when I apprehend him, I'll make damned sure Lamb Chops is nowhere near.

Chapter Nineteen: The Six Jolly Porters

Fickett's shock-Richard-Darwin-into-confessing strategy went into effect at nine o'clock Monday. He and Richard were sitting across from one another at a small round table in a dingy, low-ceilinged parlour towards the back of The Six Jolly Porters. Richard faced the only window, giving Fickett, aided by the low winter sun, an excellent view of his suspect's face.

After the briefest of pleasantries, Fickett thrust the locket in Richard's face.

'M... my wife's?'

The hoarsely whispered question was followed by a nod from the inspector, a sharp intake of breath from his prey, a snake-like dart of his hand to grasp the gold chain, a shaky-fingered fumbling to open the locket, a quick look, and a second sharp intake of breath.

'You... you've found her?'

'Believe so, sir.' Not exactly a lie, but said so authoritatively it conveyed more certainty than warranted.

'Dead?'

'Murdered,' was the brutally blunt response. Shake him up, that was the plan. And it was working. Fickett saw shock blanching Richard's face, then panic. Got him! He's going to blurt it all out. Instead of a wife-free, suspicion-free life, he's landed in his worst possible nightmare, her corpse identified, her murder under investigation, and he, suspect number one. Fickett edged forward on his chair.

'I want to see her,' Richard said.

Damn! Not the words the inspector wanted to hear. No confession, despite the guilt Fickett had seen in his eyes. Might still be a chance, though. Seeing the body might do it. Let's see how he reacts when he's confronted by the gory consequences of the savaging meted out to his wife on his instructions. 'Very well. Come, I'll show you.'

Leaving the hostelry, the pair followed a short path to an old wooden shed behind the pub. Inside, on a makeshift table was a human form under a sheet. Fickett whipped back the cover.

Revulsion, Richard's first reaction, fractured his features, his face like a mosaic of mismatched pieces. His second, relief, was there for only a second, seen for an instant, then gone. Revulsion was to be expected. Anyone viewing that wreck of a human being would be sick to the stomach. But why that glimpse of relief? The question had barely formed in the inspector's mind when Richard pivoted on his heel, and like a lunatic in full-moon frenzy, rushed out of the shed and back across the flagstones to the inn.

The inspector followed hard on his heels, entered the parlour and saw his quarry bent over, hands to mouth as though fearing an upsurge of half-digested breakfast. Fickett's constable manhandled the overwrought wretch into a chair, and a tot of rum, brought by the landlord, was soon burning its way down Richard's throat.

As the liquor took effect, the moans and groans slowly subsided to a barely audible mumble, but Fickett heard nothing that could be remotely described as self-incrimination. Impatient though he was to question the man, he waited until his suspect was sufficiently calmed before beginning. And then: 'Dr Darwin, is that your wife?'

No answer, no sign Richard even heard the question.

'Sir, is that your wife? I must have an answer,' Fickett pressed.

'I… I don't know.' Richard looked up slowly, not making eye contact, but the inspector spotted the crafty look that crept across his features. 'How can I identify that… that *thing* as my wife when I can't even recognise it as a human being? It's nothing, *nothing* I tell you, like the wife I loved with all my heart.'

That was when Fickett understood the flash of relief in Richard's eyes on seeing the state of his wife's face and body. Before entering the shed, he'd feared her corpse would be recognisable, exactly what the inspector had led him to believe. But when he saw the pulpy mass of flesh and bone left by his hired assassin, he saw his way out. No one could identify that *thing*, as he called it, as his wife, and without a positive identification, there was no proof Henrietta was dead, and no reason to investigate him as her killer.

Fickett marvelled at the man's coolness under pressure. In that second, that instant of reprieve, he'd formulated his strategy – keep insisting he couldn't identify that *thing* and he was in the clear. And he was right.

Fickett had hoped to have Richard arrested and the case neatly wrapped up before morning's end so that he could report a successful outcome to Henderson. Well, that was not going to happen. Fickett cursed his ill-fortune – *the fellow was more resilient and resourceful than I gave him credit for* – but then rallied. Richard might have won this round, albeit by the skin of his teeth, but the inspector was in for the long haul. He was close to fathoming how Richard had pulled off his trick and 'miracled' Henrietta's body out of Down House. Once he had that, he'd have his man.

Unable to force a confession, Fickett had sent Richard on his way. He was putting on his overcoat ready to leave when he heard raised voices from the front of the public house. He stepped outside and found his constable doing his best to placate a woman remonstrating loudly, her left arm raised to give force to her words, the right bent at the elbow and hidden under the short cape of her winter coat. He couldn't see her face, only a glimpse of pale skin between fur hat and Pashmina muffler, but she was clearly a lady of standing. 'Perhaps I can be of some help, miss.'

The woman turned towards the speaker. 'Ah, Inspector Fickett.'

'Miss Moxley.' He stared at her in surprise. 'What are you doing here?'

Fickett had interviewed the lady, Henrietta's sister, at Down House, but only briefly. Since she'd arrived there well after Henrietta's disappearance, she could contribute little to the investigation so he'd not paid her much attention. Now, he regarded her afresh. In her early thirties, he estimated. Her face was pleasantly attractive but lacked that upward tilt of the lips' right side, the feature that added a touch of allure to her sister's. Estelle, yes that was her name. Estelle Moxley, the woman supposedly in an on-off romantic relationship with Mivart. At least, that's what that fool Line had claimed.

'Where's Richard? I want to see him at once,' she demanded. 'I understand he was brought here on *police business,* or some such nonsense. He promised to call on me at nine sharp this morning with any news about my sister. When he didn't arrive, I inquired at his club and was told he'd been escorted from the premises and carted off like some... some common criminal. Where is he?'

'I'm afraid he's already left,' Fickett replied. 'If you would be so kind as to come inside, I'll endeavour to explain.'

He directed her to the same parlour where he'd interviewed Richard and gestured to the chair her brother-in-law had occupied. She cast a disapproving eye over the shabby furnishings, flicked her glove across the seat as carelessly as a bored maid swishing a feather duster and perched uncomfortably upon the edge.

Keen to be on his way, the inspector briskly informed her about Richard's summons to The Six Jolly Porters to view a body thought to be that of his wife. 'My sister!' gasped an anguished Miss Moxley.

Fickett instantly regretted his abruptness, and hastened to assure her that Richard had not been able to identify the corpse, mumbling something about the unfortunate state of the remains. It was then that the conversation took a decidedly bizarre turn.

'Inspector, if I understand this terrible situation correctly, you have a body that has been, well... rendered unrecognisable. Am I to take it that the poor woman's face has borne the brunt of this savagery?'

'Miss Moxley, please let me spare you the gruesome details. Suffice it to say—'

'No, no, I must know. Was it just the face?'

'Afraid not, miss. Body as well.'

'I see. And the feet?'

Fickett stared at the woman. What strange questions. Was she deranged?

Some perverse fascination with the macabre? This has to be handled delicately.

'I've not seen the lower half of the corpse myself, but according to the doctor the... the damage was from the hips up, but I don't see how this—'

'The hips up, you say. Then, I believe it should be possible to establish that this... this outrage to humanity is *not,* as I pray it's not, my poor sister.'

What? How on earth can she do that? wondered Fickett. The lady was clearly mad. Best send her on her way fast as I can. 'Miss Moxley, I really can't allow you to be exposed to this barbarity. Seeing the body will only cause you the greatest distress and not advance us one iota.'

'I appreciate your concern, inspector, but have no fear, I believe there's a way forward that will avoid any affront to my female sensibilities.'

'And what might that be?' Fickett didn't know what to make of the woman, but her assured demeanour and tone were enough to hold his attention.

'Let me explain. My sister and I grew up on the family estate outside Carlisle. We had the run of the place, including an old barn where we liked to clamber on the rafters.'

'Miss Moxley, I fail to see—'

'Allow me to finish, inspector, and you *will* see.' Miss Moxley raised her left arm to silence him. 'One day, when I was six, my sister eight, we were sitting on one of these beams when it started to give way, tilting and tipping us forward. Before I knew it, I was plummeting towards the hard-packed earth of the barn's floor. Plunging face-downward, I saw the ground rushing to meet me and naturally thrust my hands out in front of me to break my fall. I landed heavily on my right arm.'

Fickett's eyes involuntarily swivelled towards the right-angled shape beneath the coat's short cape. Yes, he remembered now what he'd been told at Down House. A local doctor had set the badly fractured bone, but either he did a poor job or there was severe nerve damage because when the splint was removed, Miss Moxley couldn't straighten her arm and it had remained bent at the elbow ever since. He quickly willed his gaze back to her face.

Miss Moxley didn't seem to notice, caught up as she was in her memories.

'My sister falls feet first,' she continued, unconsciously switching to the present tense, no doubt visualizing the incident in her mind's eye. 'Older and stronger, Henrietta hangs on for a second and then falls feet first. I think she's going to be unhurt, but just before I pass out, I see it, the tip of a nail, protruding from her foot.' She looked at the inspector to see if he'd grasped the significance of her last remark. He had.

'I learned later,' she resumed, 'that she landed on a six-inch iron nail sticking point-upward out of a wooden plank. It went right through her left foot. She has two scars, one on the bottom of the foot, the other on the top. There, is that enough for you? Can you take a look and tell me... *please, please tell me*... that the dead woman's left foot is *unmarked*? That the body you've found is *not* my sister's?'

'Wait here,' ordered the inspector, courtesy forgotten in his haste to check the corpse's left foot. One minute later he was back. He'd practically broken into a smile as he emerged from the shed, but now he sobered his expression, readying himself to impart his news to Henrietta's sister.

'Miss Moxley, please prepare yourself. I'm afraid I have bad news. It is your sister. The scars were exactly as you described. I'm so sorry.'

Estelle Moxley stared at him before crumpling forward on to the tacky table, huge sobs shuddering her body. Fickett watched in alarm, unsure what to do until he recalled the landlord's liquor-curative. Brandy, though, for the lady, not rum. The order was dispatched and a few minutes later, the innkeeper's wife was tending to Miss Moxley, encouraging her to take a sip of the restorative. Fickett left the women to themselves.

He was right. He knew it all along. It was Henrietta's body and Richard murdered her. He didn't get the confession he'd hoped for, but at least the positive identification was something he could report to the commissioner, enough to keep Lamb Chops off his back for the time being. And, Richard had conveniently forgotten to mention those telltale scars. One more corroborative nail in his evidentiary coffin. Yes, on balance, a passable morning.

Chapter Twenty: The Inquest

L ine's fifth folder arrived at Meadowlark Cottage mid-morning on Thursday. Keen to learn the latest developments, Dunston put aside the newspaper he'd been about to read and dived into the enclosed report.

Case No. 1-1872

Inquest, Wednesday, January 31

I'd been pleased and relieved to see Charles Darwin's retraction in Monday's Times and hoped that the kidnappers had kept their side of the bargain and released his daughter-in-law. Today, however, I learned the shocking news – Henrietta Darwin was dead.

Henrietta dead! The folder slipped from Dunston's hand to the kitchen table. He too had seen Charles Darwin's retraction and, having heard nothing to the contrary in the three days since, had assumed Henrietta had been returned safely to her family. But now this dreadful news.

How tragic. Heartbreak for her husband. And for the elder Darwins, losing a daughter-in-law *and* seeing their main hope for another grandchild expunged as easily as a brass snuffer extinguishes a candle's flame. Sadness cloaked him, but his natural curiosity could not be held in check for long, and, half-reluctantly, half-instinctively, he picked up the report, wondering what else Line had learned at the inquest…

Line, dressed in his usual everyday jacket and one-and-only tie (navy), took a seat in the last row of chairs in the public bar of The Six Jolly Porters in Great Hermitage Street. It was a good-sized room, well used to holding inquests. Today's was sparsely attended, just the coroner seated at an oblong table, then, facing him, the jurors and behind them a handful of witnesses, two constables and a spattering of spectators including a veiled Mrs Darwin and, several seats away, Inspector Fickett in full uniform as usual.

The family had managed to keep Henrietta's death out of the newspapers, a singular achievement in news-hungry London, but one that was not going to last long, a few reporters, sharks with pencils, in attendance. The power of the Darwin name was also evident in another respect; Richard Darwin, the deceased's grieving spouse was not present. The coroner had conceded to Mrs Darwin's request for him to be excused, presumably confident that there was ample evidence at hand to determine cause of death, the sole purpose of the inquest, without putting Richard through the agony of testifying.

The proceedings were brief. The coroner began as usual by instructing the jury to view the body still laid out in the shed behind the inn. The jurors marched out in orderly fashion through a side door, only to return a few minutes later looking decidedly the worse for wear. Clearly a gruesome sight had greeted them, as was confirmed by the first witness, Mrs Geraldine Hawksby, who testified to the severe beating meted out by a single assailant in Nightingale Lane around one in the morning of Friday, January 26.

The second witness, a studious, bespectacled man in his late thirties, was Dr Matthew Cullingworth who informed the jury that the victim had died from a fractured skull with many of the other injuries sustained after death. He also reported that the deceased's wedding ring was missing – he'd seen the indentation it had left on her finger – and that he'd found a gold locket in her skirt pocket.

To Line's surprise, Grace Trewin, maid at Down House, came next. Smartly dressed for the occasion in a light blue frock and matching bonnet, she testified that the locket was a present from Mrs Emma Darwin to her daughter-in-law, Mrs Henrietta Darwin.

A wave of whispered questions swept through the saloon: Henrietta

Darwin? Charles Darwin's daughter-in-law? Her locket on the waterfront? What was it doing there? Stolen? Or... or what?

Grace stepped down, and Miss Estelle Moxley was called to the stand. Guided by the coroner, she described in a quiet but firm voice how she identified the corpse.

'And the name of the deceased?' prompted the coroner.

'Henrietta,' sobbed the witness. 'Henrietta Darwin.'

To a man, the small contingent of reporters sprang to life, furiously jotting down those incomprehensible squiggles and swirls, the shorthand much used in their profession. Seconds later they rushed off, each desperate to be the first to inform Londoners that the daughter-in-law of England's foremost scientist had had her brains bashed out in one of London's most unsavoury districts.

Once the hullabaloo of the news hounds' exit had died down, Miss Moxley was escorted out, and the jury was led to one of the smaller rooms at the back of the inn to consider their verdict. While waiting for their return, Line digested Miss Moxley's testimony. She'd said little about the long-ago mishap that caused the childhood injuries, but the clarity and precision of her description of the scars left little doubt that the mangled remains laid out in the shed had, before death, been the living, breathing Mrs Henrietta Darwin.

He was saddened for the Darwins, to be sure, but his detective brain was also at work, pondering the puzzling timing of events. Two dates struck him – Friday, January 26 when Henrietta was killed; and Monday, January 29 when Darwin's retraction appeared in The Times.

The question they raised was this: Why did the kidnappers kill Henrietta *before* the retraction had been published? It would have made more sense to keep her alive until Darwin's recantation of his theory was made public. Killing her removed the threat hanging over Darwin's head. So why do it?

Line saw only one explanation for this sequence – Henrietta's death was *unintended*, perhaps the unfortunate result of an attempt to escape. It was easy to imagine what happened – her captors dropped their guard, she slipped away, and a chase ensued, ending with a heavy blow from a cudgel, one powerful enough to crush her skull.

What was the kidnapper-in-chief to do now that the bait, Henrietta, was dead? The retraction had not yet appeared in The Times so the entire effort was wasted, *unless he could cover up her death*. Hence the after-death battering to prevent identification. Not knowing Henrietta was dead, Charles Darwin went ahead and publicly renounced his entire body of work, exactly as the kidnapper wanted.

Line smiled, satisfied. The facts, the foundation of any Line investigation, always tell a story if you let them, and in this instance, the tale they told was of the abductor's last-gasp effort to salvage his plan to extort a retraction from Charles Darwin.

The jurors were soon back, and the coroner announced their verdict – murder by an unknown person. Everything seemed cut and dried, but in his many years as a policeman, Line had always made a point of tying up any loose ends, and the inquest had left two. First, the body. A Line investigation was not complete without an examination of the corpse, and he'd not yet seen it. And second, the childhood mishap. Miss Moxley had rightly focused on the scars, her sister's distinguishing marks, without really describing the accident in any detail.

Since the corpse was at hand, now was Line's chance to cross item number one off his list. The jurors had gone out through a door on the left side of the saloon on their way to inspect the body so he followed their path. He found himself in a passageway. He turned right towards the rear of the hostelry, exited the inn, and followed the paving stones straight to a small, stand-alone shed. Guessing that nobody would be guarding the corpse, Line opened the door and entered.

The sight that met his eyes when he pulled back the top half of the sheet covering the body, shook him to the bone. The top of the woman's skull had been flattened like a lump of dough kneaded into submission by a heavy-handed pastry cook. The doctor was right – the blow that caused this damage was more than enough to kill her. Line gave the rest of the wounds a cursory glance, enough to confirm that someone had gone to a lot of trouble to make Henrietta unidentifiable, exactly as he'd surmised.

He pulled up the bottom part of the sheet and examined her left foot, the object of interest. The circles of scarred tissue, now some twenty years old, were faded, but Line could see they were as described by Miss Moxley. Closer inspection revealed that the top one was about the size of a bronze farthing, the other perhaps half that size. He was about to replace the sheet when he heard the one voice he least wanted to hear.

'Looking for the privy, are we?'

'Ah, Inspector Fickett, no, not the privy.' Damn! Caught red-handed. The blasted fellow's going to make the most of my discomfort, fretted Line. 'Forgive me, but I thought this might be a good time to take a quick look at the corpse.'

'Yes, well, no harm in that,' Fickett responded expansively.

Line was caught off guard by the inspector's surprisingly gracious dismissal of the intrusion. Not like him at all. Given the man's good mood, Line decided to take a chance and push for information about the sisters' fall in the barn, the other item on his need-to-complete agenda. 'Well, um, thank you for your understanding. I was particularly interested in the scars on the foot. A childhood accident, I understand. Haven't heard all the details myself but I imagine you know what happened.'

'Of course.'

Ah, that's more like the Inspector Fickett he'd come to know. 'If it's not too much of an imposition perhaps I could ask you to enlighten me.'

'Not much to tell,' replied the inspector guardedly. He quickly went through what Miss Moxley had told him about how she damaged her arm in the fall and how Henrietta landed feet first on a nail, causing the scars Line had just examined.

'I see. Well, thank—' Line broke off.

'What is it?' asked the inspector, instantly alert.

Line didn't reply. Something in Fickett's account of the accident was off. Probably nothing, but the detective always followed up any odd detail, no matter how small, and this one would have to be squared away. 'Um, nothing.' He felt a little guilty about his fib, Fickett having on this occasion been unusually obliging, but all was fair in love and sleuthing. 'Let me not

97

take any more of your time,' he said, moving past the inspector and out of the shed, interested now in having a word with Mrs Darwin.

He caught up with her in the parlour and asked her about the sisters' fall, but she couldn't offer anything beyond what he already knew. She did however suggest one person who might be able to help – Betsy Smurkle, the sisters' nanny. Line noted the name, bid Mrs Darwin a safe journey back to Down House and took his leave.

Back in Meadowlark Cottage, Dunston raised his eyes from Line's report. After the shock of reading about Henrietta's death, he'd thought the remainder of Line's report would be dull as ditch water, but nothing could have been further from the truth. Line's neat reconciliation of that odd sequence of events – the lady's death *before* the publication of Darwin's letter – was a virtuoso performance. Like Mozart teasing a heart-melting melody out of a few notes, the master detective took two dates and turned them into a scene-by-scene frieze of Henrietta's final moments.

Dunston was less impressed with Line's performance in the shed. The sisters' mishap in the barn had obviously caught his attention, but it didn't seem to Dunston like a particularly promising avenue for further investigation. Surely, the solution to the crime lay in explaining how Henrietta was keylessly spirited out of a locked-up Down House, something about which Line seemed totally in the dark, as, Dunston had to admit, was he.

Chapter Twenty-One: The Lord Chief Justice

Moving with the joint-creaking slowness of an octogenarian, the stooped man slowly approached a well-worn, leather armchair, and lowered himself onto the soft-cushioned seat, its dual depressions perfectly contoured to his skinny buttocks. Befitting his age, he had only the sparest wisp of white hair; extra folds of flesh pulling down his jowls; and weak, bleary eyes. But don't be fooled. This boneless sack of watery blood and weary tissue was Sir Winston Grissick, Lord Chief Justice, the most powerful man in England's judiciary.

Grissick had spent his eighty-plus years relentlessly pursuing a single objective – to make himself the most influential force in the country's judicial system. A lifelong campaign of systematic promotion of his sons, nephews and male cousins, strategic marriages for his daughters, and blatantly lenient treatment of anyone of standing who foolishly ran afoul of the law, had led to his current position as the unquestioned patriarch of England's courts. Key appointments, assignment of major cases, even sentencing in high-profile trials, all fell within the ambit of the man presently arranging himself for maximum comfort in his favourite chair.

A knock on the door, a sharp 'Come', and Metropolitan Police Commissioner, Sir Edmund Henderson, and his Chief of Detectives, Inspector Jeremiah Fickett entered Grissick's private chambers in the High Court of Justice on the Strand. The former offered a 'Good Morning' – no reply – while the latter glanced around the spacious, wood-panelled room. He barely noticed the bookcases stacked with dusty tomes recording the statutes of the land, his eyes fastening first on the magnificent, full-length portrait of Grissick in wig and fur-edged, red robe, and then shifting to the handsome, over-sized oak desk. Dreams, no doubt, swirled in the inspector's head about *his* office once Henderson was put out to pasture.

Grissick was not in his ceremonial robes today, wearing instead a black frock coat, waistcoat and stripped trousers. He waved his guests toward the two straight-backed, wooden chairs on the other side of his desk. He closed his eyes, leaned his head on his right hand, and without a word, signalled them to begin.

The two policemen – Henderson in civilian clothes, Fickett, as always, in full uniform – had come to see Grissick that Monday morning following their own meeting on the preceding Friday. Hearing that Fickett was close to arresting Richard Darwin for his wife's abduction and murder, Henderson had decided to pull the reins in on the glory-grabber.

Fickett had grudgingly laid out his case against Richard, including his explanation, now fully fleshed out, of how Henrietta had been conjured out of Down House, a clever deduction on Fickett's part, as even Henderson had to admit. The evidence Fickett presented was compelling, and arresting Richard would not be unreasonable in normal circumstances, but these were not normal circumstances – the individual to be charged was the son of one of England's most prominent figures.

Henderson, a man who had come up through the ranks on merit, had witnessed first-hand how easily the upper crust of English society bent the laws of the land to their advantage. While he didn't know Charles Darwin, he knew that the scientist had enough clout to cause a fuss should his son be apprehended, and, if found innocent, every right to savagely berate in courtroom and broadsheet the man responsible, namely himself, for such a travesty.

And there was a hole in the case against Richard: no motive. Juries liked to understand the why of a crime before convicting. No, an arrest at this point was premature.

Henderson opted for the time-honoured tactic of pushing the decision up the chain of command, a neat way of ostensibly supporting his inspector while leaving the final say to a third party. The third party he'd decided on was the Lord Chief Justice, someone whose past behaviour strongly suggested the outcome would be exactly what the commissioner wanted – no arrest, at least not yet.

Henderson began by expressing his thanks for the meeting, explained why they were there, and then handed over to Fickett. The inspector laid out the evidence against Richard, starting with the reference to Aesculapius in the first anonymous letter and ending with the scars on the victim's foot, making sure to stress his own role in each development especially the highlight of the investigation – his solution (and his alone) to the mystery of Henrietta Darwin's disappearance.

Grissick's eyes remained shut throughout the recital, but as soon as the inspector was finished, he opened them and posed a single question. 'Are you sure, young man, that nobody other than Richard Darwin could have, shall we say, *levitated* Henrietta Darwin out of Down House?'

The commissioner stepped in quickly. 'Hard to say for sure, Sir Winston, but Fickett's explanation is the only one we've come up with so far.'

'Hmm. Tricky case. Abduction, blackmail, murder, all rather bewildering.' The eyes closed. 'Let me think.'

After ten minutes of apparently deep thought, Grissick opened his eyes and delivered his ruling, his hard stare at the commissioner underscoring that he expected his wishes to be carried out to the letter.

'Arrest Richard Darwin.'

Henderson couldn't believe his ears. He'd been sure Grissick would bend over backwards to avoid offending someone of Darwin's stature. What's going on?

'Thank you, sir. I'll get right on it,' an obviously delighted Inspector Fickett said. 'I'll be at Down House first thing tomorrow to make the arrest.'

Grissick turned his eyes toward the younger officer. 'Good man.'

'Perhaps, Sir Winston,' the commissioner said cautiously, 'it would be best not to be too, um, hasty. We don't want to upset the Darwins unless we're absolutely convinced of Richard Darwin's guilt, and to date we've not come up with a motive.'

'Motive, yes, very important.'

Henderson breathed a sigh of relief. 'Just thinking aloud,' he continued, 'but the anonymous letters look like a crusade to force Charles Darwin to renounce his anti-religious theories. Points to someone who embraces the Bible's version of creation, and that's not Richard Darwin, he's a firm supporter of his father's theory. There's one man, Sir Winston, who better fits the bill – George Mivart.'

Although the commissioner believed he'd successfully warned off Mivart when they'd met two weeks ago, the man did have a grudge against Darwin and pointing that out may give Grissick pause. 'Mivart's a recent convert to Catholicism,' he explained, 'and currently engaged in a highly acrimonious dispute with Darwin. Given the importance of motive, we should perhaps take a look at him before—'

'George Mivart, you say,' cut in Sir Winston. 'Hmm, supported his election to the Athenaeum, you know. Sent those Darwin hounds packing. Powerful judicial lobby in the club, by Jove, and this George Mivart, not in the legal profession himself, silly boy, comes from a long line of lawyers and judges, more than enough backers to squash Darwin and his cronies.' Grissick smiled at his guests, savouring the victory, small though it was compared to many others in his life, but a victory is a victory.

Damn and blast! Henderson was furious with himself. He'd forgotten that the entire Mivart family, except George, held various important positions in the courts, a circumstance that had apparently been enough to tilt Grissick in favour of Mivart in the membership dispute. But that was about joining a London club; this was about murder!

'Trust my confidence in the young man wasn't misplaced,' said Grissick with a look that made clear it most certainly was not. 'Still, you're right,' he continued, giving the commissioner a snippet of hope, 'we should have a motive, but injecting one for someone other than the younger Darwin could confuse jurors and thwart the pursuit of justice. The solution, gentleman, is obvious – *unearth Richard Darwin's motive.*'

As usual when England's judicial overlord was involved, an arthritic but supremely legal thumb had pressed the scales of justice in his preferred direction.

'Arrest Darwin and sweat it out of him if you have to,' he told them. 'Once they feel the shackles tight around arms and legs, even the toughest crooks can be persuaded to confess. Need to get this villain to trial quick as you like. Good day, gentlemen.'

Chapter Twenty-Two: His Only Hope

Lucy had spent the whole day after rescuing her baby inside the shack tending the infant, resting as best she could, and anxiously considering her options. Knowing she could never return to her family in Cornwall with a child in tow, she decided to make her way back to London in the vague hope that Eyesore Annie would let her spend a few nights in Shoreditch Workhouse while she looked for a more permanent arrangement.

But London was ninety miles away, and with no money, the journey was daunting. She was debilitated from childbirth; still hurting from the beating dished out by Fingers and mate; weakened from lack of food; incapacitated by a hand that hurt so much she couldn't even use it to hold her son; each made her undertaking difficult enough, together they posed a challenge that might well be beyond her. No matter, she had to try.

Willing herself out of the shack, she set off Saturday afternoon with only the shawl 'borrowed' from the workhouse to protect them from the cold. She trudged through the snow and slush of country lanes and by-ways, the wind's icy blast chilling her to the bone, the baby growing heavier with every step. She'd managed barely two miles, already unsure whether she could go much further, when she spotted a big-wheeled, garishly painted vardo. Gypsies! She'd been brought up to steer well clear of Romany travellers but in desperate need of help, she didn't hesitate to approach.

The hugely pregnant Roma woman in a brightly coloured headscarf and heavy woollen shawl pinned at the bosom, took pity on a mother in distress and bid Lucy join them for supper. Seated around a small cast-iron cooking stove inside the wagon, Lucy shared their meagre evening meal – a heavily spiced stew of root vegetables and rabbit. The quarters were cramped, but the woman said Lucy could spend the night on the built-in bench towards the front of the caravan, while she and her husband would sleep in their stow-away bunk at the rear, their usual resting place.

The next morning, after a scanty, gruel-like breakfast, Lucy saw husband and wife in a heated discussion. The man shrugged and walked off, muttering to himself. The woman approached Lucy seemingly unperturbed by her husband's surly behaviour. 'He said you're velcome to travel vid us, *rakla,* if you vants.'

Lucy didn't know what to say. She could hardly believe her good fortune. The gypsies were doglegging across southern England on their way to a Romany spring festival on the east coast – first, east towards Brighton, then north towards London before branching off east again to their destination. This suited Lucy perfectly. She reached out, her good hand finding the Roma's, a simple gesture, yet full of meaning for mother and mother-to-be.

Journeying with the Romanies proved uneventful, and Lucy quickly adapted to the daily routine. The man, reins in hand, sat in the driver's seat while the two women walked beside the caravan. The baby, named Joey after Lucy's father, was safely settled in the vardo. Lucy was more than happy with the dozen or so miles covered each day, every milestone passed a measure of how far she'd come but also a dispiriting reminder of how far she had to go. By the time they stopped each night she was exhausted, barely able to stand let alone walk.

It wasn't just the walking that was taking a toll. The gypsies ate sparingly as it was, and Lucy's presence was clearly putting a strain on their limited food supplies, the portions served by her hosts getting smaller and smaller until they were hardly sufficient to keep body and soul together. Instead of building up her strength, Lucy was wearing down, becoming gaunter with each passing day. More worryingly, she wasn't producing any breast milk, and the pap-like mixture the woman fed Joey wasn't enough to put any flesh on his tiny bones.

On the ninth morning of travelling together, the Romanies headed off to their festival, leaving Lucy on the outskirts of Caterham, a village on the flint and chalk hills of the North Downs, still twenty miles from London. Lucy sat on the grass, her back against a milestone, her son tight to her breast, and waited for a passing hay wain or cart that could take them the rest of the way to the capital.

The morning wore on without a single passer-by, giving Lucy ample time to think. Even when she was with the gypsies, she'd begun to have serious second-thoughts about her plan. Now, cold, hungry, weak, and still unable to feed her baby properly, new doubts began to creep into her mind, and once there, they stuck with the cling of a leech. If she reached London, what then? Eyesore Annie might provide a roof over her head for a few days, but then she'd be back on the streets, starving, penniless, at the mercy of the likes of Micus Loman and Fingers.

She needed a better plan. Where else could she go? Down House where she'd maided was only a few miles away. Could she go there? Throw herself on the mercy of Mrs Darwin? No, Jarke, the butler, would never allow it. That mean-spirited tyrant would send her on her way with a cuff around the ear long before she got anywhere near the lady of the house.

Still… maybe there was another way… yes, perhaps there was. But the idea had barely formed when it was just as quickly suppressed. She pushed it away, no, *never*, too unthinkable, too unbearable. But… if there was no other option…

Lucy set off for Down House, but the going was hard. The brutal severity of the weather ushered in by the new year had abated, but it was still February-cold, bitter enough to sap what remained of her strength. And she was hungry. She pushed aside her own need for something to fill her belly, but she couldn't shut out Joey's piteous cries, a constant reminder that her son was starving to death. His little body – thin parchment over baby bones – weighed nothing, yet her one good arm ached from the awkward way she had to hold him.

The afternoon was a series of stops and starts, the stops becoming longer and longer, until Lucy couldn't take another step. She'd covered about three miles, barely half way to the house, but she couldn't go any further without rest. She stumbled into a barn by the roadside and buried herself and Joey in the hay stacked in a corner. There, she shivered her way through the night, hoping that sleep would reinvigorate her enough to continue her trek.

The next day she felt weaker yet more determined than ever. Lucy pressed on until, late in the afternoon she finally found herself back at the gates through which Jarke had sent her packing seven months earlier. She gave the house a wide berth, circling around to the back, and slipped inside the tool-shed, intending to spend the night there before launching her plan.

The night hours dragged by. Joey was feverish and hungry, and wouldn't settle. Lucy was still not producing any milk, and could do nothing except cradle him to her breast and hope her body heat was enough to keep him warm. She hung on as best she could through the small hours until she guessed it was about five in the morning. Then, with Joey in her arms, she slipped out of the shed. Feeling her way in the inky darkness, she crept around to the front of the house and gently placed her child, wrapped in her shawl, her only outerwear, on the doorstep. She kissed him and said a prayer over him, kissed him again and stole away. She'd done what she had to do.

She hid behind a yew tree beyond the iron gates at the end of the short driveway. From there, she could see the front door and watch her baby's fate unfold before her eyes. Just after dawn, the door opened and a house maid – Milly, if Lucy remembered correctly – appeared in white bib apron and mob cap, broom in hand. With a squeal of surprise, the brush was cast aside, the bundle picked up, whisked inside, and the door shut. Now, all she could do was wait... and hope.

For the next several hours nothing happened to suggest the household had acquired a new member. But then, when the morning had almost slipped away, Lucy saw Milly leave the servants' quarters and set off in the direction of the village. Yes, her plan was working. Milly had been sent to fetch everything little Joey would need – cot, baby clothes, wet-nurse, whatever the household lacked for a tiny stranger.

It was late afternoon when Milly returned... *empty-handed*.

Oh, no! Had she miscalculated? Lucy was sure that Joey, a motherless, helpless infant, would be taken in and cared for. But that was not what was happening. Jarke must've seen her, guessed the baby was hers. First thing tomorrow, he'd make sure Joey was packed off to the nearest workhouse. Probably the one in Cudham, no more than a mile away. Lucy gasped – *that* was where Milly went, to make arrangements for his admittance.

It was dark by five in the evening when she returned to the tool-shed, frantic with worry. With only a couple of gunny sacks for warmth, Lucy suffered through another long night, but this time wide awake, desperately thinking how to recover the son she'd just given away.

By morning, lack of sleep, no food, the frigid weather, her aching hand, all were taking their toll. Many a mother would have given up by now, but not Lucy. She'd seen children sold for half a pint of gin in London, but her son was everything to her and she would get him back no matter what it took. She summoned the last of her energy and dragged herself to the yew tree in time to see the sun rise.

Mid-morning brought a bustle of activity around the door to the servants' quarters. Lucy, waking from a half-doze, struggled to make out what was happening. She saw a cart stationed at the door, ready to take Joey away. This was her chance. She willed God to give her strength, but with or without His help, she must act *now*.

Armed with a fallen branch, she stumbled forward, only to stop in her tracks. Where was Joey? She couldn't see him. All she saw was the same maid, Milly, and two men, two delivery men, unloading packages of all shapes and sizes. She couldn't believe her eyes. Was her plan working? She prayed for it to be so, begging the Lord to grant her wish, still uncertain, not convinced until… until a young woman marched through the gates and approached the group with a cheery wave – the wet-nurse! Yes, of course! Milly was sent to order everything needed for Joey, and now it was all arriving. Her plan had worked! Her Joey was safe.

The hardest part was over, and just as well she thought, not sure how much longer she could hold on. Nonetheless, she stayed at her post in the freezing cold all day to make sure nothing went wrong. By the time darkness fell, Lucy was exhausted, on her last legs, barely able to stagger back to the tool-shed. She crawled under the gunny sacks and curled her body into the mother-perfect shape to cocoon a baby. Even though little Joey was no longer there to fill the space, her heart swelled to a newfound fullness, aching with love for him.

She closed her eyes.

Chapter Twenty-Three: In Haste

Late afternoon on the same day that Lucy kept her final vigil by the yew tree, Line was in the Railway Hotel's lobby in Carlisle waving a note in the air to dry the ink. He'd travelled up to the town on the border with Scotland to see Mrs Smurkle on the day after Mrs Darwin had mentioned her name at the inquest. He'd found the nanny's cottage easily enough, but the lady herself was absent, visiting her sister in Sunderland.

Line had been obliged to spend the best part of a week checking at her cottage each day and otherwise twiddling his thumbs or rambling over the Cumberland moors. He also browsed the newspapers. Only one item caught his attention – Richard Darwin's arrest for the murder of his wife. The article went on to say that the trial was scheduled to start at the Old Bailey on Friday, February 9. Today was Thursday, and it was only around noon that he'd finally managed to meet with Mrs Smurkle.

He placed the note on the small writing desk and read through the quickly penned message.

Carlisle,
4 PM, Thursday, Feb 8

My dear Burnett:

Apologies once again for leaving you to your own devices for so long. In my defence, I can say that my trip to Carlisle has been most productive as I've uncovered vital information in the Henrietta Darwin case. Cannot

110

write more at the moment, must get to the post office before it closes. Want to get this off to you and send a telegram to Fickett telling him I'll be at Scotland Yard first thing tomorrow morning with the new evidence.

In the meantime, take a close look at my account of the inquest and what I <u>saw</u> and what I <u>heard</u> in the shed behind The Six Jolly Porters.

In haste,

Your absentee host,
Archibald Line

Line addressed the envelope to Dunston at Meadowlark Cottage, unaware that he had already left for London earlier that morning to attend Richard's trial. Even had Line known his letter wouldn't reach Dunston for some days, he wouldn't have been concerned. His telegram would be on Fickett's desk within hours, and that was what mattered.

Chapter Twenty-Four: The Telegram

A slouch hat, broad brim pulled down over the face; a nondescript overcoat, collar turned up; shoulders hunched; head lowered; that was all to be seen of the slightly built man who exited the last house on Dane Street late Thursday evening. He could be old, judging by the stooped posture, or a younger man trying to be inconspicuous. He glanced left and right, and set off eastward along High Holborn. On reaching Lombard Street, a mile later, he paused, repeated the left-right routine, and headed for The George and Vulture.

He entered the inn, rapped on the counter to draw the landlord from the back room, and ordered the house ale. He checked the taproom – low-ceilinged, dingy-walled, a scatter of scored tables and rickety chairs, but no customers. Mug in hand, he crossed to the corner settle where he'd have a clear view of any newcomers, sat down, and waited.

He'd barely supped his beer when the door opened and another man, this one taller and straighter, a black cloak covering him from chin to knee, entered and scanned the room, his gaze passing disinterestedly over the slouch-hatted drinker. The rapping on the counter was repeated, the landlord appeared and another mug of ale was purchased. He took a sizeable draft, wiped his mouth with the back of his hand, and ambled over to the table in front of the settle.

Slouch Hat sat in silence as the new arrival placed his hat on the table, sat down across from him without a nod or word of greeting, and made himself comfortable. He took another hefty swig of his beer, and, apart from smacking his lips, matched the other's silence. Minutes passed. Then, he spoke, his words directed towards the sawdust on the floor: 'Waitin' for someone?'

'Maybe,' Slouch Hat replied. 'Who's asking?'

'Don't 'ave time for silly games,' the newcomer said. 'Gaffer said someone would be 'ere who'd pay well for what I've got. So, you 'im or not?' He fixed the other with a hard stare.

'Happens I am expecting some information, but not from you,' Slouch Hat said.

'Gaffer ain't coming. Laying low right now. Sent me instead.'

'And who might you be?'

'You can call me... *Mr* Migston.'

'*Mr* Migston, it is then.' Slouch Hat did not attempt to keep the sarcasm out of his voice.

'Don't take liberties with me or it'll be the worse for you!' Migston snarled, taking instant offence. He lunged across the table, his right hand a blur as it sped from tankard to Slouch Hat's throat. 'Be careful, my fine friend. Easy as blinking to finish off the likes of you. Just one good squeeze...' He tightened his grip on Slouch Hat's windpipe, shutting off the airflow. His point made, he released his hold and settled back as though nothing had happened.

Coughing, spluttering, and gulping oxygen, Slouch Hat needed a full minute before he could speak. 'Alright... alright,' he gasped, 'let's get on with it and be done.'

'Whoa, there. Not so fast,' Migston said. 'Afore we goes any further, let's see the colour of yer blunt.'

'Five guineas, if the information's any good.' Slouch Hat laid five coins on the table, but kept his hand over them.

Migston reached into his waistcoat pocket, pulled out a piece of paper and handed it over. Slouch Hat unfolded it and read the short message.

ATTN. INSPECTOR FICKETT

FOUND NEW EVIDENCE. RICHARD DARWIN INNOCENT. TRIAL MUST BE STOPPED. TAKING OVERNIGHT TRAIN

TO EUSTON STATION. WILL BE AT YARD TOMORROW
MORNING.

ARCHIBALD LINE

Only a few words but enough to drain the blood from Slouch Hat's face.
Seeing his chance, Migston lifted the hand covering the coins and quickly
pocketed them. But the real business was yet to come.

'What yer going to do 'bout that, then?' Migston demanded. 'Told us the
Nightingale Lane job would be a cinch, bash her sodding brains out and
that'd be that. Well, that wasn't how it worked out, was it? Scufters was all
over it like flies on cow dung. Gaffer weren't too happy, me neither, *'cos
I'm the one what done her*. But then, the crushers got their hooks into this
Richard Darwin feller. Long as he ends up on the gallows, and our names
don't come up, me an' the Gaffer's in the clear. Now this,' he rasped. 'If Line
can get him off, nex' thing you know, scufters'll be sniffing 'round us. So,
what yer going to do?'

'How d'you get this telegram?' Slouch Hat asked.

'None of yer bleedin' business.'

'Has Fickett seen it?'

'Nah. Got to the Yard late this afternoon, but never reached Fickett.'

'Good. Let me think.'

Migston snorted, got up, sauntered over to the bar and yelled for more
beer.

RICHARD DARWIN INNOCENT. TRIAL MUST BE STOPPED. How could
this be happening? The trial's *tomorrow*. Think! There must be a way…

Migston returned to his seat, refilled mug in hand. 'Time's up,' he said.
'Let's hear how you're gonna keep us outta Newgate.'

'Know this Archibald Line, d'you?' Slouch Hat asked.

'Aye,' was the sour reply. 'Bastard was one of the top brass at the Yard 'til
he shot some serving wench by accident, and the silly bugger just up and
quit. Haven't heard a dickey bird 'bout him since…'til now.'

'Alright. Listen to me.'

The pair talked for another five minutes, Slouch Hat issuing instructions,

Migston bargaining every step of the way. Negotiations apparently concluded, more coins found their way from Slouch Hat's hand to Migston's pocket. The newly hired killer swilled down the last of his ale, picked up his hat and took his leave, followed a little while later by his paymaster.

Chapter Twenty-Five: Outside Euston Station

The train shuddered to a stop at Euston Station, jolting Archibald Line out of a semi-doze. He'd not slept on the overnight journey from Carlisle, partly because he couldn't get comfortable in his second-class seat, but mainly because his mind kept replaying what Mrs Smurkle, the sisters' nanny, had told him. He'd been right to follow up what had struck him as odd in the shed behind The Six Jolly Porters after the inquest. Yes, it always paid to check every detail, no matter how insignificant, another of the former chief of detective's cardinal rules.

Thanks to Mrs Smurkle, he now had conclusive proof of Richard's innocence. She'd unwittingly presented him with a chance to right a wrong, to save a guiltless man from the gallows. And perhaps make partial amends for that other wrong – taking the life of an innocent young maid, killed by the only shot he'd ever fired in his entire police career. He never again carried his revolver on a case, but the remorse... *that*, he carried everywhere. Perhaps today, if he could save Richard...

The task now was to get to Scotland Yard as quickly as possible. He stood up, slipped his hand into his jacket pocket, and felt for the sliver medallion with its engraved *R* and *M*. He squeezed it between forefinger and thumb once and then once more, his never-neglected, be-back-soon promise. The ritual complete, he pulled on his overcoat, collected his carpet bag and disembarked. He exited the station quickly, worried he might not find a cab at this early hour.

The locality was safer than many in London, but knowing he held a man's life in his hands, he was not about to take any risks, especially in the half-darkness of a winter morning. He glanced around him as he walked, his policeman's instincts slipping into high gear. Passers-by were few and far between so he was able to keep track of anyone who strayed too close.

He'd barely left the station, still on Euston Road, when he heard a gruff voice call out from behind him:

'Need a cab, guv? I'm free.'

Line turned and saw the reassuringly solid shape of a carriage emerging out of the gloom, the cabbie prodding his horse forward, clearly hoping for his first fare of the day. What luck, Line thought. Should be at the Yard in half an hour. Time enough to review my notes on the way and collect my thoughts before meeting with that pipsqueak Inspector Fickett. He smiled at the prospect of bursting the pompous ass's bubble… and righting the fool's flawed investigation.

'Jump in then,' the cabbie urged him. 'Ain't got all day.'

'Right-ho,' said Line opening the half-door and tossing his carpet bag inside. About to climb in, he paused. Odd. Cabbie didn't ask me where I wanted to go. Line turned towards the driver, but before he could say a word, his vocal cords were severed.

He hadn't heard the soft footsteps coming out of the shadows of a doorway; nor the knife snapping open. He didn't feel any pain either; he was dead before his body hit the cold pavement.

Line's assailant bent over the corpse, pulled open his victim's greatcoat and grabbed the two or three sheets of notepaper tucked in the breast pocket of the dead man's jacket. 'Move it, Gaffer,' he shouted to the cabbie as he hopped inside and settled in the seat that Line had thought was to be his.

Chapter Twenty-Six: Opening Statements

The Lord Chief Justice, Sir Winston Grissick, took great pride in the speed at which the British legal system dispensed justice and meted out punishment. Nowhere in the world, he liked to say, was a murderer dispatched to the gallows more quickly than in London, the scaffold in Horsemonger Lane only a few steps from the Old Bailey.

He was surely pleased then that the trial of Richard Darwin for the abduction and murder of his wife was already underway, only four days after he'd pressed for the fellow's arrest. The morning newspapers were full of what promised to be one of the most sensational cases ever tried in London's most famous court, a journalist's dream come true, and Grissick, ever ready to promote himself, had decided to preside. Resplendent in long, white wig, red, ermine-trimmed robe and gold chain, he regarded the courtroom from his dais as though surveying his personal kingdom.

Dunston was seated in the packed spectators' gallery, the tiered balcony running around three sides of the courtroom. Having failed to find a rational explanation for Henrietta's 'miraculous exit' from Down House, he'd decided that his best hope of solving her murder lay in the evidence to be presented at Richard's trial. He craned forward, intent on absorbing every nuance, as Mr Smythe, counsel for the Crown, rose. The white-wigged, black-gowned prosecutor stood at one end of the semi-circular mahogany table in front of the judge's podium, jury to his left, defendant to his right, and began his opening statement.

'M'lud, gentlemen of the jury, the task before us today is a challenge of the first order. We are dealing with one of the most devilishly clever murderers I have ever encountered in my thirty years at the bar. The accused, Richard Darwin, devised a scheme for doing away with his wife, Henrietta, so cunning that no one would even suspect a murder had been committed. How was this astonishing feat to be accomplished? By means of misdirection. The defendant set out to make everyone believe his wife had taken her own life.

'To this end, he shrewdly chose January 17 of this year as the day for Henrietta's disappearance. Why? Because on this very day, three years earlier, Henrietta's much cherished eighteen-month-old son came down with a seemingly minor ailment. His father, a doctor, administered his usual tonic and left to visit a patient, leaving the child in his grandmother's care. He was only gone an hour but by the time he returned, the infant had passed. This heart-breaking tragedy bore constantly on the now childless mother, but especially on the anniversary of that cruel event. A sorrowful Henrietta went to bed early that evening *and was never seen again*.'

Mr Smythe let his words settle in the minds and hearts of the jurors. He was a beanpole of a man with the hunched shoulders and lowered head of one who'd spent his life stooping to fit in with his shorter brethren. He liked to gesticulate with his right arm, its movement matching the modulation of his speech: arm up, voice high; arm down, voice low. His features – narrow face, sharp chin, hooked nose – brought to mind Mr Punch from the popular puppet show, yet this in no way undermined the authority of his deep and cultured delivery.

'The family,' he continued, 'feared a grieving Henrietta went out into the winter's night to end her life, exactly what the accused intended. To complete the deception, he arranged for his kidnapped wife to be bludgeoned to death so brutally that her identification would be impossible. The police, he reasoned, would eventually call off their search, and her disappearance would be ruled a suicide, body never recovered. There in a nutshell, you have it – Richard Darwin's perfect crime.

'All went well for our ingenious wife-killer until he learned that the detectives of the Metropolitan Police Force were as clever as he, and had seen through the fake suicide. He realised at once that suspicion would now fall on him.

'In such circumstances, most men would confess or run. Not so the defendant. He masterfully devised a second and even more baffling means of misdirecting would-be investigators. He presented them with an apparent impossibility – the removal of Henrietta's body from Down House, with all exterior doors securely locked *and* all keys accounted for.

'The defendant believed the police would never fathom how the abduction was accomplished and, missing that all-important link in the chain of evidence, a conviction would be impossible, and he, a kidnapper and murderer, would sit untouched by suspicion, completely in the clear.

'The ploy almost worked. The police were indeed flummoxed... except for Chief of Detectives, Jeremiah Fickett, who brilliantly unravelled the keyless vanishing trick *and* identified the only person,' arm up, voice raised, 'who could have pulled it off. And that person, gentlemen of the jury,' finger pointing at the defendant, 'is none other than... *Richard Darwin.*'

Mr Smythe sat down, having squashed, or so it seemed to a fretting Dunston, any hopes of acquittal for the defendant. The lawyer had painted a compelling picture of a vicious, scheming villain, a portrait so dark and distressing, the horror of it was etched on every juror's face. They'd listened spellbound, absorbed every word, and been thoroughly convinced.

Dunston glanced at Mrs Darwin on the opposite side of the court and saw an ashen face, teary eyes, and quivering mouth beneath her dun-coloured bonnet, clear signs she knew she was losing her son. He searched the rows of spectators for Line, anxious for a reassuring nod or smile, but didn't see him. Where was the man? Nothing from him since the inquest.

At the other end of the mahogany table, counsel for the defence, Mr Matheringly, rose to his feet. A robust figure with square shoulders and barrel chest more befitting a circus strongman than a lawyer, he took a bulldog stance and glanced confidently around the courtroom. Dunston's spirits lifted, only to plummet as soon as he heard his high-pitched voice – more mouse-squeak than lion-roar – and oddly toneless delivery. Dunston feared the worst.

'My learned friend has spun an interesting tale,' the lawyer began. 'A story of a wife's brutal, premeditated murder orchestrated by her husband, whom we are told, is amazingly clever. Now, I'm not a clever man, yet even I can see the gaping hole in the Crown's case – motive.' He placed not an iota of emphasis on this last, seemingly important word. Instead he paused, apparently his way of signalling that what he'd just said was worthy of attention.

'A husband,' he resumed, 'who planned his wife's murder as carefully and coldly as the villain depicted in the Crown's fairy-tale must surely have a powerful motive. Yet my learned friend omitted to mention it. And with good reason. There isn't one.' Another pause. 'Richard Darwin has no reason to want his wife dead. In fact, the motive behind this crime has nothing to do with murdering Mrs Henrietta Darwin, but everything to do with coercing her father-in-law, the eminent scientist, Mr Charles Darwin, to act against his will.'

Seeing that his extraordinary claim had electrified juror and spectator alike, Matheringly skipped his usual pause, and carried on in his reedy, humdrum tone.

'You see, Mr Darwin Senior is involved in an academic dispute with a young biologist, a devout Catholic by the name of George Mivart. Make no mistake, this is not a mild disagreement. This is science pitted against religion in a life and death battle for the minds and souls of man, a feud charged with such ferocity, it culminated in a deadly ultimatum – Charles Darwin must retract his theory...' pause '...or his daughter-in-law dies.'

The lawyer's words had the jury hanging on every syllable. Even so, he remained silent for a few seconds to make sure that no one had missed the cornerstone of his argument.

'Here, then, we have motive, not to murder Henrietta Darwin, but to force Charles Darwin to renounce his theory of evolution. Yes, you may say, but the lady ended up dead, brutally battered. True, but, having understood the motive, we can now grasp how events transpired. Imagine the scene. Henrietta Darwin, held captive in some hole in London, escapes. Her captors race after her, running her down in Nightingale Lane, and, in the ensuing scuffle, she's killed. Not intentionally, perhaps, but she's dead nonetheless.'

Ah, Line's theory of the botched kidnapping. Dunston's round face beamed with pride as he recalled the former inspector's 'virtuoso performance' in The Six Jolly Porters. He must have mentioned it in his weekly case reports to Mrs Darwin, and she in turn must have shared it with the lawyer.

'Now, with Henrietta dead,' Matheringly continued, 'the threat the kidnapper was holding over Charles Darwin was gone, but the villain who masterminded the abduction was not done. He realised that as long as no one knew the bait, namely Henrietta, was dead, he could proceed with his ransom demand. So, what did he do? He had her beaten beyond any likelihood of recognition.

'With no reason to think his daughter-in-law dead, Charles Darwin continued to believe she was in grave danger unless he acted, and act he did, his retraction appearing in The Times of Monday, January 29, exactly what Mivart wanted.' This statement was followed by the longest pause so far.

'Had the prosecution considered motive more carefully, they would have realised we are not dealing with a premeditated murder, but with a bungled kidnapping. Instead of accusing Richard Darwin, a man who had no reason to murder his wife, we should be trying George Mivart, a man who had every reason to kidnap her. Thank you.'

Amazing, marvelled Dunston. The same set of facts, yet two totally different versions of the crime. The pendulum, which had veered far in the direction of a runaway victory for the Crown, had now swung back to vertical. The jurors, all of whom had worn expressions that said GUILTY in large letters after the prosecution's opening statement, now had faces contorted into a dozen confused question marks. Well played, Mr Matheringly.

A solid recovery, but matters were still delicately poised, and Matheringly had done nothing to fill in the gaping hole in his version of events – how Mivart managed to extricate Henrietta from Down House – whereas the Crown prosecutor claimed to know exactly how Richard Darwin did it. Very worrying.

Chapter Twenty-Seven: The Anonymous Letters

Dunston usually took a short nap after lunch. But not this afternoon. Instead, he was perched on the edge of his uncomfortable courtroom seat, all ears and eyes. He followed closely as Mr Smythe, counsel for the Crown, used the first hour of the afternoon session to acquaint the jurors with the basics of the crime beginning with the discovery of Henrietta's empty bedroom.

He then took them through the evidence that led the police to suspect abduction rather than suicide. He covered the whiff of chloroform in the bedroom (a Line observation), the footprints outside the backdoor (Line's explanation of the single-track trick), and the absence of a body in the surrounding area despite a thorough search. He next turned to the evidence of murder: Geraldine Hawksby's account of the beating in Nightingale Lane; Dr Cullingworth's report (death from a fractured skull); and Estelle Moxley's identification of her sister's remains by means of the scars on her left foot.

The police investigation, Smythe summed up, indicated that Mrs Henrietta Darwin was drugged, removed from Down House via the backdoor, taken to London, and there bludgeoned to death. Matheringly remained seated throughout, evidently quite happy for the Crown to establish that Henrietta was abducted, this being perfectly consistent with his botched-kidnapping defence. Dunston too was pleased – Line might not be in court, still no sign of the fellow, but his stamp was all over the evidence.

Proceedings took a more interesting turn when Smythe introduced the first of the two anonymous letters. He read it aloud to the jurors ending dramatically with, *I swear by Aesculapius that the Hounds of Hell will feast on your flesh for all eternity!*

'This letter,' the prosecutor continued, 'arrived at Down House on December 24 of last year. Note the reference to *Aesculapius*. Odd, you might think, to mention a Greek god in a statement about the true God's creation of the world. Well, perhaps not if you're a doctor, because, as I'm sure you all know,' he said, well aware that the clodhoppers in the jury would know nothing about ancient-world mythology, '*Aesculapius* is the Greek god of medicine, usually depicted carrying a rod encircled by a coiled snake, the symbol still used by the medical profession.

'Now the writer wanted us to believe that this note was sent by someone who vehemently disagrees with Charles Darwin's theories, a clever move to divert suspicion from himself, but the reference to *Aesculapius* gives him away, signals it was written by a doctor, and the defendant, may I remind you,' voice and arm raised, 'is a doctor.' Smythe stared at the man in the dock for a long minute and then sat down.

Matheringly was not going to let this pass unchallenged. He rose to his feet. 'I suppose,' he said, making clear that this was not at all what he supposed, 'that since *Aesculapius* is the god of medicine, the sender of this letter could indeed be a doctor, but since *Aesculapius* is a Greek god, one might with equal justification conclude the sender is... a Greek.'

Half-stifled giggles interspersed with the occasional guffaw broke out around the courtroom. Not usually given to humour, even Dunston joined in with a chuckle, his fat jowls bobbing up and down, pleasantly surprised by Matheringly's clever retort. Lowbrow humour trumped intellectual arrogance every day of the week, he thought.

'Neither inference,' the lawyer said when he had everyone's attention, 'is founded on hard evidence, they're just mildly interesting speculations that have no place in a court of law. Here, we deal exclusively with facts,' he affirmed, unwittingly chancing on words that might have come straight from Archibald Line's mouth. 'And the facts are these: the sender used notepaper from the Athenaeum Club; the words were clipped from The

Times; and the letter was posted in London. Any number of gentlemen could have managed this with ease. Let me mention one who fits the bill, someone who, by the way, recently became a member of the Athenaeum Club – Mr George Mivart.'

Dunston nodded approvingly. Matheringly had delivered a telling blow, and kept Mivart's name front and centre.

Counsel for the Crown, though, seemed unperturbed. Calmly picking up a second piece of paper, Smythe said: 'Let me turn now to the anonymous letter that arrived at Down House on January 23 and which, as my learned friend kindly pointed out, contains a threat to Henrietta Darwin's life if Charles Darwin does not retract his theory of evolution.' He read the letter aloud, stressing the final, sinister words – *your daughter-in-law will perish.*

'The police initially thought that Richard Darwin had also written this one, but new evidence has come to light. The Crown calls George Mivart.'

A torrent of whispered questions sluiced through the court. Mivart? The man the defence believed was the kidnapper? Whyever was the prosecution calling him? Concern clouding his face, Dunston glanced at Matheringly – what was going on? The lawyer was doing his best to maintain an unruffled exterior, but there was no hiding his shock.

Dunston watched the witness take the stand. He saw a short, slump-shouldered man, his slight build lost in the large witness box. In a dark, well-tailored suit, with a navy blue cravat set against a white shirt, he looked like any other gentleman. The face, though, caught Dunston's eye. The man must be forty, yet his cheeks, chin and upper lip displayed hardly a trace of stubble. Either he had the sharpest razor in England or he was one of those men who never sprouted much by way of facial hair.

'Mr Mivart,' began Smythe, 'do you recognise this letter?'

'I do.'

'How so?'

'I sent it.'

Gasps of disbelief erupted at this astonishing admission. After banging his gavel twice to restore order, Grissick motioned Smythe to continue but, to the bewilderment of the entire courtroom, the lawyer sat down, and with a casual wave invited Matheringly to cross-examine.

The defence lawyer looked nonplussed at what he'd just heard. The prosecution had all but proved Mivart's guilt. If the witness sent the ransom note, as he admitted, then didn't that make him the kidnapper? Yes, it did, and there was a way Matheringly could nail the point.

He rose, taking his time before speaking, no doubt choosing his words for best effect. 'Mr Mivart,' he began mildly, 'did you send the first anonymous letter?'

'No, I did not.'

'Yet, you claim to have sent the second one. Am I right?'

'Indeed, you are, sir.'

'Good. Now, as I recall, this second letter arrived at Down House on January 23, so it must have been posted in London no later than January 22. Would you agree?'

'I would.'

'And Henrietta Darwin's bedroom was found empty on the morning of January 18, so we have four days between her disappearance and the latest possible posting of the letter. During that time, news of the kidnapping was kept out of the newspapers so the abduction was not general knowledge. In fact, the only people who knew about it were the immediate Darwin family, Mr Darwin's household staff, the police, and… the kidnapper. Do you follow me?' Matheringly's tongue flicked from side to side, like a snake's before it strikes.

'I do.'

'Then, Mr Mivart, since you are not a member of the Darwin family, nor a servant in Mr Darwin's household, nor an officer in the Metropolitan Police, the only way you could have known of Mrs Henrietta Darwin's abduction is if you orchestrated the kidnapping yourself.' Pause. 'In short, sir, by confessing to sending the ransom demand, you have, I submit, confessed to kidnapping.' The snake had struck.

Matheringly delivered his knockout blow in his usual tedious drone but its effect was as though he'd shouted it from the rooftops like a *muezzin* calling the faithful to prayer. Much banging of the gavel was required before

Grissick could quiet the afternoon's third and noisiest outbreak. Silence restored, Smythe rose to his feet.

'Mr Mivart, my learned friend has accused you of kidnapping. What is your response?' Smythe asked.

'My response is this, sir. I did not kidnap Mrs Henrietta Darwin nor harm her in any way. Nor did I send the first anonymous letter. I confess *only* to sending the second one, and apologise most abjectly for doing so. Let me explain how it happened. I was in the Athenaeum Club with Sir Edmund Henderson, Commissioner of the Metropolitan Police. It was *he* who informed me that Charles Darwin's daughter-in-law had been kidnapped.'

This time the courtroom was absolutely silent, spectators and jurors alike realising they'd heard a crucial piece of evidence but struggling to grasp its significance. Not so Dunston. He knew at once that Matheringly had blundered, fallen into a neat trap laid by the prosecution. There was no way out. Mivart learned about the abduction from the Police Commissioner – the *Police Commissioner* for goodness' sake!

'An odd conversation, I thought,' resumed Mivart, every eye fastened on him. 'The commissioner and I had never talked before and all of a sudden he was sharing confidential details about an otherwise undisclosed crime. And then it struck me. *This must be God's doing.* The Lord had seen fit to bring Darwin's vulnerability to my notice, to present me with an opportunity to end his blasphemous attacks on the true teachings of the Catholic church. Convinced I was doing the Lord's work, I prepared the ransom demand and sent it later that day.

'I immediately regretted my shameful behaviour and prayed for God's forgiveness. What I'd done was not a Christian act, it was not His wish, just my own desire to prove my point and discredit Charles Darwin. When I saw his retraction in The Times, I knew there was only one honourable course of action – I had to make amends. I swear on my oath that I will apologise to Mr Darwin privately and publicly, and hope with all my heart that he will have the goodness and grace to forgive me.'

The silence after this sorrowful outpouring of self-condemnation was different, respectful, reverent almost.

'Perhaps, this would be a good time for me to address the court,' announced the Lord Chief Justice, emerging from his listening pose, eyes twinkling in anticipation of one of his jury-nurturing moments. The English judicial system was evolving, as Darwin would say, with judges slowly relinquishing their role as the ultimate authority in the courtroom for that of neutral arbiter. Grissick was the exception, a legal dinosaur thriving long after the rest of his species was extinct, still willing to inject views reflecting his own singularly personal interpretation of justice.

'I've observed many witnesses in this court and, sadly, many a time listened to lies, deceptions and insinuations. It is, then, wonderfully refreshing to have before us an honest man. Mr Mivart, under no obligation other than that of his conscience, has confessed to what is a despicable act. His intentions may have been virtuous, noble even, but the deed itself must be condemned. Now is not the time to dwell on the appropriate punishment for his transgression, but it is the time and my duty to consider the implications of his confession for this trial.' Like sheep ready to be led, the twelve good men and true listened carefully to their shepherd.

'Gentlemen of the jury, it will no doubt have occurred to you that having admitted to sending the more threatening of the two anonymous letters, Mr Mivart had no reason not to confess to sending the other. That he did not, has, I imagine, led you as it has me, to suspect that some other person is responsible for that first abomination.' Grissick paused, slowly turned his head and stared hard at the defendant. Dutifully following his lead, the sheep trained twelve pairs of hostile eyes on the accused.

'But that's not all,' continued Grissick, eyeing his flock. 'You will also, I'm sure, have wondered whether a murderer would willingly confess to sending a letter that portends the death of his victim. I have no view on this point, but let me leave it with you and trust you will give it its proper weight in your deliberations.'

Grissick's beady eyes shifted to the witness. 'Mr Mivart, the court condemns your actions but commends your honesty. You may step down.'

Dunston watched in disbelief as Mivart, with the hint of a smile – relief? or something else? – playing about his lips, walked out of the courtroom.

Chapter Twenty-Eight: Bad News

Dunston and clothes did not go together well. Suits were a particular problem. Of the two he possessed, both dark grey, one was overly long in the body, the jacket reaching too far down his heavy thighs; the other unduly tight around the torso, the buttons of his waistcoat threatening to pop off at any minute. To make matters worse, the sleeves on both were a tad short, the material thus saved apparently applied to the trouser legs which puddled around his ankles unless constantly hitched up.

Most customers would have demanded that the offending garments be replaced or at least re-tailored. Not so Dunston. The tailors in question were Scutters and Sons, Strood's leading gentleman's clothier, and complaining to them was something that didn't even cross Dunston's mind. Better to keep the ill-fitting suits than cause a fuss.

Nor did Dunston have a good relationship with the usual sartorial refinements of a gentleman's attire, especially the bowtie. Instead of forming a neat, straight line gracing the centre of his collar, Dunston's ended up with one side askew or else both sides drooping like a bloodhound's ears. Still, Dunston took solace in one of the sayings of William Horman, a sixteenth-century headmaster at Eton School – *manners* maketh man.

As he took a corner table in the Adelphi Hotel's breakfast room on Saturday morning, the hang of his suit and the alignment of his bowtie were the last things on his mind. It was the day after Grissick had delivered his extraordinary extra-legal guidance to the jury, and the trial's events were uppermost in his thoughts. He feared the cards had been stacked against Richard, convinced the diabolical pair of smooth-as-silk Smythe and conniving Lord Chief Justice Grissick stage-managed Mivart's testimony.

By casting Mivart as an honest, God-fearing man who'd made a mistake, Grissick had exonerated him in the eyes of the jurors and effectively undercut the defence Matheringly was mounting. Thanks to the prosecution's artful manoeuvre, Matheringly hadn't even had a chance to bring up the abrupt termination of Mivart's courtship of Henrietta's sister.

Still, Crown counsel hadn't come up with a motive for Richard to kill his wife, and juries placed great weight on motive. Nor had the prosecution offered anything to substantiate their claim that they knew how he removed Henrietta's body from Down House. Without establishing why or how the crime was committed, surely no jury would ever convict him. Dunston was cheered by this thought and the timely arrival of breakfast.

He was finishing his coffee when Nick appeared with the day's Times.

'Ah, thank you. I'll take it up to my room and read it later.'

'Best look at it now, sir,' Nick said. 'Page five. Bad news.'

Slightly put out, Dunston opened it, gave it a good shake and started to read. 'Good Lord!'

LONDON'S FORMER CHIEF OF DETECTIVES MURDERED

Archibald Line, the Metropolitan Police's first Chief of Detectives, was murdered, his throat slit, shortly after six o'clock Friday morning outside Euston Station.

Dunston slumped back in his chair, the newspaper slipping to the floor.

'Sir, you alright?'

'I... I need a few moments by myself.' He started for the exit, stopped, turned back, scooped up the newspaper and left the room.

He stumbled up the stairs, lurched into his bedroom, and sank into its only armchair. He fumbled the paper open and read the page-five article in full. Written to make the morning edition, the report did not have much more to say about the crime, other than noting that the police suspected a revenge killing and were calling for any witnesses to come forward. Most of the piece summarised Line's career, highlighting his arrests of some of London's most notorious murderers, his successful breakup of the infamous Scutters gang of burglars operating in Kent, and his unintended shooting of an innocent bystander, a seventeen-year-old maid, the incident that led to his resignation.

The article's last paragraph, however, switched to his personal life. As he read, Dunston's face turned ghost-white, his fingers gripped the edges of the newspaper, his eyes teared, blurring the newsprint… except for a handful of ugly words that jumped off the page – *wife, Rose, and ten-year old daughter, May, both lost to cholera on July 17, 1850.*

'Good Heavens!' Dunston muttered. '*R* and *M*! The two letters on the medallion he always carried. His wife and daughter.' Dunston had only glimpsed the initials once or twice, and Line had never explained them. Until he saw those dreadful words in the newspaper, he'd no idea Line had been married or fathered a child. Dunston sat there, motionless, a sack-like bundle of rumpled clothes.

He remembered the epidemic well, one of the worst in London's history, thousands dying in agony. A terrible end to life for the afflicted, and tragic for those left behind. For Line to lose his two dearest… and on the same day… what an unbearable loss! The man must have been devastated.

Now I understand, thought Dunston, why Line, like me, led such a solitary existence: for him, a response to life's mindless cruelty; for me, always there from my earliest memories. Whatever the cause, it was surely as heavy a burden for him as it was for me, but, strange as it seems, that was what brought us together, provided the common ground from which had sprung those first tentative sprouts of friendship. Sad to say, with Line's death, that fledgling plant was uprooted from the earth, and gone from Dunston's life forever.

Dunston would grieve for his friend today, tomorrow and for all the tomorrows to come, but for now, he would put his mourning on hold. He wiped nose and eyes and turned his mind to the murder itself. Who on earth would do such a thing? His first thought, prompted by the newspaper article, fastened on the remnants of the Scutters gang, vicious characters like Snatcher and Stingo Pete, who would gladly cut Line's throat first chance they had. Or maybe someone close to the young maid he'd shot, had taken revenge.

But they were in Line's past. Why would anyone wait until now for vengeance? No, this was not retribution for some deed from Line's time in the Metropolitan Police Force. That left the cases he'd taken on since becoming a private inquiry agent in Kent a year and a half ago. Only a few as Dunston recalled, and in his letter inviting him to visit, the city-hardened policeman had spoken disparagingly about them, nothing but country-bumpkin crimes – minor pilfering, the occasional break-in, a stolen sheep, except...

Except for his current case. That must be it. Line's death must have something to do with Henrietta Darwin's abduction and murder. If he'd found evidence that proved Richard innocent, then... then someone else was guilty, and that someone butchered Dunston's friend.

Dunston had been intrigued by the Darwin case from the start. Henrietta's seemingly impossible removal from Down House presented a serious intellectual challenge, and he dearly wanted to be the first to solve the puzzle. That was then. Now it was personal.

Anger burned through him like a wind-whipped forest fire racing through drought-dry undergrowth, boiling his blood, searing his resolve until it was white-hot and battle-ready. From this moment forward, Dunston was a man on a mission, his entire being focused on only one goal – to find whoever bludgeoned Henrietta to death because, that done, he'd have the scum who slit his friend's throat.

Chapter Twenty-Nine: Mrs Annabelle Curdsley

Archibald Line's murder gnawed at Dunston's insides for the rest of the weekend, robbing him of sleep and dulling his usually healthy appetite. He'd spent Saturday poring over Line's reports, striving to replicate the logical, step-by-step progression that Line had no doubt pursued to find whatever it was that proved Richard's innocence. But that took him nowhere; it was not how Dunston's mind functioned.

On Sunday, he switched tactics, shuffling the facts like playing cards, randomly dealing them out, and hoping his idiosyncratic, dot-connecting intuition – his extra half-sense as Line called it – would point him in the right direction. But still no joy. Either Dunston was missing something, or Line had unearthed new evidence in the nine-day gap since his last report.

After his wasted weekend, Dunston returned to the Old Bailey for the second day of the trial, massively more energised now that his investigation had vaulted from solving a lady's disappearance to finding his friend's killer. More desperate than ever to pick up some clue or at least a hint from the day's testimonies, he'd arrived early at the courthouse and grabbed a front row seat. He'd been in place for a full hour, when the prosecution counsel, Mr Smythe, summoned the morning's first witness.

'The Crown calls Mrs Annabelle Curdsley.'

The spectators, many of whom were still settling into their seats, paid scant attention to a witness whose name no one recognised. It wasn't until she'd taken the stand that eyes turned toward the lopsided-looking woman and fastened with morbid curiosity on the enormous mass of flesh on the right side of her neck. Wearing a gawdy day dress with a puff-sleeved bodice, her thin, grey hair tucked up under a garish bonnet, the old fussock looked more like a street-worn trollop than the respectable matron she'd no doubt been aiming for.

'Please state your name,' recited Mr Smythe.

'Annabelle Curdsley, tho' everyone in the spike calls me Eyesore Annie. Can't for the life of me understand why, 'cos ain't nothin' wrong with my eyes, it's my neck what's sore,' she said, fingers tenderly stroking the disfiguring goitre, 'and if them numbskulls can't see that, must be something wrong with *their* eyes.'

'Indeed, Mrs Curdsley, I take your point,' conceded the prosecutor with a curt nod, obviously keen to move on to the meat of her evidence. 'Am I to understand that when you say 'spike', you're referring to Shoreditch Workhouse in Kingsland Road?'

'Well, aren't you the clever one? That's right, dearie.'

'Very good. Now, Mrs Curdsley, I'd like to take you back to Monday of last week when I believe you visited the residence of Mr George Mivart.'

George Mivart! The name was once more on everyone's lips, questions flying around the courtroom – Mivart, again? Didn't the judge dismiss him? The judge in question raised his gavel but before he could bring it down, the gallery fell silent, everyone anxious to hear what connection Mrs Curdsley could possibly have with George Mivart.

'Could you please tell the court the purpose of your visit?'

'Yes, sir. The why an' the wherefore of it was this. This bloke was in my usual watering hole, magging on about some clever clogs, name of George Mivart, who was in a big brouhaha with another brain-box. Something 'bout where we all come from, and how gorillas and chimpanzees and such are our brothers an' sisters. Can you believe that? Load of donkey droppings, you ask me.'

Her words were greeted with a few cheers from the spectators, but a stern, get-on-with-it glare from Smythe. 'Anyway,' she continued unabashed, 'according to loudmouth, Mivart cursed the other fellow up an' down, said he'd give his right ball— oops, sorry sir, just slipped out. Funny tho', now that I think 'bout it, how it's always the right one, ain't it? Never the left. Makes no sense, all look the same to me.'

'Yes… a very illuminating observation, for which the court thanks you, but could you confine your remarks to the events leading up to your visit to Mr Mivart?'

'As you like,' replied Annie equably. 'Well, when I heard the other bloke's name was Charles Darwin, I couldn't believe me ears, 'cos it so happened, I knew something what might help Mivart steamroll old Darwin into the dirt. So, I asked blabbermouth where Mivart lived, and next day went to see him.'

'And was Mr Mivart interested in what you had to say?'

'Was he ever. Listened real careful, never said a word, then handed over four sovs when I'd finished. Can you believe that? *Four sovereigns.* I was that flabbergasted, a baby's fart could've knocked me flat on my back.' Eyesore Annie's eyes bugged at the memory of her unexpected windfall, her face aglow, the bulge on her neck quivering with delight.

'I see. And what was it that warranted such a princely sum?'

'Usual story, sir. See, this young woman, girl really, no more than twenty, came into the spike with a belly round as a beer barrel.'

'She was with child?'

'That she was.'

'And when was this?'

'Middle of January.'

'And her name?'

'Don't remember, sir. See, girls like her come in all the time to drop their babies. Some give their real name but most don't, so over the years I've learned to take no heed of what they call themselves,' Annie explained. 'Said she was from Cornwall, if that helps.'

'Very well. Please continue.'

'Yes, sir. Trouble was, she was a slip of a thing, and the mite wouldn't come out. Real difficult birth, blood everywhere, the girl's face getting whiter an' whiter, and then she stopped breathing. We was in a real state, left with a dead mother and a live babe.'

'A sad tale, Mrs Curdsley, but not uncommon. Perhaps, if it's not too much trouble,' Smythe's exasperation with the woman's digressions was evident, 'you could tell us what was so interesting to Mr Mivart?'

'Haven't come to that bit yet, sir. See, she weren't as dead as we thought, came back from the beyond, she did. Then, a few days later, the ungrateful little slug stole some clothes and took off to find her son.'

'Any idea where she is now?'

'Could be anywhere, for all I know.'

'Very well. Then let us return to the question of Mr Mivart's interest in this sad tale,' instructed the prosecutor for the third time.

'Right, sir. Even after she came back to life, she'd still black out every now an' then, sometimes out to the world, sometimes wide awake as, well, as you, sir.'

'Yes... um... thank you. And did she say anything?'

'Well, sir, if I asked her anything 'bout herself when she was wakeful, she'd shut up like a clam. What Mivart paid me for, she let slip when she was passed out. Called her my Sleepin' Beauty 'cos in her little dreamworld, she'd spill her guts like nobody's business, babble away nineteen to the dozen.'

'I'm not sure the jury need hear every detail,' directed Smythe. 'Just those that bear on the case.'

'That's what I'm trying to tell you if you'll only let me,' Annie complained with a shrug of her shoulders that caused the great, fleshy protuberance on her neck to concertina.

'Of course, Mrs Curdsley,' said the prosecutor through gritted teeth. 'Forgive me. Please take your time.'

'Thank ye kindly,' replied a mollified Annie. 'Well, she went on about the butler where she maided, so I thought he was her little'un's father. Easy as pie for butlers to take advantage of them lower down the ladder, but that ain't what happened. Girl was mad with him 'cos he threw her out soon as her belly showed, but he wasn't the father.'

'Mrs Curdsley, perhaps you could tell us who *was* the father rather than who *wasn't...*'

'Well, if that's all you want to know, here's what I can tell you. The father was a gentl'man, judging by the way she spoke 'bout him. Don't know how she met him, but she fell for him head over heels. Called him her darlin' Richard.'

Every eye in the courtroom, even Matheringly's, converged on the man in the dock. What about Mrs Darwin? Dunston pulled his gaze away from the son and looked at the mother. She was sitting on the other side of the court from Dunston, as close as she could possibly be to Richard. Despite what she'd just heard, she was smiling encouragingly at her firstborn, doing her brave-faced utmost to buck him up, but not with much success judging by his lowered head and slumped shoulders. She might still be hoping for the best, but he, Dunston sensed, was fearing the worst. As was Dunston.

'And he was the father sure as eggs is eggs,' continued Annie. 'Many a time, blacked out as she was, her hand would go to her tummy as though the babe was still there and Sleepin' Beauty would say,' she softened her voice, *'your father may not be here, little one, but you will forever be my darlin' Richard's son.* That's word for word what she said.'

'So, this Richard is the father. Very good. But there must be hundreds of Richards in England,' said the lawyer, feigning bemusement.

'S'ppose so. Never had cause to count 'em. And no need to 'cos I know which Richard she was talking 'bout. One of the last things she said 'fore she woke up proper and clammed up for good, was the words what fetched me four gold'uns from Mr Mivart's kind hand.' Annie switched back to her Sleeping-Beauty voice, *'You, my little love, may never carry the name, but always remember you're a Darwin by birth.'*

Mr Smythe turned to the jury, embracing them with his gaze, and solemnly said, 'Gentlemen of the jury, we have our motive.'

Chapter Thirty: A Courtroom Demonstration

Dunston took his seat in the courtroom after lunch and glumly reviewed the morning session. Without actually spelling it out, the Crown counsel had made Richard's motive crystal-clear. With his wife out of the way, Richard would be free to marry the young woman and be a father to their child, a son to replace the one he'd lost. What a disastrous morning. Still, things couldn't get any worse.

'The Crown calls Grace Trewin,' announced Smythe.

Excellent, thought Dunston. Line viewed her favourably, so perhaps she'll be more sympathetic to Richard's cause. And maybe there'll be something in her testimony that will finally open a line of inquiry into my friend's death.

'Miss Trewin,' began the Crown counsel, 'the police have determined that Henrietta Darwin was drugged, carried down the backstairs, and taken out of Down House via the backdoor. Since that door had to be unlocked by the kidnappers for them to enter and then relocked after their exit, they must have acquired one of its three keys. Two of them – the master's and the butler's – were too well secured to have been used. That leaves the third key, the one belonging to your mistress. Could you please tell us what you know about that key?'

'Yes, sir,' said Grace, once again smartly turned out in her light blue frock and bonnet. 'The key's kept in a cubbyhole behind a false panel in the mistress's vanity, and that's where it was found on the Saturday after her disappearance.'

'But the disappearance was discovered on Thursday morning,' Smythe pointed out, 'so why wasn't the key found before Saturday?'

'You have to insert two little brass figures into slots on the front of the vanity to release the panel and to close it, sir' answered Grace. 'My mistress has one. Hers was on top of the vanity where she often left it, but Mr Richard's was with him in London, saw him put it in his waistcoat pocket when he was getting ready to leave on Wednesday morning. Without his, the panel couldn't be opened. Had to wait for his return on Saturday.'

'And when he returned, what happened?'

'I saw Mr Richard and the inspector go upstairs. Mr Richard looked ghastly, barely able to put one foot in front of the other. They went into my mistress's bedroom and I slipped in behind them to watch. Mr Richard was all fingers and thumbs, but he managed to take his brass figure out of his pocket, pick up his wife's, insert them in the slots and the panel dropped down. He was standing a little to one side so I could see the opening to the cubbyhole plain as day. I saw Mr Richard reach in, find the key and pull it out.'

'Thank you, Miss Trewin.'

Dunston grimaced. The maid had repeated exactly what she'd told Line, nothing more. He'd had high hopes for her testimony – a fresh detail about the brass figures perhaps, or a just-remembered trifle about the vanity's locking mechanism, something he might have missed when he examined the dressing table – but nothing. Nothing to snap his standstill investigation into life. He was disappointed but not deterred, determined to see it through to the end.

Smythe called his next witness, Jeremiah Fickett. The inspector took the stand, assured, cocky almost, like a prize fighter confident of victory before the bout's even started. The silver buttons on his full dress uniform shone so brilliantly, they must surely have been polished that day.

'Inspector Fickett, we've heard from Miss Trewin that both brass figures are required to open and close the cubbyhole, and that the defendant had his with him in London from Wednesday morning to Saturday afternoon,' Smythe said. 'So, *before* his departure, the cubbyhole could be opened and the key removed. But, *after* it, until his return, no one, I repeat, no one could get into the vanity to replace the key, yet that is where it was found on the Saturday after Henrietta Darwin's disappearance. Did your investigation shed any light on this apparent impossibility?'

'Indeed, it did, sir,' replied the inspector, in total command of himself and the courtroom. 'This is what happened. The defendant removed the key from the vanity before leaving Down House and passed it to his henchmen. They abducted Henrietta Darwin, and handed the key back to him in London.

'He returned to Down House on Saturday, intending to plant the key on the path outside the backdoor. When it was later found there, perhaps with some help from him, it would confirm that his wife had opened the cubbyhole before his departure for London using the two brass figures, her husband's borrowed without his knowledge, and taken the key. After he'd left, she exited Down House and wandered off into the night to end her life, the key falling from her hand as she stumbled along.'

'Forgive me, Inspector Fickett,' said Smythe, his bemused expression back in place, 'but Miss Trewin testified that the key was found in the vanity, not on the path from the backdoor.'

'Miss Trewin's testimony is accurate as far as it goes, sir, but to find the truth we must delve deeper. With your permission,' said Fickett, addressing Lord Chief Justice Grissick, 'I would like to conduct a demonstration.'

Grissick signalled Fickett to proceed. The area in the semi-circle formed by the mahogany table was quickly cleared and the vanity brought in and placed facing the jury.

'The vanity you see before you,' Fickett explained, 'is the one from Henrietta Darwin's bedroom. It's positioned so that your view is exactly the same as I had when I asked the defendant to open it. If you please, I will now assume the role of the defendant. Watch closely.'

Fickett stepped up to the vanity, took the brass figures from his jacket pocket, inserted them, and the panel dropped. He was standing slightly to one side, allowing the jurors an uninterrupted view of the cubbyhole. After slipping the figures back into his pocket, he reached in, felt around for a second, then withdrew his hand and showed the jury the key, right there on his palm.

'Inspector Fickett, I watched closely as you requested,' said the Crown's counsel, 'and as far as I can see you've proved that the key was indeed in the vanity's compartment as Miss Trewin testified. Am I correct?'

'No, sir. When the vanity was brought in and placed in full view of everyone, *the key was in my pocket.*'

The courtroom erupted in a frenzy, spectators on their feet, abuzz with exclamations of utter disbelief – Impossible! How can that be? What's going on? Grissick didn't try to quiet the unruly crowd, he was too experienced for that. He waited until the outburst was running out of steam, and only then brought his gavel down and called for silence.

'Do you mean to say, inspector, that, when you reached into the cubbyhole, the key was already in your hand?' asked Smythe.

'Exactly so,' replied Fickett, now back in the witness box. 'And that, sir, is how the defendant managed to fool us. Once he'd used the two brass figures to open the panel, he paused to take out his handkerchief and wipe his brow before returning it to his trouser pocket. That's where the key was, the business with the handkerchief merely a pretext for him to get hold of it. With the key concealed between index and middle finger, at least that's how I did it, he reached in, then withdrew his hand, and, hey presto, there it was on his palm.'

Dunston scanned the courtroom, grimly noting the jurors' nods of understanding. The inspector was indeed a convincing witness, very much the man to deliver the prosecution's second blow of the day, this one fatal.

'An interesting theory,' Smythe kept his tone noncommittal, 'but why would the defendant stage such an elaborate charade if, as you argued, his intention was to drop the key on the path?'

'Planting the key on the path was the *plan*,' responded the policeman, almost salivating at the prospect of nailing the son of England's most prominent scientist. 'But life has a way of intervening in inconvenient ways. The inconvenience in this instance was my meeting him directly on his arrival at Down House, and informing him that we'd ruled out suicide and were treating his wife's disappearance as an abduction.

'My news completely ruined his plan. The consequences of that switch – from suicide to kidnapping – flashed through his mind as we climbed the stairs to his wife's bedroom to open the vanity and find what he knew was an empty cubbyhole. That was fine for the defendant as long as we believed his wife had used the key to exit Down House and taken her own life, but not if the disappearance was being treated as kidnapping, as it then was.'

'Let me see if I've grasped your point,' said Smythe. 'Once the police suspected kidnapping, they'd conclude from the empty cubbyhole that the *kidnapper*, and not Henrietta Darwin, took the key. Correct?'

A nod from Fickett.

'But then, why should this worry the defendant?'

'Because, sir,' replied Fickett, 'only the accused and his wife had access to the brass figures and, since his wife was the kidnap victim, he instantly grasped that we'd mark *him* as the kidnapper. In a split second, his world was turned upside down. Instead of being the grieving widower of a wife who'd died by her own hand, he was about to become the sole suspect in her kidnapping and murder.

'He was desperate, but the man kept his nerve and in those few seconds as he went up the stairs, he conjured up a fiendishly cunning plan, the only possible way of saving his skin – *he'd pretend to find the key in the vanity's cubbyhole*. He hadn't had time to place it on the path so there it was still in his pocket. If he could replace it in the vanity and withdraw it in one motion, as I did, then we'd be fooled into believing it had been there all along. We'd have no idea how the crime was committed, and no reason to suspect him. We'd be left clueless; he'd be in the clear.'

'But you were not fooled, inspector.'

'To begin with I was,' conceded Fickett. 'But not for long,' he continued smugly. 'And once I'd detected how the trick was pulled off, I knew who was behind Henrietta Darwin's abduction and murder... the defendant, Richard Darwin.'

Dunston shrank into his seat. This was damning evidence; Richard was doomed. A glance at Mrs Darwin told him she'd reached the same dire

conclusion. He'd watched the interplay between mother and son throughout the trial: she positive, uplifting, determined; he resigned, full of doubt, fearful. The inspector's words had shattered that uneasy equilibrium. Now, Mrs Darwin was withdrawn, knowing that even a mother's love was not enough to save her son. And he was shrivelled into himself, sensing his fate all but sealed.

Smythe was about to continue when a single raised finger from the bench stopped him cold. When the Lord Chief Justice signalled you to be quiet, you became a mouse.

'I see you have no further questions for this witness, Mr Smythe,' Grissick said, and the mouse sat down. 'I'm sure you have some questions, Mr Matheringly, but perhaps it's best to leave your cross-examination until the morrow. Given Inspector Fickett's remarkable testimony, it might be of some small service if I summarise the main points before we retire for the day.'

Oh no, thought Dunston, not again. Judging by the twinkle in Grissick's watery eye, the master of legal ceremonies was about to point the jurors in what he considered the proper judicial direction.

'Gentlemen of the jury, you are all rational men and as such have no patience with explanations of Henrietta Darwin's disappearance from Down House that rely on hocus-pocus, wizardry or devilry. I'm confident, therefore, that you have concluded a key was used to open the backdoor and close it again once the kidnappers had exited with their captive. Furthermore, of the three backdoor keys, two were too secure to have been purloined by the kidnappers, leaving only the third key, the one kept in the lady's vanity.

'With this in mind, I'm sure each of you has listed everyone with access to the two brass figures required to open and close the cubbyhole. The list is short; only two names. One of them, Henrietta Darwin, was the kidnapping victim and, therefore, hardly likely to have taken the key. And even if she had, there is no way it could have been returned to the vanity during her husband's absence since he had one of the figures in his possession. This, I'm sure you'll agree, rules *her* out and, by default, leaves her *husband* as the only remaining candidate.

'What do we know about *his* access to the cubbyhole? It's clear the defendant could have acquired the key before departing for London but, and this is the question on which the case turns, could he have replaced it *after* his return?

'This question has been convincingly answered by Inspector Fickett's brilliant demonstration of how the key found its way back into the vanity. Of course, none of us ever really thought we had anything so spiritually uplifting as a miracle on our hands, and now we've seen that it was nothing but a trick, an artful sleight of hand to be sure, but a trick nonetheless.'

Grissick ran his eye over the faces of the jurors, apparently assessing the impact of his words. With a satisfied smile, he resumed. 'I trust this summary does justice to the evidence as presented, and hope it will guide you when you come to deliberate the defendant's guilt... or innocence.'

And with that, the Lord Chief Justice brought his gavel down on its wooden base and, to all intents and purposes, on Richard Darwin.

Chapter Thirty-One: Back to Down House

Mrs Emma Darwin stepped down from the brougham and brushed past Milly, her parlour maid – highly unusual behaviour for a lady who prided herself on treating all, whether street beggar or peer of the realm, with equal consideration.

'Ma'am, what hap—'

'Must see the master,' she said curtly, hurrying into Down House.

The horror of the trial's heart-breaking final session yesterday morning had taken its toll. She'd sat there, cringing as Matheringly did his utmost to cast Richard in a favourable light by calling several character witnesses, but the jury wasn't moved, an outcome as predictable as King Canute's failure to stay the tide.

In a last-ditch attempt to sway the jurors, he'd put Richard on the stand. What a colossal mistake! Instead of generating sympathy, his sorrowful expression came across as shifty and suspicious. If his fate wasn't determined before his testimony, it was by the time he stepped down. Even so, Mrs Darwin was still stunned when the jury delivered its guilty verdict and that sinister old lizard in his black hanging cap condemned her favourite child to a barbaric death.

She entered her husband's study, styled after his book-lined rooms in Christ's College, Cambridge, removed her cloak and bonnet, and told him, as gently as she could, that his son had been sentenced to hang at ten o'clock on the following Monday, only five days away. Charles, in a heavy winter dressing gown, still unwell, was devastated but did his best to hold his sorrow in check. When *his* favourite child, Annie, their firstborn daughter, had succumbed to tuberculosis aged ten, he'd been left physically sick and emotionally lost for well over a month. This was different. Richard was in terrible trouble but he was *alive* – action, not grieving, was called for.

Darwin was seated in the oversized, upright armchair specially made to accommodate his long legs. He placed his cloth-covered writing board across the chair's arms, picked up his pen and bade his wife tell him everything that happened at the trial.

She'd barely finished, when her husband's one-word pronouncement – *Appeal!* – sent a ray of glorious light bursting through her darkness, a small, circumscribed shaft of brightness to be sure, but a beam full of hope, nonetheless. He handed her his jottings, and she eagerly read them. Two flaws! He'd identified two weaknesses in the Crown's case.

> *Prosecution claim*: Richard impregnated maid.
>   *Fact:* Woman never testified; baby never confirmed.

> *Prosecution claim*: Richard hired killer.
>   *Fact:* Murderer never found.

She was over the moon, giddy with delight that her husband had been able to bring his dispassionate, analytical skills to bear on such a personally painful matter, and find a way forward. Next steps were quickly decided. He would telegraph Matheringly, asking him to come to Down House to prepare the appeal. She would return to London in hope of seeing Richard.

Milly, in white bib apron and mob cap, her freckles and pale skin tell-tale marks of her Irish heritage, was waiting for Mrs Darwin as she came out of the study. 'Ma'am, need to speak to you. Would've done so second you arrived but you had other things on your mind.'

'Indeed, I did, but the master has eased that concern to some extent, so tell me now. But please be brief, I have much to do.'

'I'll try, ma'am,' began Milly, 'though truth is, a lot happened while you were away. Best if I show you.'

Milly led her mistress upstairs, knocked on one of the bedroom doors, peaked in and then stood aside to let Mrs Darwin enter.

'Oh, it's you, ma'am,' said the wan young woman in a white shift propped up on pillows, the relief in her voice tinged with an undertone of apprehension.

'Lucy… Lucy Kinsley!' exclaimed Mrs Darwin. She'd been very upset when Lucy just upped and left last summer without a word to her, but she'd always been fond of the girl. 'Didn't expect to see you back at Down House, but I'm pleased you're here. Why are you in bed? Are you unwell, my dear?'

'Much better now, ma'am, but if it hadn't been for your gardener, I'd have been done for. He found me in the tool-shed, barely breathing, stone cold. He reckoned another hour and I'd've been a goner.'

'Oh, Lucy, that's terrible. Whatever were you doing in the tool-shed?' asked an incredulous Mrs Darwin.

'Well, ma'am,' Lucy began, 'after I'd left my little darling on your doorstep, I waited two days, watching and praying he'd be welcomed into your home. When I was certain he was safe, I went back to the tool-shed for one last night before leaving in the morning, but I must've blacked out.'

Her little darling? On the doorstep? A baby, Lucy's baby in the house? 'Lucy, I had no idea… The master… he never mentioned a… a new arrival.'

'He wasn't told, ma'am,' Lucy said diffidently.

Mrs Emma Darwin's eyebrows shot up, twin arches of disapproval, the mistress's *look,* as the servants called it.

'Milly said master was really sick, and thought it best not to disturb him,' explained Lucy quickly. 'Said she'd handle things 'til you got back and could decide what was to be done.'

Eyebrows restored to their customary position, Mrs Darwin nodded, pleased and thankful Milly had been so thoughtful. Still, Charles must be told. With a parting smile, she was about to take her leave, when something in Lucy's look rooted her to the spot. Woman's intuition, a mother's understanding, whatever it was, Mrs Darwin knew in that instant exactly what Lucy was silently telling her.

How stupid I am. Should have guessed, she scolded herself. It was all there in Eyesore Annie's testimony – Richard's son born to a maid... like Lucy; from Cornwall... like Lucy. She hadn't made the connection then, but now she knew. *Lucy was the mother of her grandchild.*

'Your little one, he's Richard's, isn't he?' More an affirmation than a question. Mrs Darwin reached out and took the young woman's left hand, the heavily bandaged right one unseen under the covers. Their clasp signalled a silent pact, an unbreakable bond between mothers, to do everything they could for Richard and his son.

Still holding Lucy's hand, Mrs Darwin briefly reported the outcome of the trial.

'Oh, ma'am. How can that be? Richard wouldn't hurt a fly, let alone a fellow human being.'

She calmed down a little on hearing the plan to appeal the verdict, and then said: 'And my son... wh-what will happen to him now?'

By this time, the bold idea that had been taking shape in Mrs Darwin's mind was fully formed. 'Lucy, my dear, listen to me,' she said. 'I feared I'd never again hear the noise and laughter of another little one in the house after I lost my grandson three years ago. But God has answered my prayers. Lucy, I believe your child was *destined* to grow up here at Down House... as part of our family—'

'Oh, ma'am, really? That would be wonderful. How can I ever thank you?'

'Wait, there's more,' said Mrs Darwin, 'I want *you* to stay as well... as his *nanny*—'

'His nanny? Oh, my goodness. That's so kind, so—'

Like a sudden change in the weather from bright sunshine bathing the countryside to heavy clouds darkening the landscape, Lucy's happy glow vanished, replaced by a steely resolve. 'No... no, I can't.'

'Why ever not?' asked a baffled Mrs Darwin.

Lucy glanced nervously towards the bedroom door. The girl is skittish, thought Mrs Darwin, like a child who's sneaked into the circus tent without paying, constantly fearing an official hand on her shoulder. Something's bothering her.

'Ma'am, I can't. I'm really, *really* grateful to you for letting my little boy live here at Down House but *I* have to leave. It's the only way. If Jarke—'

'Jarke?' queried Mrs Darwin. 'What's the butler got to do with this?'

'He was the one who sent me away, ma'am, soon as he found out I was with child.'

So that's why she ran off last summer without a word to me.

'Told me never to come back or it'd be the worse for me. If he sees me, he'll know the baby's mine, and the spiteful beast will do everything he can to ruin my darling son's chance for a good life or, Heaven forbid, harm him in some way…' She was sobbing now. 'That's why I have to go away, even if it means never seeing my child again. I'm so sorry…'

'Lucy, Lucy, listen to me. Jarke will *never* bother you or the baby.'

'Ma'am, you don't know him. Nice as pie with you and the master, but treats us servants like dirt.'

'Well, I may know him better than you think. Fact is, I'd become so dissatisfied with his service, I had the master dismiss him first of the year. Jarke is gone. And *you*, Lucy Kinsley, *will* be your son's nanny.'

Chapter Thirty-Two: The Appeal

Dunston did not see Line's letter, the one he posted from Carlisle on Thursday, February 8, until Sunday, February 18. He'd stayed in London for his friend's funeral, not returning to Meadowlark Cottage until late on the seventeenth, and had only found it the following morning.

A glance was enough to recognise the writing. Dunston held the envelope with its message from the grave in his hand for several seconds as though weighing the memory of the man who'd given his life in pursuit of justice. At the funeral, Line's colleagues had praised his detective skills, his knowledge of London's underworld, and his relentless pursuit of felons. That was impressive enough, but it was the reading of the will that most affected Dunston.

With his wife and daughter passed, and no other relatives, Line had bequeathed his cottage and modest savings to the family of the girl he'd shot. Dunston had marvelled at the unbounded decency of the man, the former inspector still striving to make amends for his one mistake even after his death.

The only other bequest – a silver medallion – was left to none other than Dunston himself. He'd examined the coin's markings, feeling, as Line had done so many times, the engraved *R* and *M*. Line's keepsake! His memorial to wife and daughter! Knowing from the newspaper account what those letters meant for Line, Dunston had been overcome, genuinely touched that the detective had left his most precious remembrance of Rose and May to him.

Dunston, who'd last heard from Line two weeks ago, was anxious to learn the letter's contents. The envelope opened, the single sheet of notepaper extracted, Line's words leapt off the page – *uncovered vital information.* Good Lord! Line did find something… something that got him killed.

The letter didn't say what that something was, but it did say Line had sent a telegram to Fickett. Why wasn't this mentioned at the trial? Did the police withhold evidence? Evidence that could have saved Richard? The Darwins had to be informed at once. Dunston rushed to Down House, only to learn that Mr Darwin was too sick to see him, and Mrs Darwin had gone to London.

Dunston took the afternoon train and caught up with Mrs Darwin at the Adelphi Hotel late Sunday evening, and together they spent several hours debating the letter's significance. The next morning, they were joined by Richard's lawyer, Matheringly. They sat at breakfast, eating not a scrap, intent on finalising their assignments for the day: Matheringly to deliver Line's letter to the Home Secretary; Dunston to find out what happened to the telegram; Mrs Darwin to see Richard. Plans settled, chairs were scraped back, and the three set off with one goal in mind – to stop the hanging, the appointed time of ten o'clock only hours away.

8.00 AM: Dunston was a master of delay rather than a man of action, yet he accosted Groggins, the desk sergeant at Scotland Yard, so strenuously that the poor fellow finally decided the only way to get the pleading, wheedling pest off his back was to do as asked and see if Inspector Fickett would spare him a few minutes. With Dunston on his heels, he entered the inspector's office and announced the uninvited visitor.

'Mr Burnett, believe I saw you at Line's funeral,' said Fickett. 'What can I do for you, sir?'

Dunston briefly explained about Line's letter and its delay.

'Then, please take a seat and tell me what Line has to say.'

Fickett listened carefully as Dunston recited the contents verbatim, and then said, 'Well, Line was murdered before he reached Scotland Yard so I have no idea what new evidence he might have unearthed. And, as far as a telegram is concerned, sorry, but I never received anything from him.'

Dunston stared at him, open-mouthed. What? No telegram? What's going on? Before he could collect his thoughts, Groggins knocked and poked his head in.

'Home Secretary wants to see you, sir. 8.30 sharp.'

'Right, on my way, sergeant. 'Fraid you must excuse me, Mr Burnett. Duty calls. By the way, where's this letter now?'

On hearing that Matheringly was delivering it to the Home Secretary, Fickett swore silently. And then aloud, 'Thank you, Mr Burnett.'

With that, he was gone.

8.15 AM: As soon as she arrived at Newgate prison, Mrs Darwin was led straight to the cells for the condemned where she found her firstborn sitting on a wooden bench, hunched over, shrunken and hollowed out, lost in his arrow-stamped prison jacket. They hugged silently, words hard to come by, their few muttered exchanges steered by her towards her hopes for the appeal, by him towards explanations meant only for a mother's ears. He swore he had no hand in his wife's ending – a certainty his mother had never questioned – before he stumblingly admitted he'd broken his marriage vows.

The mother did not have to be told; she knew exactly what happened. Her son, always needy, had to feel loved, and if he couldn't find the tenderness he craved with his wife, he was weak enough to take it wherever it was offered. Not a mean bone in his body, just no spine. But it didn't matter to her; she loved her firstborn fiercely, always had, always would.

'But Mother,' he breathed into her shoulder, 'as God's my witness, I never knew she was with child. What… what will happen to them?'

'It's alright, my son. Please don't worry,' Mrs Darwin said as firmly as she could. 'Lucy's safe. She's at Down House. She will stay with us, as will Joey.'

'Joey? Is that… is that my son's name?'

'Indeed, it is. Lucy named him Joey after her father. His full name, though, will be Josiah Richard Darwin, Josiah after grandfather Wedgwood, Richard after you, and Darwin because he *is* a Darwin.'

'Oh, Mother, that's wonderful. I-I can't thank you and Father enough.' His eyes were closed, but tears squeezed out anyway.

He fell silent, the threat of the noose robbing him of speech. The mother instinctively tightened her arms around her trembling son, comforting him as best she could, though when the guard called time, all she could offer, all any mother could offer, was her undying love.

8.30 AM: 'Sit down, Fickett,' said Sir Rufus Smethurst, the instant Fickett entered the Home Secretary's office in Westminster. Dressed in his customary dark jacket, high-collared white shirt and burgundy cravat, Sir Rufus was a small, fidgety man, his hands flitting from the papers on his desk to his moon-lensed spectacles, sideways to each ear, down to his lap and then off again on round two. He had a worried frown on his terrier-like face.

'It's the Darwin business,' he said, unnecessarily. 'Police Commissioner has already had a word with me. Fears we may have acted a little rashly.'

Damn Lamb Chops, thought Fickett. The old boy's out to cut my legs from under me, still furious I shut him out of the arrest.

'And now it's Darwin's lawyer,' continued Sir Rufus. 'Left an appeal at my office on Friday – haven't had a chance to do much more than glance at it – then came by this morning with a letter sent by your predecessor to some fellow called Burnett. Damned inconvenient. Still, it's my duty to determine if there's anything in their submission that might warrant a pardon. Have to get a move on, fellow's to hang in an hour or so.'

Fickett nodded, well used to the hasty decision-making that determined whether a man lived or died, the English justice system's endemic callousness of no concern to him… except in this instance. The inspector had a personal stake in the fate of the man convicted in this case – to put it bluntly, if Richard Darwin hanged, Fickett's career would take off, and Lamb Chops would be out of a job.

'First issue,' began Sir Rufus. 'The appeal claims Richard Darwin didn't have any motive to kill his wife because the liaison with this serving girl was over and he had no idea she'd given birth to his child. What do you say to that?'

'Exactly what you'd expect him to say, sir,' responded the inspector, sure of his ground.

'Hmm, yes. Still, the point is that the girl, who apparently is staying with the Darwins at Down House, something you remarkably failed to discover, confirms both the separation and Richard Darwin's ignorance of the child, and *she*, as the appeal points out, wasn't called to testify at the trial.'

'True, sir.' Fickett knew his case was solid. All he had to do was make sure Mr Twitchy didn't fret himself into allowing some trifle to sway him. 'Fact of the matter is, sir, we didn't ascertain her whereabouts until after the trial but, even if we'd found her before, a serving wench of blatantly loose morals would carry no weight as a witness. Crown counsel would have ripped her apart.'

'Ye-e-es, suppose you're right.' Hands reined in from their roaming, Sir Rufus made a note in the margin of the appeal. Fickett couldn't see what he'd written, but he was certain his argument had prevailed.

'Time's pressing,' said Sir Rufus, 'so let's move on. The appeal further points out that Crown counsel never established any link between Richard Darwin and the person who actually killed his wife and notes that the police – that's you, Inspector Fickett – have no idea who did batter Henrietta Darwin to death. Correct?'

'Correct, sir,' acknowledged Fickett. 'But, if I may, the jury was well aware of this, and *still* convicted Richard Darwin for *arranging* his wife's murder.'

'Quite so, but it's unfortunate the murderer hasn't been apprehended. Had he testified to Richard Darwin's role in the crime, then the conviction would've been absolutely solid. As it is… well, it's all rather troubling.' The Home Secretary wrote another comment in the margin, underlining this one twice. Fickett's self-assurance sank with each stroke.

'Yes, decidedly troubling, and we've yet to come to the most worrisome issue.' Sir Rufus waved the letter brought by Matheringly in Fickett's face. 'This says Line was on his way to you with new evidence when he was killed. The letter didn't reach this Burnett fellow until several days after the verdict had been rendered so it could not have been introduced at the trial. But it clearly mentions a telegram from Line to you, a telegram that should have arrived at Scotland Yard *before* the trial began, and Mr Matheringly wants to know, as do I, why it was not submitted for the jury's consideration. Pray enlighten me.'

'Sir, the telegram never reached my desk. Never saw it.'

'WHAT!' The Home Secretary's restless hands came to an abrupt halt, shocked into mid-air immobility. 'Whatever do you mean?'

'Not sure, sir. Only heard about this half an hour ago. Haven't had a chance to check with the post office yet, but, if it was delivered to Scotland Yard, then—'

'Then you have a leak,' cut in Sir Rufus. 'And if the telegram cleared Richard Darwin, then we also have a wrongly convicted man on our hands.'

'I don't think so, sir,' Fickett said quickly. 'Believe I know what Line discovered,' he asserted with more confidence than he felt, sensing that his once-secure conviction was beginning to crumble around the edges like a day-old scone.

'Well?'

'Think of his record, sir, all those arrests, all built on his knowledge of London's criminal world and his tenacity in running down suspected felons. In this instance, we already had the man pulling the strings, Richard Darwin, under lock and key, so what did Line do? He went after the thug who actually did the dirty deed, and Line, being Line, *found Henrietta Darwin's killer.'*

'Very ingenious... and plausible, I suppose,' conceded the Home Secretary. 'Yet far from conclusive. Fact of the matter is we have no idea what new evidence Line discovered. Much food for thought here, Fickett.'

Damn, he's not convinced, thought the inspector, fool's going to pardon a man who's guilty as hell. 'Sir, if I may—'

'No, you may not. Here's what you *may* do, Inspector. First, track down Henrietta Darwin's killer, who, if the telegram did indeed identify him as you suggest, almost certainly ended Line's life. That is, after all, your job. And second, make damn sure you plug the leak in what I'd always thought was the safest place in England. Now, if you'll excuse me, I need a moment to order my thoughts. Good day to you.'

Sir Rufus waited for Fickett to leave. As soon as the door closed behind the inspector, he dipped his pen in the ink-pot. He usually scrawled *PROCEED* across the official execution authorisation without a moment's thought; occasionally, very occasionally, he'd write *PARDONED.* This morning he paused, nib inches from paper, then wrote his decision and signed his name. He glanced at his fob watch. Good, enough time for his ruling to reach Horsemonger Lane Jail before ten o'clock.

10.00 AM: The official executioner for the City of London, a stickler for proper procedure, always waited until the last moment before releasing the trapdoor in case the prisoner received an eleventh-hour pardon. Today, the Home Secretary's one-word instruction reached the hangman only seconds before the appointed time of execution. Never one to question an official order, he did exactly as directed.

After he'd pulled off the convicted man's hood and removed the noose, he signalled to two prison dogsbodies. They stepped forward and carted off Richard Darwin's broken-necked corpse.

Chapter Thirty-Three: Fickett Rebounds

Inspector Fickett called the meeting to order at ten o'clock. It was the morning after Richard Darwin's execution and though he was well-satisfied with that outcome, he felt chastened by the dressing down delivered by a tetchy Home Secretary. The inspector, though, was not a man to sulk. When events turned against him, he rolled up his sleeves and did his utmost to set matters straight. In this instance, to plug the leak in his office and put the man who clobbered Henrietta Darwin and sliced open Line's throat behind bars.

He and Line might have rubbed each other the wrong way, not surprising given their respective positions, but Fickett was duty-bound as an officer of the Metropolitan Police Force to spare no effort in chasing down his predecessor's killer. And it didn't escape the inspector that doing so would give his career a further boost, as well as earning him credit with his officers. 'Gentlemen,' he began, 'today we will avenge the death of former Chief of Detectives, Inspector Line.'

As expected, this announcement was greeted with a chorus of Aye's and Right's from the three, plainclothes officers present.

'This morning, I got a tip from one of my narks, and lads, *I know where to find Line's killer.*'

'Good work, chief,' said Beresford, a burly fellow with hands so massive they looked capable of tearing the killer to pieces. Ruggles, the youngest officer present, nodded vigorously, ever eager to be fully involved. He had the build of an athlete, lean but powerful, useful attributes for anyone who wanted to be in law enforcement, and brought an energetic enthusiasm to every task assigned to him. Fickett had already concluded he'd have to watch this fellow. He had no intention of allowing Ruggles to do to him what he was doing to Lamb Chops. For now, though, the lad had his uses.

'Can't trust those snitches, sir,' said the third officer. 'Lie all the time. Turn their own mothers in for tuppence.' A dour Scot, wide in the shoulder with grey-streaked, red hair, McWhirter was the oldest and most experienced present. He was not given to speaking often, but when he did, everyone including Fickett listened.

'True enough,' Fickett agreed. 'This time though, I think we've got the goods on our man.'

'Can't wait to get the bastard,' declared Ruggles. 'Where is he?'

'Hold it right there,' snapped the inspector. 'You'll know soon as I want you to know and not before. Can't have the scoundrel getting wind of this before we're ready to act. McWhirter, call in Groggins.'

McWhirter opened the door and shouted for the duty sergeant.

'Yes, sir!' Groggins saluted smartly on entering Fickett's office.

'Tell the ordnance officer I want two revolvers, one for me and one for McWhirter. Understood?'

'Yes, sir.' Groggins paused, waiting for further instructions. When none were forthcoming, he asked, 'What shall I say they're needed for, sir?'

'Got Line's killer in our sights,' blurted out Ruggles. 'Going to—'

'That's enough, Ruggles!' Fickett glared at the blabbermouth. 'Have you forgotten? This stays under wraps 'til I say otherwise.' The inspector's anger was clear to see but fortunately for the loose-lipped novice, short-lived. On seeing the lad's crestfallen face, he softened his tone and added, 'No harm done this time.' But then, to make sure the young man knew he was in the doghouse, 'I'll speak to you later. Now, back to business. Groggins, tell the ordnance officer we need the weapons because our suspect is likely to be armed.'

'Yes, sir,' said the sergeant, saluting again.

'Alright, men. Dismissed. Except you, Ruggles.'

Fifteen minutes later, Fickett spotted their quarry. With Ruggles by his side, Beresford and McWhirter right behind, they watched the man, face half-hidden by the collar of his cloak, turn into Little Earl Street's confusion of run-down taverns, seedy pawnshops and squalid boarding houses. The filth clogging the thoroughfare – foul-smelling rags, carthorse droppings, scraps of rotten food, night soil, some stale, some fresh – found its match in the human scum plying shady deals and illegal trades in dark corners and broad daylight alike with little regard for the arm of the law.

The spied-upon man took a quick look up and down the street, and knocked on a small door partially concealed from prying eyes by a low-slung canvas awning. The building was no more dilapidated than its neighbours, but its shuttered windows and cold dank exterior put casual passers-by on notice that they were unlikely to receive a cheery welcome should they stray across the threshold. A second later, the door opened and the caller was spirited inside, vanishing as though he'd never stood on the doorstep.

'Ruggles, stay here with me,' Fickett commanded, using the break in the action to position his men. 'We'll cover this end of the street. Beresford and McWhirter, up to the Shaftesbury Avenue end with you, quick as you can. Keep out of sight and wait for my signal.'

A good deployment, it would seem, trapping anyone emerging from the house between the two pairs of officers, but even the best laid plans of mice and police can go awry. Before his men had a chance to move, the door opened and Groggins stepped out, followed by another.

'Crushers,' yelled Groggins to his companion. 'Run for it.'

'Damn it, they're on to us,' muttered Fickett. 'Close in! NOW!' he barked.

'You bloody shit-head,' hissed Groggins' mate. 'Led the soddin' scufters straight to me! Furkin' peach on me, would yer?' A hand-to-pocket blur, a glint of steel and a bright red spray spurted from Groggins' gashed cheek. The knife-wielder balanced himself for a second strike, a finisher aimed for the liver, but the sound of fast-approaching footsteps persuaded him otherwise. 'I'll cut yer cods off, yer poxy bag of piss,' he yelled at Groggins, and took off.

Ruggles was moving sinuously as a leopard, rapidly closing in on the fleeing man, the inspector some distance behind. The fugitive, sensing his pursuer was almost upon him, suddenly turned and jabbed his knife at the youthful policeman's face, causing him to check and lose his balance. The feint worked; the real assault, a swift lunge to the officer's exposed ribs, followed so fast Ruggles had no chance to defend himself.

The knife sliced easily into the flesh of the detective's left side, but before it could slip between the ribs and pierce the heart, the policeman hurled himself to the right. With a snarl, the cutthroat ripped his blade from the meat and muscle around the ribcage and readied for another thrust.

CRACK! The sound of a single gunshot was quickly followed by the thud of a body hitting the ground and the clatter of a knife skittering across the cobblestones. Keeping his revolver trained on the downed man, Fickett rushed to Ruggles, concerned to see him slumped against the wall, face chalk-white, blood seeping through the fingers clutching his left side.

'You alright?' Fickett asked.

'Only a… nick, sir.'

'Bit more than that, I'm afraid,' the inspector replied, pulling open the blood-sodden front of the injured man's coat and examining the damage. 'You'll live, but you're bleeding like a pig. Here, hold this over the wound, tight as you can.' He pushed his scarf into his officer's hand.

Ruggles half nodded, barely listening, still caught up in the excitement of the moment, adrenalin blotting out the pain. 'Think he's our killer, sir?'

'Looks like.'

'Good. You got him, sir.'

'Yes, I did.' The inspector grinned, already assuming full credit, even though the outcome wasn't all he'd hoped for. He'd wanted the murderer alive, but he'd had little choice, had to shoot quickly, didn't want a young officer knifed to death on one of his operations.

'My plan worked well,' Fickett said. 'Your little bit of playacting in my office was all it took. Groggins swallowed your bogus gaffe about us knowing the whereabouts of Line's killer like it was gospel.' Fickett had suspected Groggins was the snitch – he was the first to see incoming telegrams, and he'd been nosing around a lot the last few weeks – but Fickett needed some way of getting the desk officer to reveal himself. 'Got him and Line's murderer to boot, two birds, mole and killer, with one stone, couldn't have worked out better.'

'Yes... sir...' The fledgling detective was starting to fade, but still managed a small smile, pleased everything had worked to his chief's satisfaction.

The pavement-pounding clomp of flat feet alerted Fickett to Beresford's approach. 'McWhirter's... got... Groggins,' he gasped, gulping down enough oxygen to put everyone else in the vicinity at risk of asphyxiation. 'Didn't give no trouble,' he managed. 'Bit of a scratch on his face, nothing more.'

'Good. Hail a hansom and get Ruggles to the police surgeon. Our junior sprint champion needs a few stitches. I want a word with Groggins.'

Fickett trotted back down the street to find Groggins, his police uniform visible beneath his partly open cloak, pressed up against the building's clapboard siding by the bear-like McWhirter. 'Thought you were the leak, Groggins. Couldn't prove it, but you were stupid enough to walk straight into my little trap. What d'you have to say for yourself?'

'Sir, I can explain. Feller you shot threatened my nippers and the missus, swore he'd cut out their tongues unless I did exactly what he told me.'

'When was this?'

'Several weeks back. He was waiting for me when I come out of The Adam and Eve. Pushed me 'gainst the wall and had his knife at my throat quick as a flash. Said I was to keep him posted 'bout the investigation into the Nightingale Lane murder, else it'd be the worse for my family.'

'Should've come to me; we could've sorted it out.'

'Know that now, sir, but thought I could handle it. I was pretty sure he killed Henrietta Darwin, so I figured he wanted to check if you were on to him. Didn't sound like he wanted much and I was right, least to begin with. Then, when Richard Darwin was arrested for arranging the murder, he got real nervous, until I told him the Darwin bloke was denying everything, claimed he had no idea who done the killin'. That satisfied him, and he said he had no more need of me unless something turned up that changed matters.'

'And something did turn up, didn't it? The telegram.'

'Yes, sir. From Line, it was.'

'And what did it say?'

'Said Line had proof young Darwin was innocent—'

'WHAT!' Fickett exploded. He couldn't believe his ears, the case was watertight... *is* watertight. Line couldn't possibly have found something that cast doubt on the investigation.

'Ended up with something 'bout Line arriving at Euston Station early in the mornin' and going straight to Scotland Yard,' said Groggins. 'Those were his final words.'

'Indeed, they were his final words. Since Richard Darwin never gave up the name of the man who actually did the killing, the murderer was in the clear. The last thing he wanted was new evidence upsetting that applecart. Taking the telegram to that piece of shit over there was as good as signing Line's death warrant. Didn't you think of that?'

'No, sir. Thought he'd bolt, scared out of his britches he'd be fingered if the investigation was reopened. And that's what I told him day before the trial. Leg it out of here, I said, for yer own good.'

Groggins looked at the inspector, hoping for a few words of understanding, but all he got was a cold-as-ice 'Get on with it, Groggins.'

'Yes, sir. With him off my back and my family out of harm's way, I was ready to tell you the whole story. But then, as I was coming into the Yard next mornin' to 'fess up, I heard Line had been shivved, and I panicked. Decided the only thing I could do was keep my mouth shut.'

'Damn you, Groggins,' Fickett spat. 'Line is dead because of you and Richard Darwin may have been hanged for no reason.' Fickett did not believe this last part for one second. Richard Darwin got what he deserved, the evidence was as clear as daylight, but Line... 'Legally, you're an accessory before the fact in Line's murder. The man I just shot wielded the knife, but you're as much a murderer as he. You'll swing for your trouble, my fine friend. God have mercy on your soul, because I won't. Best you tell me what else you know.'

'N-not much to t-tell, sir,' Groggins stammered. 'Bloke mentioned someone called the Gaffer once or twice, think he was some sort of go-between, there to pass instructions on to Migston.'

'Migston? That the killer's name?'

'Yes, sir, though his mates called him Fingers.'

Chapter Thirty-Four: The Nanny

Dunston could feel the self-doubt closing in on him. It was Friday, four days after Richard's execution, and Dunston was at a loss, still without any clear idea how to move his investigation forward. Had he bitten off more than he could chew? Would he ever find Line's killer? Not sure what to do next, or even if there was a next, he sat in the kitchen at Meadowlark Cottage staring glumly at Line's five reports laid out on the table.

He'd already been though them a dozen times. He was debating whether or not to have one more go, when Line's words of eighteen months ago came back to him – *Would that my former colleagues were as astute and persevering as you, Mr Burnett*. Persevering, that's what Line had called him. And persevere he would. He grabbed the first report – Meeting with Mrs Emma Darwin, Down House, December 28 – and dug in.

Nothing there. Nor in the next three reports, but in the fifth, he spotted a possible line of inquiry. After hearing about the sisters' accident in the barn, Line had developed a sudden interest in Mrs Betsy Smurkle, their nanny. Dunston had given this short shrift on previous readings, but it wouldn't hurt to talk to her, and surely someone at Henrietta and Richard's funeral service, scheduled for that afternoon at nearby St Mary the Virgin, would know the nanny's whereabouts.

After lunch, Dunston waited with the other mourners in the graveyard until man and wife had been laid to rest, and then approached Mrs Darwin, dressed head to foot in mourning black. Condolences first, he'd decided, then his query. 'Mrs Darwin,' he began. But that was as far as he got. Seeing

164

the pain behind her fixed expression, the phrases he'd rehearsed so carefully flew out of his head. 'So… yes… uh… very, *very*… uh… my sincerest…'

Mrs Darwin stared at him, her face registering first confusion and then understanding. 'Well, yes, thank you, Mr Burnett.' She gently touched his arm before moving on.

The query! Dunston lunged after her, pushing forward until he was close enough to ask if she knew Betsy Smurkle's current address. She was too preoccupied, however, with her fellow grievers to catch his question, and even Dunston, England's Duffer-in-Chief as far as society's rules of etiquette were concerned, realised he couldn't press her further.

He'd have to inquire of someone else. He looked around and spotted Grace, Mrs Darwin's maid. She proved a more fruitful source of information, readily supplying the address of the sisters' childhood home outside Carlisle. 'But,' she continued, 'the house was sold to pay off creditors when the sisters' parents died. The two girls had to move out, and Mrs Smurkle returned to her village. No idea where that is. Sorry.'

Dunston's ears had pricked up at Grace's mention of Carlisle. Line's letter, the last he ever wrote, was from Carlisle. And in it, he claimed to have uncovered *vital information* in the Henrietta Darwin case. From Mrs Smurkle? First thing tomorrow, he'd be on the Royal Scot speeding up the West Coast Main Line on the eight-hour run to the border city.

He spent the night of his arrival in Carlisle at the Railway Hotel, as had Line, then called at the sisters' former home early the next morning. There, he was informed that the nanny now lived in Coomsdale. He was given directions to her house – over the moors, past the lane to Liddel's smithy, and there, next to The Bogwort Inn, he'd find it, sure as day follows night. In Dunston's world, however, day did not always follow night as a matter of course, and an hour after starting out, he'd found himself in… Coomsdell.

'Ye need to know yer *dales* from yer *dells*, young feller, if ye wants to go trampin' 'round these parts,' he was told by a villager, a farmhand judging by the sour smell of working-man sweat and overpowering stink of dung. Dale and dell, however, were only a few miles apart, and an hour's walking over Coomsmoor brought him to Nettle Leaf Cottage, Mrs Betsy Smurkle's home.

His knock on the front door was answered by a shrunken female, a heavy shawl wrapped tight about her bent form and a knit cap pulled down low on her head. She looked up, her watery eyes slowly taking in the figure on her doorstep. Dunston's heart sank to the bottom of his boots at the sight of this ancient creature, who must be sixty-five if she was a day, and hardly likely to remember what happened yesterday let alone events that took place two decades ago. Still, since he was here...

'Mrs Betsy Smurkle?'

'Eh?'

'I'm looking for Mrs Betsy Smurkle.'

'Ahh, Betsy. Why didn't yer say so? It's Ma you want.'

'Your mother?' he exclaimed in disbelief.

'Aye. I'll fetch her. She's out back, feeding the sow.'

Stamping his feet and rubbing his hands, his greatcoat and deerstalker barely keeping the cold at bay, Dunston waited impatiently, increasingly annoyed with himself. 'Shouldn't have come, complete waste of time,' he muttered under his breath. 'Her mother? Dear Lord, however old can she be?'

'Eighty-seven years on this piece of God's earth, young man, if it's any of your business.' So spoke Mrs Betsy Smurkle, a twenty-years-older version of her daughter, dressed in identical shawl and cap. 'Three score an' ten, that's what it says in the Holy Book but that's only for men. Women, leastways up here in the north country, live a damned sight longer than any of the menfolk, and work a good deal harder,' she announced, all the while casting her eye over her visitor, apparently assessing his prospects for an early grave.

'Remarkable, Mrs Smurkle, if I may say so.'

'Can if yer like, but ain't got all day. Miss Matilda's waiting for me and lady pigs don't take kindly to being kep' waiting. Neither do I, so best get on with whatever brought yer to Nettle Leaf Cottage.'

'Yes, quite. Um... I wonder if you remember my... my associate, Mr Archibald Line... came all the way from London to see you?'

'Mr who? Oh, you mean Archie,' said the old woman, her face warming into a smile. 'Aye, I remember him. So sad him being killed. An' such a nice man. We had a luv'ly chat an' a cuppa cha. What of him?'

Archie? Lovely chat? Cup of tea? Didn't sound anything like the rather austere investigator familiar to Dunston. Whatever did Line do to be treated so cordially? No tea for me, he noted ruefully. Still, he was not here to savour Betsy's brew; he was here for information.

'Yes, well, you see, I believe Mr... er, I mean, *Archie* learned something important from you and I'm hoping you'll be willing to tell me what you... *chatted* about.'

'Well, let me see. Nursing, aye, that was it.'

'Nursing? You talked about... first aid?'

'Not that kind of nursing, you fool. *Suckling*, that's what we talked 'bout.'

'Suckling?'

'Aye. Archie was worried 'bout Miss Matilda. Got seven piglets she have, and with seven of 'em sucking at her day an' night there's a lot of wear an' tear on her teats.'

'Yes... I imagine there would be. Um... was there anything else?'

'Now that I think 'bout it, he was interested in... hmm, how best to put it? Let's just say, *having a bit of muffin*,' she stage-whispered, her eyebrows rising to make a come-hither. coquettish arch any twenty-year-old flirt would be proud of.

'What? He wanted a muffin with his tea?'

'Don't be daft, man. *Stuffing the muffin*... planting the parsnip... burying the weasel... riding St George. Bless my soul, you city folk don't know much 'bout the ins an' outs of country life, do yer? Mathilda can't *suckle* if she ain't been *mated*, now can she?'

'Um, no, I don't suppose she can.'

Surely Line talked about something other than breeding and rearing swine, thought a frustrated Dunston. Have to get her off this animal husbandry track and on to the sisters' accident. Line must have done it somehow.

'Fascinating, Mrs Smurkle. I had no idea Archie was so interested in... um... livestock. I imagine though you talked about other matters? The two girls, Henrietta and Estelle, the ones you nannied, did you talk about them by any chance?'

'Aye, that we did. Archie was interested in their mishap in the old barn. Wasn't my fault, I told him. Those two was a real handful, always getting into mischief. If I told 'em once, I told 'em a thousand times not to go in that barn. Hadn't been used for years and I was afeared it'd collapse on 'em. Death-watch beetles been eating through joists an' beams like they was bone-dry shortbread for goodness knows how long. Well, ramshackle old thing didn't collapse, thank the Lord, but this rickety old rafter they liked to sit on gave way. Didn't break, mind you, just tilted, but that was enough.'

Yes, that's exactly how Inspector Fickett described the mishap to Line, Dunston noted, squares perfectly with his account. Nothing odd here. Line was barking up the wrong tree if he thought there was something suspicious about the sisters' fall. Must be something else he found out from Mrs Smurkle. Before he could ask, though, Betsy was moving on with her story.

'Estelle, poor little mite, come a real cropper, falling on her arm and mangling it bad. Passed out, she did. Henrietta was scared witless but somehow still got herself up to the house screaming her head off, not for herself, mind you, but for her sister. She was like that with Estelle, and Estelle the same with her. We sent for ol' Diddlesford – local doctor, dead now – but the silly fool messed up the girl's arm even worse. Never was right after that.'

'I see. That's very helpful,' Dunston said disingenuously. 'Anything else?'

'Not really, just bits an' pieces 'bout the girls, and that was that. Reckon Archie had chatted enough by then 'cos it was plain he was keen to be off. Said he had to get back to London but, give him his due, he was nice enough to take a minute and ask if the girls had kep' in touch with me after the house was sold. Told him yes for Estelle, no for her sister. Last saw Estelle when she came up here just before Henrietta's weddin'. All excited 'bout this dressing table she was having made as a weddin' present. Knew this Chinaman in Carlisle who made these fancy tables with secret drawers an' suchlike.'

'Really…' Dunston was suddenly all ears.

'Oh, aye. Stayed here in the cottage when she came to pick it up. Couldn't wait to show me this tiny cubbyhole hidden behind a false panel. Had to use two brass figures to open it. One was shaped like a man for Richard, Henrietta's husband to be, and the other like a woman for Henrietta. Never seen anything like it in all me life.'

An interesting titbit of information, Dunston thought, but otherwise not that enlightening. Maybe not, but her next words bowled him over, tumbling his mind into a topsy-turvy world of somersaulting brass figures and pinwheeling cubbyholes.

'What was that you said, Mrs Smurkle?'

Betsy dutifully repeated her remark, this time a little louder and a little slower for the benefit of the apparently hard-of-hearing, half-witted city gent.

Dunston stared at her, open-mouthed. Good Lord, *this is it*. This is the *vital information* that led Line to rush back to London... and his death. Dunston had to get away, calm down, think this through. 'Um... I... I fear I've kept you too long from... from Miss Matilda...'

'Won't die but, aye, best be getting back. I bid you good day, young man.'

'And I you, Mrs Smurkle.'

Chapter Thirty-Five: Justice for Lucy

Inspector Fickett knew he had to explain the missing telegram to the Darwins but he dreaded facing the parents of the man whose execution was largely due to his efforts. He'd only done his duty, he reminded himself, and in the end, it was the jury who convicted Richard Darwin, and the Lord Chief Justice who passed sentence, but still… The funerals of Richard and Henrietta had provided an excuse to defer the discomforting meeting, but the pair were buried last Friday and the unpleasantness could be postponed no longer.

Having asked via telegram when it would be convenient to visit, he'd received a curt reply suggesting Monday at two o'clock. Today was Monday, the hour approaching two. The inspector braced himself and stepped up to the front door of Down House.

Inside, three ladies, all in mourning dress, sat in the drawing room, their sombre mood a measure of how much each had suffered at Friday's funeral: Emma Darwin, heart bleeding, had grieved silently as son and daughter-in-law were laid to rest; Estelle Moxley, on edge, watched sorrowfully as her sister's coffin was lowered into a cold February grave; and Lucy Kinsley, out on her feet, had wept openly as the father of her son was placed in the ground.

A light knock and Parslow, Mr Darwin's manservant now serving double duty as butler, entered. 'Inspector Fickett, ma'am,' he announced.

'Inspector, I confess I'm surprised to see you again at Down House.' Mrs Darwin did not rise to greet him, nor invite him to sit. 'You must surely know that this is an extraordinarily difficult time for us and, frankly, your presence is very upsetting. Still, you're here, and as any hostess must, regardless of the circumstances, I'm obliged to receive you.'

Fickett was taken aback to find himself in the presence of three women, sedate enough, as befitted well-bred English ladies, but to the policeman, caught-off-guard, they might as well be Gorgons bent on turning him to stone with their baleful gaze. He tugged at the collar of his uniform, suddenly too tight. 'My apologies, Mrs Darwin, for disturbing you,' he said. 'Perhaps I could speak to your husband?'

'Out of the question. He's much too sick for… visitors, for reasons I'm sure you understand. Whatever you have to say, you can say to us. I believe you already know Miss Estelle Moxley, Henrietta's sister. The third member of our party is Miss Lucy Kinsley, mother of my fatherless grandchild.'

Fickett flinched at her choice of words, his stomach clenching as he realised he was face-to-face with Richard's paramour. Best get on with what he had to say, he decided, and leave as quickly as possible. 'I have no doubt my visit is an unwelcome intrusion, Mrs Darwin, but I felt duty-bound to report in person. I'll be as brief as possible, but first allow me to offer my sincerest condolences for your loss. And, if I may, assure you that my officers and I did only what we are trained to do, to follow the evidence wherever it takes us. I hope—'

'Inspector, forgive me,' Estelle interrupted, 'but perhaps you should move on.'

'Yes, of course, Miss Moxley. Let me, then, come to the point. Mrs Darwin,' he said, 'I believe you have seen the letter to Mr Dunston Burnett from former Chief of Detectives Inspector Line, saying that Line sent a telegram to me claiming he'd uncovered new evidence in your daughter-in-law's case. That telegram should have arrived at Scotland Yard in time to have been presented in evidence at the trial. I'm here to report that it was intercepted *before* it ever reached my desk.'

'Well, isn't that convenient,' Mrs Darwin said acidly. 'Information that might have saved my son, disappearing into thin air, just like that.'

'Er… yes… very unfortunate, but we tricked the culprit who stole it, my duty sergeant I'm sad to say, into leading us to the thug who ended your daughter-in-law's life. I hope it will bring you at least some comfort to learn that the man paid for his sins. He died during the arrest.'

'Yes, good news of a sort, I suppose,' Mrs Darwin said. 'And are we allowed to know this villain's name?'

'Migston, ma'am, commonly known as Fingers.'

'Fingers!' Lucy jumped out of her chair like a Jack-in-the-Box.

'Lucy, whatever's the matter?' Mrs Darwin asked.

'Fingers,' she breathed. 'He's the beast who beat me up, twice; nearly killed me the second time.'

'Can you describe him?' the inspector said.

'Yes, I'll never forget him. He chopped off my finger.' She held up her right hand, the light bandaging around the palm and over the stump leaving in full view the empty space between thumb and middle finder. She let her hand drop and gave the inspector a detailed description of Fingers' features and dress including his bowler hat.

'Yes, that's him. We think another man was involved, Migston called him the Gaffer. Know anything about him?'

'I'm afraid not, but I know who Fingers worked for – a real scoundrel, runs a flower-selling business, at least that's what he calls it, but it's a cover for trapping young women into selling their… their… well, you know what I mean. Micus Loman, that's his name. He could be the Gaffer.'

'Thank you, Miss Kinsley, that's very helpful. We'll be on the lookout for him, I can assure you. Well, perhaps it's time I took my—'

'No need to look for him,' Lucy cut in. 'Don't know the address, but I know the house. Never forget that horrible place.'

For the first time since the inspector's arrival, he and Mrs Darwin made eye contact, each assessing Lucy's surprising news, and her offer. Fickett could see from her expression that their expectations, like trains leaving the same station but on diverging lines, had ended up miles apart: he, counting on Micus Loman to confirm Richard Darwin's guilt; she, confident he'd exonerate her son.

'I hesitate to ask, Miss Kinsley,' Fickett said, not hesitating for one second, 'but would you be willing to come to London and help us lay hold of this

Micus Loman?'

Lucy looked to Mrs Darwin who nodded her acquiescence and the young woman promised to make herself available on the morrow.

Inspector Fickett met Lucy when she arrived at Charing Cross Station early the next morning, accompanied by Estelle Moxley. Asked by Mrs Darwin to see that no harm came to the young woman, Estelle had willingly obliged, her only reason for being at Down House – to attend the funerals – now passed. Lucy guided Fickett to Loman's modest house in Brew Crescent where she and Estelle were left in the safe hands of Officer Beresford while the inspector hammered on the front door. The surprised occupant took one look at the inspector, turned and bolted out of the back door… straight into the waiting arms of Officer McWhirter. London's crooks never learn.

An hour later, Fickett stepped inside a holding cell in the bowels of the Yard. The dingy, windowless pit reeked of unwashed bodies and piss, turning Fickett's stomach and leaving a foul taste at the back of his throat. 'Time for you and me to have a little chat.'

Micus Loman, now dressed in standard prison garb of white jacket and trousers, both stamped with the broad arrow signifying crown property, was seated on a low bench set against the far wall, iron shackles tight about wrists and ankles. After a long worrying hour in jail, his naturally pale face was a shade or two whiter, and his habitually low-key composure was decidedly ruffled and panicky. But the man had weathered his fair share of encounters with the law and he was not about to give up anything to this nobody without getting something in return. 'What's there to chat about?' he asked sourly.

'Two murders: Mrs Henrietta Darwin's and Inspector Line's.'

'Don't know nothin' 'bout 'em.'

'Not what your henchman says. Fellow by the name of Fingers Migston, chained up in a cell just like this one,' Fickett lied, Migston's body having been removed from Little Earl Street long since and dumped in the nearest pauper graveyard.

'Migston? Bah! Won't get a word out of him.' Loman smirked as he spoke but he was clearly rattled.

'I wouldn't be so sure. McWhirter has a gift for making our... guests blabber like babies. The lads call him the 'Squeezer' because he can wring the last drop of truth out of any poor sod he questions. Wasn't necessary this time, though; your Mr Migston was more than willing to spill his guts.'

'Don't believe yer,' Loman said loudly but the smirk had been replaced by a shadow of doubt.

'Maybe a little sample will convince you. He calls you Gaffer, doesn't he?' Fickett knew he was chancing his arm but his stab in the dark proved to be right on the mark judging by Loman's scowl. 'How'd you think I know that if the Squeezer didn't squeeze it out of him?'

Loman shifted uneasily on the bench, his Adam's apple bobbing in his throat like a cork on the open sea. Ha, got him, Fickett thought.

'And that's not all he squeezed out. Migston owned up to both killings, quick as you like. Knows he's for the long drop so nothing to lose and no reason to lie. Little squealer claims you were the go-between, got the instructions from Richard Darwin and passed them on to him. Right?'

'Filthy piece of dogshit's lying thru his teeth. He done that woman and Line, right enough, but I never had nothin' to do with the killings, I swear.'

Fickett stared hard at him, but stare as hard as he liked, Loman wasn't going to budge. Finally, the inspector looked away.

'Well, now, seems as though we have a bit of a stalemate, your word against Migston's. No way I can prove who's lying and who's telling the truth, so let's move on to something I can prove. And what I can prove, Loman, is that you *run a whorehouse.*'

The sudden switch took Loman by surprise, but he'd been down this road many times before and quickly recovered, his sturdy stockade of denials and lies back in place before his defences could be breached. 'Don't know what you mean. Selling flowers, that's my business – violets, dried lavender and the like, that's all. Nothin' to—'

'Don't waste my time,' snapped Fickett. 'After McWhirter carted you off yesterday, I had a look around your house, including the attic and what did I find? Half a dozen strumpets, sorriest looking trulls I've ever seen, but trulls just the same.'

'Those girls? They're flower-sellers. Ask 'em, they'll tell you.'

'I did, and they all claimed they'd been tricked into whoring by a certain Mr Micus Loman.'

'Bah! Those bitches lie outta their arses, say anything you want 'em to say.'

'Maybe, maybe not. Anyway, doesn't matter because I've got Martha, your so-called housekeeper, in custody and she's willing to talk. And if that's not enough, I've got Lucy Kinsley. Remember her? She can't wait to put you behind bars.'

'Damn her. Nothin' but trouble, that one, ever since I laid eyes on her.'

The sheen of sweat on Loman's brow, the tremble in the hands, the up-and-down cork in his throat, told Fickett all he needed to know; his bird was nicely cooked and ready for carving.

'You're done for, Loman.' Fickett let his words sink in before dangling the clemency carrot in front of the fettered donkey. 'Maybe I can be persuaded to turn a blind eye to this business with the trollops, and let you walk out of here scot-free,' the inspector said, his prisoner destined for Newgate no matter what, 'but only if you answer a few questions about Richard Darwin. Agreed?'

Fickett watched as Loman digested the proposal. The fellow obviously couldn't believe his good fortune, as intended. And he had no reason to give a fig about Richard Darwin, someone who'd been strung up over a week ago. Loman nodded his agreement.

'Good. So, who paid you to kill Henrietta Darwin and Inspector Line?'

'Whoa, hold on. Told you, I had nothin' to do with no murder.'

'Yes, I know what you told me. Look, I can't prove you were involved in committing the murders so you're safe, but we both know you took the instructions from Darwin and delivered them to Migston, so no more messing around. If you want to avoid jail time for putting young girls on the street, you'd be wise to tell me what I want to know. Now, last chance, was Richard Darwin the man who gave the orders?'

'Alright, alright. Truth is, I don't know. He never said his name. Read in the papers that Richard Darwin had been hanged for it but that was later.

At the time, had no idea who he was.'

'Still, you must've seen the man.' Fickett removed Richard Darwin's portrait from Henrietta's locket, borrowed yesterday from Mrs Darwin, and showed it to Loman. 'Is this he?'

'Nah, nothin' like him,' Loman replied.

'What do you mean?' a shaken Fickett demanded.

'Bloke in the picture,' Loman nodded at Richard's portrait, 'sits up straight, broad in the shoulders, full-face beard. Bloke I met was the exact opposite. Short fellow, round shoulders. Wore a slouch hat, pulled down over his brow, but I could see his face clear enough. No whiskers, cheeks an' chin smooth as a baby's bum. Muffin-face, I called him.'

Good God! MIVART!

Chapter Thirty-Six: Putting the Pieces Together

The day after his tea-less conversation with Mrs Betsy Smurkle, Dunston tracked down the Chinese cabinet-maker in Carlisle and verified what the nanny had told him. Unaware Groggins had been exposed, he decided against sending a telegram with his findings to Fickett, fearing it might go astray. Instead, he took the overnight train, arriving at London's Euston Station in the pre-dawn gloom of a frosty Tuesday morning and followed in Line's footsteps, the last the private inquiry agent ever took, towards Scotland Yard.

Gruesome images of Line's slashed throat hurried Dunston through the semi-darkness of Euston Road to a just-awakening Tottenham Court Road, where he prayed he'd find a hansom cab. His luck held. Two gold sovereigns, a huge fare any time of the day or night, persuaded a bleary-eyed cabbie, on his way home after an all-nighter, to take him to police headquarters, only to learn on arrival that Inspector Fickett had just left to meet Miss Lucy Kinsley, and was unlikely to be back for several hours.

When Dunston returned after an early lunch, Officer Ruggles, confined to desk duty while his wound healed, waved him through to Fickett's office where the visitor, having knocked twice, tentatively opened the door.

'Inspector Fickett…?'

Receiving no reply, Dunston stepped inside. The odd mix of furnishings – an elegant, buffed-mahogany desk, incongruously surrounded by a meagre supporting cast of two heavy, straight-back chairs for visitors and a wall of wooden shelves stacked with files – was exactly as Dunston remembered. The same could not be said of its sole occupant. Seated sideways, torso bent at a forty-five degree angle, head lowered, uniform crumpled, the inspector looked as downcast as an old sheepdog newly bereft of its lifelong master.

The silence lengthened, until Dunston, anxious to share his news, tried again, this time a little louder. 'Um… inspector, are you alright?'

No response. He was wondering whether he'd better leave and try again later, when he saw Fickett's lips move as though mouthing a silent prayer. A moment later, the policeman looked up, only then becoming aware of another's presence.

'Ah, Mr… er… Mr…' he said, sitting a little straighter, but still remote, as though cut off from the world by an invisible wall of his own making.

'Dunston Burnett, inspector.'

'Ah, yes…' A listless arm motioned his visitor to sit.

Dunston removed his greatcoat, placed it on one of the chairs in front of Fickett's desk, and seated himself on the other.

The inspector began speaking but in a lifeless tone, more to himself than his caller. 'Should've known Line was right, should've listened to him. Wouldn't have made such a terrible hash of it if I had. Too late now. Career's ruined.'

'Not sure I follow you.'

'It all fitted,' said the policeman, still in his private cocoon. 'Had all the proof I needed. Yet somehow… somehow it was all wrong. My evidence… nothing but worthless rubbish. If only… if only Line's telegram had reached me, I'd have known… known that Line could clear him.'

'Richard? You mean Richard?' Dunston almost sprang out of his chair in excitement.

'Of course I mean Richard,' Fickett sighed. 'Line had the evidence. Wanted the trial stopped. That's what his telegram said. Groggins told me.' The inspector stopped abruptly, as though only now seeing his caller. His eyes, suddenly sharper, ranged over his visitor's round face, round body, and poorly cut, dark grey three-piece suit, obviously trying to place him.

'Ahh, Line's contact,' he finally said. He straightened his jacket and cleared his throat. 'Ahem… forgive me, these last few hours have been, well… shocking, absolutely shocking.'

'My Goodness, whatever happened?'

Fickett eyed Dunston glumly, shaking his head as though loath to go over events that had obviously left him scarred and tormented. But then he took a deep breath and began in a dry-throated monotone to recount what led up to that sucker-punch moment when his future went up in flames and came down in ashes. He started with how Migston, Henrietta's murderer, and Line's, was caught and killed, and ended with Loman's identification of the man who hired him – *Mivart*.

'Mivart!' exclaimed Dunston. 'Loman identified Mivart?'

'Not in so many words. When I showed him the portrait of Richard from Henrietta's locket, he said it was *nothing* like the man who'd paid him.'

Fickett passed the locket to Dunston, Richard's portrait now back in place alongside Henrietta's. Dunston looked closely at both likenesses, especially hers, the first time he'd seen her face with its appealing surround of dark ringlets, and that captivating upward tilt of the lips' right side, before returning it to the inspector.

'He didn't know the man's name,' Fickett resumed, 'but the description he gave fitted Mivart perfectly – short fellow, round shoulders, no facial hair. He was always wearing a low-brimmed slouch hat, but Loman swore he saw his face well enough. I was desperate not to believe him, but the man has nothing to gain by lying. Mr Slouch Hat is Mivart alright.'

Dunston was pleased to hear that Richard had been vindicated, but devastated that an innocent man had been convicted and hanged. He could only imagine how the Darwins would feel, the same emotions as he, no doubt, but felt a thousand times more keenly.

'Line was right,' the inspector said morosely. 'Clever bastard suspected Mivart all along. Should've listened to him but I was sure Richard was my man. He was the only one with access to the two brass figures, the only one who could take the backdoor key and return it, *the only one*. It had to be him.'

Fickett fell silent, staring expectantly at Dunston, wondering no doubt what had brought this pudding-shaped fellow to Scotland Yard. Dunston knew he must apprise the inspector of his own findings, but he hesitated, not wanting to add to the policeman's burdens. Still, it couldn't be helped. 'Inspector, I don't wish to cause you further... distress... but, well, actually, Richard was *not* the only one able to access the cubbyhole. Miss Moxley—'

'Miss Moxley? Estelle Moxley? What on earth does Henrietta's sister have to do with this?'

'Frankly, I'm not sure, but let me tell you what I learned from Betsy Smurkle, the sisters' nanny, and then you can judge for yourself. You see, Estelle had Henrietta's vanity specially made as a wedding gift.'

'So? What of it?'

'Well, the what-of-it is this – according to the nanny, the vanity came with a spare set of brass figures,' Dunston continued. 'Back-ups in case one of the original figures was lost. A wise precaution, but, and this is the crucial point, Miss Moxley kept them herself, so obviously *she* had access to the backdoor key any time she wanted.'

Dunston could almost hear Fickett's detective gears locking into place. 'Hmm... Miss Moxley, interesting.'

'It is. Leaves us with a bit of a puzzle, though. The person with motive, Mivart, had no way of getting hold of the key, while the person with easy access to the key, Miss Moxley, had no reason to harm her sister. Quite a conundrum. Unless... unless... Good Lord!' Dunston broke off, gripped by one of his insights, his extra half-sense finally coming to life, sending his neural network's electrical impulses surging into dot-connecting free flow. *What if Mivart and Estelle were working together?*

Careful, mustn't get ahead of myself, he cautioned, but the warning was dismissed before it was fully formed, tossed aside like a kettle with a hole in it. He pictured what happened. Mivart carefully plotted the abduction and ransom demand, murder nowhere on the agenda, Henrietta simply a temporary bargaining chip. Estelle, still besotted with Mivart, supplied the brass figures, willing to do whatever he said, their very visible public break-up nothing but a smokescreen.

Whatever the particulars, his plan was quickly put into motion. On one of her visits to Down House, Estelle used her spare set of brass figures and took the backdoor key from Henrietta's vanity. Mivart's thugs then used it to enter Down House and grab Henrietta, later returning the key to Estelle who replaced it in the vanity on her next visit. The ransom demand completed the plan. Everything was going as intended and Mivart sat back, waiting for Darwin to comply with his ultimatum.

But then, Henrietta escaped, exactly as Line surmised, and in the chase that followed she was killed. The blackmail attempt had blown up in Mivart's face and, worse still, Estelle's sister was dead. Mivart could do nothing about that, but he did find a way to revive the extortion scheme – dump Henrietta's body on the Thames waterfront and bash head and torso so thoroughly even her husband wouldn't recognise her. The corpse would be dismissed as just another sixpenny whore who'd met a grisly end, and Charles Darwin would be left believing his daughter-in-law alive and still held captive. Very clever, Mr Mivart.

'Look like you've seen a ghost,' Fickett said, watching the array of spasm-like expressions – eyes squinting, then widening; brow furrowing, then clearing – flitting across Dunston's face.

'No... not a ghost. More like enlightenment. Inspector, *I believe I've solved the case,*' announced Dunston, astonishment and pride in his voice in equal measure. '*Mivart and Estelle were in it together.*'

Fickett listened carefully to his explanation, nodding his understanding to begin with but then switching to a puzzled frown when Dunston described how Mivart covered up Henrietta's death to keep the ransom plan alive.

'Ye-es, I see how they might have carried out the abduction,' he granted, 'but I'm not sure I agree with the bit about duping Darwin into believing his daughter-in-law wasn't dead so that the blackmail threat still had bite. I understand your reasoning, but, if you're right, why would Estelle identify her sister's body at The Six Jolly Porters? That's the exact opposite of what Mivart was trying to do, according to you.'

'You're right. Why would she do that?' Dunston was dismayed that Fickett's pinprick observation had popped his celebratory balloon, but he was not about to give up. 'Let me think. Perhaps... perhaps something happened that caused them to change tactics. Did anything occur at the inn that might have prompted her to act in this way?'

'Not that I recall. I explained why I'd brought Richard there and told her that he'd been unable to identify the corpse as his wife's. That's all.'

'Hmm, maybe something happened *before* she came to The Six Jolly Porters. Which day was this?'

'Monday before the inquest… January 29th.'

'The 29th! Ha!' Dunston's saucer face glowed with delight. 'I know what caused her to rejig the strategy. Darwin's retraction appeared in The Times *that morning*. Knowing Darwin had complied with their demand, there was no need to keep up the pretence that Henrietta was alive.'

'A clever point, Mr Burnett,' the inspector acknowledged, 'but surely, Mivart would want the body to remain nameless to hide the crime.'

'Mivart, yes…' Dunston paused, pulling his thoughts together, and then said: 'But *not* Estelle. He would have kept all knowledge of his plan to salvage his ransom scheme from her. After all, it involved bludgeoning her sister to death. So, when Estelle was suddenly confronted with the possibility that her sister's body was lying in the shed behind the inn, she was desperate to find out whether or not it was Henrietta's corpse.'

'Yes, you're right,' Fickett said slowly. But it took only a few moments for his assenting nod to switch to a glum, left-to-right shake as the consequences sank in. 'But… well… if this comes out, could be a bit awkward… for the police, I mean, and judge and jury… and me, I suppose.'

He looked away, muttering to himself, 'An innocent man… strung up by my doing… career's over… unless…' He fell silent for a moment, his eyes half closed. Then, seemingly back in command of himself, he fixed his gaze on Dunston and said, 'Mr Burnett, you've convinced me. Mivart and Miss Moxley are guilty and must be brought to justice. I trust I can count on you to keep our… er… little conversation under your hat until I have them under lock and key?'

'Of course, inspector. Won't breathe a word. But, if I may,' Dunston said, 'we don't know what proof Line had of Richard's innocence, and I'm not sure that what we have amounts to… *hard* evidence, as Mr Line would say, against Mivart and Miss Moxley, so perhaps we should—'

'Leave that to me, Mr Burnett. When those two find themselves in a Newgate cell, rats crawling over their feet, lice making themselves at home in their hair and clothes, they'll be more than ready to confess. Have no worries, I'll grill the truth out of them before they know what's hit them.'

'I… I suppose so,' said Dunston, unsettled by the sound of Fickett's proposed interrogation technique. He would have been positively alarmed had he known Fickett intended to grill much more than the truth out of them. Innocent Dunston had no idea that Fickett was planning to 'squeeze' the pair – his own brand of squeezing, not McWhirter's – until he had them begging to incriminate Richard Darwin in whatever way he wanted.

Chapter Thirty-Seven: Halfway There

Eight days earlier

The day Richard Darwin was strung up by the neck, two passengers, one wearing a slouch hat, the other a stylish, flamingo-pink bonnet, stepped down from a hansom cab at the entrance to Red Lion Square, Holborn, paid the cabby and turned into Dane Street. It was mid-afternoon and the pair were returning from Horsemonger Lane where, at precisely ten o'clock, they'd watched the final seconds of Richard Darwin's life.

A few steps brought them to a two-storey, terraced house, suitable for an up-and-coming professional gentleman or perhaps a spinster of moderate means. Once inside, they stopped in the narrow passageway to remove their outerwear, Slouch Hat taking off an overcoat with a short shoulder cape before helping Miss Bonnet to shrug awkwardly out of her wool bustle coat. After both garments had been hung on their respective wall pegs, the pair continued into the cosy, gas-lit parlour.

'Take that ridiculous thing off,' said Estelle, discarding her bonnet. 'It's done.'

'Yes, it is,' replied the other, removing the rather shabby slouch hat and tossing it on the chaise longue by the room's sole window, curtained now but on sunnier days affording a pleasant view of the square.

'Shall we have some tea?' Estelle was already on her way to the kitchen, not bothering to wait for an answer. 'I'll send the housemaid in to light the fire and attend to tea myself,' she called over her shoulder.

The housemaid, no more than eighteen or so, but a willing worker, soon had the flames dancing around the coals and, with a half curtsey, took her leave. Having watched the girl with a critical eye, Estelle's companion settled into one of the two armchairs stylishly upholstered in mauve velvet and set no more than a poker's length from the fireplace's brass fender, close enough for the occupant to reap the full benefit of the fire's pleasing warmth.

The seated person's eyes were drawn to the family photographs on the mantel, coming to rest on the grainy snapshot of two young girls, only a few years apart, posed with their nanny. She smiled at the pictured girls. 'We did it,' she whispered.

'Shows you, my dears,' Henrietta continued, softly yet firmly, 'that women can do *anything* if they put their minds to it. Even in this man's world. All it takes is careful preparation. I planned every step of my little scheme, just like playing chess with Father – from my opening move, the anonymous letter with its reference to Aesculapius to suggest my doctor husband was the writer; to the middlegame, the whiff of chloroform in the bedroom and the footprints in the snow to convince everyone I'd been kidnapped; and finally, the endgame, identification of my body by the scars, and the mysterious reappearance of the backdoor key in the vanity to incriminate Richard. And there you have it.'

'Sorry, didn't hear that...' Estelle returned with a dainty, bone china teapot and teacups on a silver tray held in her left hand, leaving the maid to bring milk and sugar. She set the tray down on an ornately carved table between the two chairs and disappeared again before her sister could reply. She was soon back with a small plate of almond macaroons, her favourite. Placing it on the table, she smoothed her pale lavender day dress and sat down across from her sister. The tea now properly steeped, she poured for both of them.

'Now, what did you say?' she asked.

'I was talking to our young selves on the mantelpiece,' owned Henrietta sheepishly, that oddly tilted smile playing across her lips. 'Silly me. I was telling them how we fooled everybody.'

'Ah, those two girls. The terrible twosome. Well, I'm sure they're not surprised. They were always a cunning pair.' Estelle peeked at the snapshot before turning back to her sister. 'Yes, we fooled everyone – police, jury, judge, the lot. A truly amazing plan, sister. Well conceived, and well executed.'

Henrietta was pleased with Estelle's praise, but her sister had never been her most demanding critic. That distinction fell to the only person whose opinion really mattered. Herself. How did she evaluate her own performance? Did everything work out as planned? Well, there were a few bumps along the way – Mivart's ransom note and Line's telegram – but otherwise her chess strategy ended up with Richard being checkmated straight into the hangman's noose, so, overall, it went extremely well.

'I haven't told you this before, sister,' Henrietta eventually resumed, 'but my first idea was to poison Richard and be done with it, even if it meant I'd end up on the gallows. But then I thought, why should I suffer for what he did? That's when I changed tack. Within a matter of weeks, I had it all worked out, a scheme to take him from cuffs to court to coffin.'

'That must be the *best* change in course *ever* – put Richard's head in the noose in place of yours,' Estelle said with a laugh.

Henrietta smiled. Then, her face clouding, 'You know what the hardest part was?'

'What?'

'The wait. Didn't want to put my plan into action until I'd manufactured convincing evidence of Richard's motive for killing me.'

'That must have been sheer torture for you,' commiserated Estelle. 'But then up popped Eyesore Annie,' she said, brightening the mood. 'What a boon she was.'

'Yes, she was. Once my inquiry agent finally traced Lucy to Shoreditch Workhouse and learned about Richard's bastard son, it was simple. A word in money-hungry Annie's ear and she couldn't wait to tell Mr George Mivart about Richard's little bastard and collect her reward. And he, as I knew he would, was just as quick to share it with the authorities.'

'With Annie primed to be a star witness at the trial, you were all set. Quite a coup, sister. Still, fortune did favour us in the way things played out.'

'What d'you mean? *Fortune* had nothing to do with it. I plotted *everything* from start to finish, *every* single detail, the *entire* plan.' Annoyed, Henrietta had spoken sharply.

'All I meant when I said fortune favoured us,' Estelle said quickly, worried her choice of words had upset her prickly sister, 'was that *Fickett* favoured us with his farcical demonstration of how Richard waved his hands like an amateur magician and seemingly drew the key out of your vanity. You must admit, that did move things along rather nicely.'

'True enough, but even if Fickett hadn't come up with his parlour-trick explanation, you my dear, the false witness with made-up evidence, would've stepped in and filled the gap with your *sighting* of Richard, key in hand, sneaking up the back stairs supposedly to replace it in the vanity before he was accosted by Fickett. And that lie, coming from you, Richard's sister-in-law, someone firmly in his corner, or so it appeared, would have been swallowed hook, line and sinker.'

'I know, and that's why I'm miffed the inspector spoiled my fun.' Estelle's disappointment was written plain on her face. 'His... inventiveness meant my playacting wasn't needed and I would have *loved* to do my bit to fool those cloddish police.'

'And I have no doubt you would've performed brilliantly, my sister-in-arms, delivered your lines perfectly and with the sweetest smile. But it wasn't to be. Besides, even though your talents were not required in that respect, you were *central* to the operation. After all, *you* identified my body, *and* took and returned the key.'

'Ah, yes. I wonder if anyone will ever work out *my* key trick. I hope not. If they do, our goose will be cooked.'

'Don't fret. No one knows about your spare set of brass figures so you're in the clear. And I'm officially dead,' Henrietta quipped, 'and dead people can't be arrested, no matter what the police discover. So, there's nothing to worry about. And, since it's all worked out so smoothly up to this point,' her fingers played with the lace collar at the neck of her maroon bodice, 'I have no doubt, my dear, the next step will go equally well.'

Estelle sighed. 'Sister, must you? I know how much this means to you but risking everything again may not be the wisest course of action.'

'Wise or not, it has to be done. We're only halfway there. One down, one to go.'

Chapter Thirty-Eight: An Arrest

The present, early Tuesday afternoon

'George Mivart, I arrest you for the abduction and murder of Henrietta Darwin, and the murder of former Chief of Detectives, Archibald Line.'

Legs braced, body tensed, Inspector Fickett was standing in the hallway of Mivart's residence in Noble Street, Aldersgate. He'd come straight from Scotland Yard after his meeting with Dunston to apprehend the man he believed hired Loman and Migston to bludgeon the life out of Henrietta Darwin and slit Line's throat.

Mivart's butler, a thickset man in his mid-fifties, had done what any butler worthy of the position would do when answering the front door and coming face to face with officers of the law. He bid them wait while he hurried off to inform his master that Scotland Yard was on the doorstep. Fickett was having none of that. He stepped inside followed by Constable Beresford, and that is where Mivart, white-faced and worried-looking, a lunch napkin still tucked in his waistcoat, found them when he emerged from the dining room.

On hearing the menace in Fickett's voice, Mivart staggered back, nervously wiping his mouth with his serviette before handing it to the butler. Steadying himself, he struggled for a more assertive stance, and then, finding his voice, managed, 'Arrest? Wh-what d'you mean?'

Fickett ignored the man's questions. He was fully into the softening-up phase of his interrogation technique, readying his prey for what was to come at the Yard. 'Your goose is cooked, Mivart. Cuff him.' He motioned with his head, and Constable Beresford stepped forward, pulled Mivart's arms behind his back and locked a pair of unusually heavy iron shackles around his wrists.

'G-get these chains off me!' Baby-faced and slump-shouldered he might be, but Mivart was not going to stand for this without at least some show of indignation. 'You... you have no right to enter my house like this and behave in this outrageous manner,' he declared hoarsely.

Fickett paid him no attention. He signalled to Beresford, and the burly policeman grabbed Mivart by the scruff of the neck, marched him out of the house and shoved him into the waiting police wagon.

Half an hour later, Mivart, still handcuffed, still in his waistcoat, was seated across the desk from Fickett in the inspector's office. The arrest had done its job, Mivart now decidedly anxious, silent and subdued. Time for Phase Two. A quick round of questioning might be enough to get a chicken-hearted milksop like this fellow to confess *and* save the inspector's career by implicating Richard Darwin enough to justify his hanging. If not, Room B4 would do the trick for sure.

'Mr Mivart, I'm going to ask you three questions.'

'Qu-questions? What questions?'

'One, did you and Miss Estelle Moxley conspire to abduct and murder Henrietta Darwin?'

'No! Of course not. I explained at the trial that I sent the ransom demand, but that was all.'

'Indeed. But now we know about your continued involvement with Miss Moxley despite your very public break-up,' Fickett lied. 'As soon as I'm finished with you, I intend to arrest her, and I'm sure she will be more than ready to place all the blame on you.'

'I-I swear I've had nothing to do with Miss Moxley since our separation, nothing!' Mivart protested.

'As you please.' Fickett was quite prepared to let this go... for now. He'd seen the flicker of uncertainty in the man's eyes, and knew he was on the right track. 'Two, did you pay Micus Loman to have former Chief of Detectives Archibald Line killed?'

'What? Certainly not. I don't know anyone called Micus Loman, and I had absolutely *nothing* to do with Mr Line's death.'

'Very strange. You see, Micus Loman is sitting in a cell in Newgate Prison and has already identified you as the man who hired him to kill Line. That slouch hat you wore was hardly an adequate disguise. Loman described you to a T.'

'Slouch hat? I haven't even got a slouch hat, for goodness' sake. I don't underst—'

'Mr Mivart, your lies will serve no purpose.' Fickett watched the man squirm. He leaned across the desk, his face inches from Mivart's. 'You have one last chance. Before you answer my final question, though, take a moment to think how what you say might help you in your present predicament. I'd think hard if I were you. This is the question. What can you tell me about Richard Darwin's involvement in his wife's death?'

'Richard Darwin? Never had anything to do with the man, so I can't te—'

'Thank you, Mr Mivart.' Not what Fickett had hoped for, but it was early days. Fellow needs a little nudge, that's all, and Phase Three will deliver a lot more than a nudge. 'Beresford!'

'Yes, sir.'

'Escort Mr Mivart to Room B4.'

Beresford's eyebrows shot up. 'B4, sir?'

'That's what I said. Move it along, man. I have to pick up Miss Moxley.'

Mivart was hauled out of Fickett's office, marched down to the basement and manhandled into Room B4, the smallest cell in the Yard, barely four-by-four-by-four. Once inside, Mivart would not be able to move an inch, or see anything in the pitch blackness; nor, thanks to the room's solid stone construction, hear a sound.

Room B4, Fickett's personal version of the Black Hole of Calcutta, could break a man's spirit in no time, and in the past had even driven the occasional poor sod raving mad. One night, that's all he gave Mivart. By morning, the snivelling weasel would be ready to incriminate anyone, the Archbishop of Canterbury even, let alone Richard Darwin, if that is what Fickett wanted.

Chapter Thirty-Nine: The Rest of the Plan

While Fickett was in Aldersgate arresting George Mivart for the murder of Henrietta Darwin, the 'murdered' woman was in Estelle's parlour in Holborn fulminating about her sister's prolonged absence. Estelle had left for Down House to attend Richard and Henrietta's funerals at St Mary the Virgin last Thursday and here it was, early-afternoon on Tuesday. The burials were on Friday so even if Estelle had felt obliged to stay through the weekend for propriety's sake, she should still have been back yesterday.

She was sitting in her armchair by the fire, a novel open on her lap, debating whether to have yet another cup of tea when she heard the front door open and slam shut. Ah, at last, Estelle was back. A moment later, the parlour door was flung open and her sister burst in, coat and bonnet still on.

'Good Lord! Whatever's happened?' Henrietta was more shocked by Estelle's white-with-fright face than her forceful entrance. Two strides and she was across the room, arms wrapping around her younger sister, gently rubbing her back and murmuring, 'There, there. It's alright,' the words she'd used in the barn all those years ago and every other time her sibling needed comforting. She knew Estelle's strengths and weaknesses as well as her own: assign her a task and she'd carry it out without any difficulty, but left to her own devices she could be easily rattled. Fortunately, as happened now, she could be pacified equally quickly by a few soothing words from big sister.

Still making sympathetic noises, the older woman helped the younger remove her outerwear, hat first, then her overcoat, carefully manoeuvring it around the right-angle of the ruined arm, trying not to grimace at the feel of its parchment-stiff flesh and stick-figure bone. She left the clothing in a pile on the chaise longue, took Estelle, still in mourning black, by her good arm, settled her in one armchair and then re-seated herself in the other. 'Now, tell me what happened,' she said firmly. Then, more gently, 'Take your time.'

'Yes, th… thank you, Henrietta. I was *so* desperate to get here and tell you my news but Lucy insisted I stay with her until she was settled on the one o'clock train back to Kent, and then I couldn't find a cab and when I finally did, the stupid thing moved through the traffic slower than a snail and all the time these terrible thoughts were crowding in on me and I… I don't know what overcame me. I must've panicked, I suppose. All I could think was that we had to flee at once.'

'Estelle dear, slow down, it's alright.' Henrietta was doing her utmost to put her sister at ease. 'Tell me what happened, then we can decide what to do.'

'Yes, I… I'll do my best.' She took several deep, calming breaths. 'It began yesterday when that Inspector Fickett, sharp as the north wind he is, came to Down House. I was in the drawing room with your mother-in-law and Lucy. Fickett reported that Migston had been tracked down and killed during the arrest. Good, I thought, he won't be able to say anything that might implicate you, but then Lucy piped up and claimed she *knew* Migston, although she knew him as Fingers.'

'Lucy knew Migston? How could that be?'

'Don't know, but from what she said he attacked her, twice, the second time hurting her quite badly.'

'So? Serves the hussy right.' Henrietta carelessly brushed a small piece of fluff off the front of her white, ruffle lace blouse. 'Honestly, Estelle, I can't see why you're fretting so.'

'That's not all,' Estelle replied. 'Before I could shut her up, the silly girl went on to say that Migston worked for Micus Loman and that she knew where Loman lived. Fickett's eyes lit up, glowing like the underside of fire-hot coals, immediately seeing his chance to get his hands on the one person who, so he thought, could confirm that Richard was behind your kidnapping and murder.'

Seeing Henrietta about to speak, Estelle held up her hand for silence, an out-of-character gesture, unusual in any entreaty from younger to older sister. 'Wait! There's more. This morning, I saw the police arrest Loman and cart him off to prison. If he talks, *he could point Fickett in your direction.* For all I know, Fickett's on his way here this very minute. Sister, we have very little time.'

'It's alright, Estelle. Let me think.' Even Henrietta, always the more stable, was unnerved by Estelle's account of Loman's capture. She'd planned everything so carefully, but not for a moment had she foreseen this development.

How much does Loman know, she asked herself? Well, he knows the woman Migston beat to death was not Henrietta Darwin, so he knows I'm still alive. Would he pass this on to Fickett? Maybe, but not likely, because if he did, he'd be admitting to complicity in murder. Same with Line's murder. No, the blackguard would deny everything, claim he was simply a go-between, passing notes, contents unseen, to Migston, the actual killer. An easy lie for him, one that would save his worthless skin and, as it turned out, couldn't be challenged since Migston was dead.

What about the last time she saw him, the day after Richard was hanged? How much did she tell him? Not an easy meeting, she recalled. At first, he'd balked at an assignment well off his London patch. Then what? She closed her eyes, picturing their exchange…

A slouch-hatted Henrietta dressed in her man-clothes sat across the table from Loman in The George and Vulture, the pub where she'd met Migston and arranged for Line's elimination. As then, negotiations were proving difficult. Henrietta thought Loman was fishing for more money, but when she put a few extra sovereigns on the table, he still shook his head. Finally, in desperation, she sketched, nothing more, the tragic story behind her request, hoping it would persuade him to accede to her wishes.

'Listen to me!' she pressed him. She began telling him what happened, becoming more and more agitated as she always did whenever she talked about that dreadful day. Her whole body started to tremble with rage and she knew she was moving dangerously close to one of her 'little fits' as Estelle so delicately called them, when she lost all control and turned into a hissing, spitting hellcat. She tried to pull back but it was too late, she was already in the grip of the ugly images whirling inside her head.

Before she knew it, she was straining across the table, her fury-fraught face no more than inches from Loman's, screaming at him, the story pouring out in a torrent of vitriol. Most of it was incomprehensible, but the hate was unmistakable, especially in her last snarled words: *'A life for a life!'*

Then, suddenly as it started, the outburst was over, her anger caged, her focus back. 'Justice *must* be served,' she insisted in her normal voice, or rather her normal, lower-register man-voice, 'and, if you put this matter to right, you'll be well paid, *very* well paid.'

Loman must have sensed his end-of-the-rainbow pot of gold was within reach because he ceased his grumbling. The final price was steep but the deal was struck. Henrietta was satisfied with the outcome, but not with her frenzied, uncontrollable eruption. Her intention had been to secure Loman's services without saying much about the assignment from fear of leaks, but she had no idea what she might have let slip in the heat of her rant. Loman's next words, though, provided some reassurance.

'Let's hear 'bout the job, then,' he said.

'You'll know when I'm ready to tell you and not before,' she told him. 'There's plenty of time. I'm planning on Thursday of next week. Be here at eleven o'clock Wednesday and you'll get your instructions.'

The scene faded away. On opening her eyes, Henrietta could see that Estelle was really frightened. Was she asking too much of her? Henrietta looked to the photograph of the two sisters on the mantel, the guardians of her conscience, seeking their guidance. Their innocence made them valued arbiters of her actions and her thoughts, the pair invariably delivering their Ayes or Nays in perfect accord as though speaking with a single voice... except today.

Was the younger one frowning at her? Yes, the girl's glower said Henrietta was using Estelle unfairly for her own purposes. Henrietta switched her gaze to the older child and there she saw firmness and determination. Her expression said, no, Estelle's a willing partner in your mission. Don't forget, she shattered her arm, but you saved her life, you caught her and broke her fall. But for you, she'd have died, busted and bloodied on that barn floor. Henrietta nodded to her childhood self. Yes, Estelle owed her and, yes, she *will* help me finish what I've started.

Henrietta carefully smoothed her periwinkle blue silk skirt over her lap. 'Sister, listen to me,' she began, giving her voice the right ring of reassurance to placate Estelle. Then, more forcefully, 'There's *no* reason for us to bolt. Fickett can question Loman as long as he likes but it won't do him any good. Loman will deny everything, it's the only way he can save himself from the noose, and, even if he does talk, there's *no* way he can connect me with any of it.'

'How can you say that? Loman knows you didn't die,' countered Estelle. 'And if he saw through your slouch-hatted disguise—'

'*Impossible*. The few times I saw him, he barely looked at me. When he did, I quaffed my ale – horrible stuff – as if I were a lifelong toper, and he never took me for anything but a man. What a dunderhead. And I didn't tell him *anything* about me. Didn't even give him a made-up name so d'you know what he called me? *Matey*, he called me matey.' A nice touch, she thought, even if a complete fabrication. 'So, no need for us to run like a pair of rats fleeing a sinking ship. Our ship is watertight... *we are perfectly safe.*'

Henrietta didn't dare look at the sisters on the mantelpiece after her untruth. Had she done so she would have seen the six-year-old shaking her head disapprovingly and the eight-year-old lowering guilty eyes. But they were innocents from a long-ago childhood. Ignoring them, today's Henrietta eyed today's Estelle, gauging the effect of her falsehood.

'Oh, I do hope you're right,' said Estelle.

'I *am*, my dear.' Henrietta breathed more easily as she saw Estelle's brow unknot. She smiled, her slightly angled lips tilting an extra degree, confident her sister's worries had been dispelled. 'No need for panic. We can still complete what we set out to do.'

'No!' Estelle's worried frown was back in place.

'Estelle, I cannot stop now. I have to complete what I started.'

'Henrietta, please, no. We should put an end to it... *now*... while we're safe,' the younger sister pleaded. 'And anyway,' she persisted, fastening on to what she saw as an insurmountable hurdle blocking her sister's foolishness, 'Loman and Migston are out of the picture so you don't have anyone to... take care of the next... the next—'

'I have *me*,' Henrietta cut in.

'You? You can't mean that.'

'Look, it's simple.' She laid out her plan for next Thursday. 'It will happen exactly as I've told you, but instead of Migston lying in wait on the Sandwalk behind Down House, it will be me.'

'No! Henrietta, you can't. I won't let you!'

Henrietta's slightly skewed lips angled a fraction more, but this time hatred twisted the usually beguiling half-smile into an ugly, murderous scowl. 'I must. I *can* do it, and I *will* do it. We'll leave for Kent at once, and then... it'll all be over by Thursday's end.'

Chapter Forty: Fickett's Message

Dunston was seated at the small desk in his room in The Adelphi Hotel, tracing the *R* and the *M* engraved on the silver medallion resting on his palm. Then, turning it sideways, he ran his finger over the already familiar date etched into the coin's rim. How many times had Line done exactly the same? Thousands, Dunston imagined, so many that the man's spirit seemed to have somehow been assimilated into the worn engravings. Dunston could sense Line right there beside him every time he touched the metal.

'You've been avenged, Archibald.' Dunston had never used the detective's first name while he was alive, but now it seemed appropriate. 'Fickett is not my favourite person, too self-seeking for my taste, but credit where credit is due, he did his job and put your killer in his grave. And now that conniving pair – Mivart, aided and abetted by Estelle Moxley – will get their just deserts for paying Migston to take your life.'

A knock on the door pulled him from his thoughts. He quickly slipped the medallion back in his waistcoat pocket. 'Come in.'

Nick entered. 'Message for you, sir. Bloke at the front desk said a young jack, name of Ruggles, brought it a few minutes ago. Asked me to bring it up.'

'Thank you, Nick.' Dunston took the note from his manservant. Ah, Fickett reporting he's nabbed Mivart and Miss Moxley, he guessed, delighted his input had landed the pair responsible for the deaths of Henrietta Darwin and Archibald Line in custody.

Tingling with anticipation, his fumbling fingers made heavy weather of unfolding the single sheet of notepaper. At last it was laid flat on the small writing table and Inspector Fickett's few scribbled paragraphs were revealed to Dunston's disbelieving eyes.

Scotland Yard
Tuesday, 6.00 PM

Attn. Mr Burnett:

Sir:

Let me begin by thanking you most profusely for your assistance in this matter. Given your invaluable help, I feel it only right to bring you up to date with recent developments.

Following our meeting this afternoon, I arrested Mivart and interrogated him for more than an hour. Naturally, he swore he was innocent, vehemently denying any conspiracy between himself and Miss Estelle Moxley. All he admitted to was the ransom demand. I tried every trick in the book, but he didn't budge an inch and, in the end, I was inclined to believe him, a view significantly reinforced by what I have to report next.

Thinking that Miss Moxley was very much the junior partner, I'd naturally focused my attention on Mivart. Now I was keen to hear what she had to say. As a courtesy to her sex, I thought it only proper to go to her house myself. It was almost five o'clock by time I got there and, much to my chagrin, I found the door bolted and the windows shuttered. The lady had made a run for it, a sure sign of guilt. Although I'd missed my chance to collar her, my visit was not for naught – a neighbour saw her leaving earlier in the afternoon with a short man wearing a slouch hat!

So, we have the mysterious Mr Slouch Hat coming out of Miss Moxley's house at the same time Mr George Mivart was under lock and key at the Yard. It doesn't take a genius to conclude that <u>*Mivart is not Slouch Hat.*</u>

WHAT? Mivart not Slouch Hat? How can that be? Dunston gasped, all his breath squeezed out of him as though his lungs had been crushed between iron clamps. Five underlined words and instead of retribution for his detective friend, he was left with nothing but the aftermath of a misguided fantasy, a fiasco of his own making. One witness and his 'solution' – the Mivart-Moxley collaboration – was cut in two, the Mivart half lopped off by some nosy-parker neighbour.

If not Mivart, then who? He willed his brain to function, but it remained resolutely defunct. Nothing there, not a single thought. Nothing in Fickett's note, either, unless… He turned the sheet over and found two more paragraphs on the back.

This development brings the case full circle. With Mivart out of the picture (I released him of course with profuse apologies), young Darwin is back as the primary suspect. I see now that the unknown Slouch Hat was simply a go-between, employed by Richard to carry his instructions to Loman, while Miss Moxley's role in the conspiracy was to remove and then replace the backdoor key using her spare set of brass figures.

Obviously, there is more work to be done. In particular, I don't yet know the relationship between Miss Moxley and Richard although a romantic entanglement seems most likely. I suspect he abandoned Lucy, the maid and mother of his child, and took up with his wife's sister. I don't know this for a fact, but I will keep digging and when I get to the bottom of it, I'm confident the evidence will show that Richard Darwin is the guilty party after all, and that the right man, thank the Lord, was charged, convicted and hanged.

With my gratitude,

Jeremiah Fickett, Inspector

OH, NO! He thinks it's Richard! Again! Or, rather, he *wants* it to be Richard. And all thanks to my 'invaluable help', fretted Dunston. What a mess.

'Sir, you alright?' Nick moved forward, not sure what to do.

No response.

'Sir, are you alright?'

Dunston stared wordlessly at his manservant, struggling to absorb Fickett's news. *Fickett can't be right, can he? There must be some other explanation. I must think. Find out what's really going on.* Then, out loud: 'Nick, I... I have to... sort this out. I need some time to work out... well, it doesn't really matter what... I just need some time. Come back first thing tomorrow. By then I hope I'll know what's to be done.'

Dunston paced his room. Sat on the edge of the bed. Paced some more. Opened the door and called downstairs for coffee. Paced up and down while he waited. Ignored the coffee when it arrived. Paced this way and that. Stared out of the window without seeing the wet thoroughfare or the evening traffic. Paced again.

Perhaps the pacing was not as pointless as it seemed; perhaps it stimulated the thinking process; or sent blood to the brain; or promoted the rearrangement of evidence into some coherent shape. Actually, none of these beneficial side-effects occurred. His mental steps were as directionless as his physical ones, his mind meandering along a winding, back-looping, go-nowhere thought-path until finally good sense – or was it faith? – intervened.

Fickett was *wrong*. Richard was *innocent*. Dunston knew it, not because he had all the evidence but because *Line said so* in his telegram to Fickett, and if Line said so, the proof must be out there somewhere, waiting for Dunston to find.

The next hour was packed with activity, this time of the non-pacing, cerebral kind. Line's telegram had been sent from Carlisle following the detective's conversation with Betsy Smurkle, so what did he learn from her that *proved* Richard's innocence?

Quickly grabbing his notes, he read his record of Line's conversation with her. He found where she told Line about Estelle's back-up brass figures, same as she told him. But that wouldn't be sufficient to convince an evidence-purist like Line, would it? While it established that someone other than Richard had access to the key in Henrietta's vanity, namely Estelle, it certainly did not *eliminate* Richard, as Fickett's letter made clear.

And anyway, according to his notes, Line was keen to be on his way *before* Mrs Smurkle mentioned the second set of brass figures. So something else triggered his sudden interest in leaving, something that came up earlier in the conversation. What *was* it?

Betsy, Dunston read, described the accident for Line, and after that told him *bits 'an pieces 'bout the girls*. Didn't sound like much, but it was immediately after this that Line started agitating to return to London. He must've heard something in Betsy's prattle that proved Richard's innocence, but what?

Perhaps Line's letter, sent from Carlisle after his visit to Nettle Leaf Cottage, would help. It was still with the Home Secretary, but Dunston remembered every word. The first sentence was an apology for Line's continued absence, and the next two, his plans for getting his findings to Inspector Fickett. Nothing by way of guidance there, but the last sentence might hold the key:

> *In the meantime, take a close look at my report of the inquest and what I <u>saw</u> and what I <u>heard</u> in the shed behind The Six Jolly Porters.*

The relevant report, packed along with the others in Dunston's portmanteau, was quickly produced and scanned. Line, he noted, didn't spend much time on the injuries to the corpse's head and body, concentrating instead on the scars on the foot. Then, Fickett, after showing up unexpectedly, recounted for Line's benefit the girls' fall in the barn. This was when something struck Line as odd.

Hmm. *Scars*, that's what he *saw*... next, the sisters' *accident*, that's what he *heard*. Ha! What bothered Line was not something about the accident by itself, but some inconsistency *between* the fall and the scars. Line, ever the professional, had travelled all the way to Carlisle to ask Betsy Smurkle about the fall *and* the scars. Dunston, still the amateur, only asked about the sisters' accident, never enquiring about the scars.

Dunston slapped his palm against his forehead. What a dolt. Should've asked Betsy to relate *all* of her conversation with Line. What did she tell Line about the scars on the corpse's foot that convinced him Richard was innocent? Only one way to find out. He'd have to make the long journey all the way back to Carlisle. Not an appealing proposition, but his own fault.

A second palm-to-forehead slap signalled a possible way out. There might be others who could tell him about the scars. Who else had seen them? Well, besides Line (dead) and Miss Moxley (on the run), Inspector Fickett had seen them. Not the best person to approach on this subject, though, since he was set on proving Richard guilty. Who else? Ah, one person… here in London. Dunston had his plan for the morrow.

Chapter Forty-One: A Consultation

Shortly after breakfast the next day, Dunston left the hotel, hailed a cab and soon arrived at his destination. He opened the building's front door and stepped inside as unobtrusively as possible. Entering a room full of people was always a challenge for him, especially if they were members of the opposite sex. In this instance, his worst fear was realised as he felt the glacial stares of a dozen women fastening upon him. They were sitting on hard-backed wooden chairs along two sad-green walls running the length of the slightly dingy, undeniably cold waiting room.

At the far end on the left was a service-hatch with a sign that read **RECEPTION**. Oh, no, he'd have to walk the length of the narrow room to get there. Modifying his usual heavy-footed tread, he tip-toed forward, twelve pairs of eyes following him every inch of the way. As he reached the service window, a woman in her late-twenties stepped into view. She was dressed more like an administrative assistant than a nurse, her grey blouse with white bow and full-length black skirt conveying a sense of professional correctness that did little for Dunston's nervous disposition.

'Yes?' she said crisply. Her query was delivered in a neutral tone, neither overly friendly nor openly hostile, but nonetheless sounded to the timid (Dunston) or the socially awkward (also Dunston) like a military command barked at an under-performing recruit. Dunston flinched.

When he'd decided yesterday to approach Dr Matthew Cullingworth, the one person in London who, having examined the corpse in The Six Jolly Porters, should be able to describe the scars and save him the long trip north, he'd never dreamed he'd have to withstand a chilling crossfire from twenty-plus flinty eyeballs and a face-to-face encounter with an assertive young woman.

'Um… well… if possible, I'd like to see the doctor.'

'Are you a patient of Dr Cullingworth?' she asked with a look that said I'm quite certain you're not.

'Not exactly, no… you see, I'm actually here—'

'Doctor's not accepting any new patients at the moment.' She was already turning away, the matter closed as far as she was concerned.

Dunston was not going to give up. He was about to try again, when the door to his right opened and an elderly woman emerged. Ha! The doctor's office. Only a step away. Seeing his chance, he pushed past the open-mouthed lady and slipped inside, a surprisingly daring move for a man usually mired in indecision.

'Name?' Dr Cullingworth was seated at his desk, head down, writing in a file, presumably the just departed patient's.

'Er… Burnett, Dunston Burnett.'

'And what is ailing you today, Mr Burnett?' The doctor still had not looked up.

'Nothing really, you see—'

Dunston was again interrupted before he could make his request known, this time by a raised hand. The patient's record complete, the doctor gave him the benefit of the serious expression Dunston remembered from the trial, now with a thinly veiled layer of annoyance. The intelligent eyes behind rimless spectacles, the refined brow and the solemnly set lips signalled that Dr Cullingworth was not a man to be trifled with. Precisely combed dark hair, clean-shaven face and sombre frock coat with grey, single-knotted tie completed his austere, resolute appearance.

'May I remind you that this is a surgery and I have many patients in urgent need of my assistance,' lectured the doctor. 'I do not have time for non-medical interruptions, so…' He gestured to the door, plainly expecting his uninvited visitor to leave.

But Dunston held his ground, another sign he was becoming, if not forceful, at least more resilient in his pursuit of those responsible for Line's murder. 'Sir, a minute of your time, that's all I ask, a minute that might right a terrible miscarriage of justice.'

'What are you talking about? What miscarriage of justice?'

'The Richard Darwin case,' Dunston said. 'You examined the corpse in The Six Jolly Porters.'

'Sir, if you're questioning my judgment,' the doctor replied with some heat, 'let me assure you the evidence was clear – the woman's skull was fractured so severely there can be no doubt about the cause of death. Now, if you don't mind, I—'

'No, no, not how she died,' Dunston said. 'It's about the two scars on the lady's left foot.'

For the first time, the doctor looked mildly interested. Dunston watched him as he silently debated whether to give his unbidden caller a few moments of his time or send him on his way. Five minutes of possibly diverting conversation with this corpulent intruder versus treatment of yet another tedious female with the vapours? Decision quickly made in Dunston's favour, the doctor nonetheless began cautiously, his natural curiosity held in check, but definitely there, just below the surface.

'The scars on her foot? Hmm.' He eyed his visitor. 'And what's your interest in them?' He gestured to the patient's chair in front of his desk and Dunston duly took the offered seat.

'Ah, yes, you see, I'm… um… acting on behalf of Mrs Emma Darwin.' The lie, rehearsed in advance, still struggled to find its way out of Dunston's mouth. Not one of the world's natural dissemblers, he reassured himself that the claim was true in spirit if not fact – he really was acting in her interests, simply not at her behest. 'She and I are concerned that her son, Richard, may have been wrongly convicted.'

'What? Surely not!' The doctor's eyebrows rose.

'I fear so. And our doubts about his guilt arise from those scars on the corpse's foot and Miss Moxley's reliance on them to identify her sister's body. Hence, my visit to you. I'm hoping that you can describe them to me because I've not seen them myself, and, if possible, tell me how they were caused.'

'Well, you've piqued my interest,' the doctor conceded. 'Here's what I can tell you. It's my practice to run my eye over the deceased's entire body before signing the death certificate so, yes, I saw the scars and examined them with my magnifying glass. They were faded, clearly many years old, most likely dating back to childhood, one about the size of a farthing, the other smaller.'

Dunston nodded. Exactly how Line described them.

'As to cause, the culprit was a round, pointed object, probably a large nail, driven through the foot from top to bottom.'

A nail, exactly what Fickett had told Line. Dunston was about to nod again when urgently clanging alarm bells brought him to full alert. 'Did you say *from top to bottom?*'

'Indeed, that's exactly what I said.'

'Are you sure?'

'Absolutely,' asserted the doctor firmly. 'When something like a nail enters a person's flesh, it leaves a larger mark at the entry point than at the exit point, if there is one. And that's not all. The tissue binds around the nail or whatever it happens to be, gripping it so firmly that considerable effort is required to extract it. The nail has to be wiggled back and forth or round and round, further enlarging the point of entry while leaving the exit wound virtually unchanged. And since the scar on the *upper* side of the corpse's foot was the larger, *that* was the point of entry. There, does that accord with Miss Moxley's account?'

'Not at all,' Dunston replied. 'In the statement she gave to the police before the inquest, she claimed her sister fell from a wooden rafter and landed on a nail protruding point-upward from a plank. If that's what happened, the nail would've entered the *bottom* of her foot and exited through the *top*.'

'Impossible,' declared the doctor emphatically. 'Had she said that when testifying about the scars, I would've spoken up, there and then. This ridiculous story of hers is totally at odds with the scarring. In my professional opinion, Miss Moxley's identification of the body is completely bogus.'

Chapter Forty-Two: No More Speculation

After thanking Dr Cullingworth, the queue-jumper braved the evil glares from the waiting-room occupants, exited the surgery and hurried back to The Adelphi Hotel. Seated in the sole chair in his room, Dunston's brain cells swarmed all over the doctor's revelation like bees buzzing around a hive. Line had already laid out the evidence when he described the scars in his fifth report: *the top one was about the size of a bronze farthing, the other perhaps half that size.* Dunston must have read that sentence at least a dozen times, yet never grasped its significance. After all, he had no idea about entry and exit wounds, but Line, a police officer, did.

Like the doctor, Line saw that the physical evidence contradicted Miss Moxley's account of Henrietta's injury. No doubt, he immediately suspected that she'd deliberately lied and that the corpse might not be Henrietta's, but the evidence-perfectionist wasn't satisfied with suspicion. There were other possibilities. Perhaps Miss Moxley had mixed up events from the past. Or simply misremembered the accident in the barn. That was certainly conceivable, considering the fall happened twenty-five years ago when she was just a young child and badly injured, to boot. Line, Dunston knew, would want irrefutable proof. Hence his visit to Mrs Smurkle.

Dunston thought about his own interview with Mrs Smurkle, and realised now he'd been far too casual. She never said that *both* sisters were actually *sitting* on the rafter when it tilted, only that they *liked* to sit on it. Nor did she mention *any* injury to Henrietta, only Estelle's mangled arm. Line's more rigorous questioning would, Dunston was sure, have established that Henrietta was not on the rafter. He would then have then asked about the scarring, and if he learned Henrietta's left foot was undamaged… Yes! *That* was all he needed to prove Henrietta was alive and Richard innocent. *That* was the 'vital information' alluded to in his letter from Carlisle.

Since Dunston didn't know what Mrs Smurkle actually told Line, he couldn't be certain that Henrietta was alive. Still, it looked that way, and if she was… Almost immediately, the familiar itch to jump ahead of the facts was prickling his skin. He tried to visualise what happened, but his mind remained blank, cells intact but empty of thought like unlit coals in a fireplace, neatly layered but generating neither heat nor light.

Nothing, not a thing, until his extra half sense, unbidden and unbiddable, suddenly burst into life. In a matter of seconds, his mind's eye saw the fiendish crime played out in a series of soul-chilling scenes from the dead body in Nightingale Lane all the way to Migston wiping Line's blood from his knife, and there, lurking in the background of each one, was Henrietta smiling her lopsided smile. *She* orchestrated Richard's conviction, payback presumably for his affair with Lucy. *And*, in her slouch-hatted, male disguise, paid Migston to kill Line because he was getting too close to the truth.

Dunston was convinced he was on the right track, but, he cautioned himself, the *only* solid fact he had was that the nail entered the foot from above. The rest of his reconstruction was speculation. And what did Line drum into him about speculation? No better than wild guessing, alright for amateurs, but not for the Metropolitan Police. Ah, Line and speculation. Well, I learned my lesson, rued Dunston, his latest disaster, the George Mivart-Estelle Moxley collaboration theory, fresh in his memory. Not again, he promised himself. He had to shore up his 'evidence'.

An hour later, an idea popped up. Yes, there was one sure way of confirming Henrietta was alive. But he needed help. Nick! Just the man. Brought up in an opium den, his formative years spent among whores, thieves and murderers, he would know what to do. 'Nick!'

'Easy as pie, sir,' Nick said after hearing his master's difficulty. 'Give me enough brass an' I'll give you the moon.' An exaggeration, perhaps, but he had a point. A few coins and London would yield almost anything the heart desired, and Dunston's immediate heart's desire was no exception.

Chapter Forty-Three: A Death Threat

'Turnkeys ain't turnkeys 'cos of the pay,' Nick explained early the next morning. 'Wages ain't enough to keep skin an' bones together. Nah, it's the under-the-table pay-offs that makes jailerin' jobs worth their weight in gold.'

As usual when it came to the seamier side of life, Nick was right. A few coins passed from one hand to another and, before he knew it, Dunston was inside the grim, grey, granite walls of Newgate Prison. The warder led him up the wooden stairs at one end of the main gallery to a second floor of cells which, like those below, ran around the four walls. They followed the walkway overlooking the interior courtyard until they reached Micus Loman's cell.

While the jailer was finding the key, Dunston peeked through the iron grille in the cell's door and found himself staring into a pair of suspicion-filled, black-as-coal eyes. Dunston jerked back as though scalded but not before seeing that the menacing, vulgar brute of his imagination looked more like a pasty-faced clerk who'd let his hair get a little unruly and forgotten to shave for a day or two. The eyes though, were not those of an honest man; dark and fox-sly, Dunston could feel them sizing him up, gauging his value for whatever purpose their owner currently had in mind, a purpose that soon revealed itself.

'Come to get me outta this shithole then, have you?' Loman asked as soon as the door was open. 'About bleedin' time. Fickett swore he'd get me out, but here I've been, stuck with the scum of the earth, for two soddin' days.'

'Alright, don't get yerself in a lather,' said the jailer, prodding Loman back until he was sitting on a small wooden bench against the far wall.

Hesitant steps carried a nervous Dunston inside. The brick-walled cell, perhaps six feet by ten, was sparsely furnished – tin basin for washing, slops pail, bedding rolled up in a corner, a tottery table beside the bench and a low shelf holding the inmate's plate and mug. The only light came from a window too high to see out of but welcome nonetheless to those unfortunate enough to spend any time at Her Majesty's pleasure.

'You're on the magistrate's docket for tomorrer,' continued the jailer. 'From what I heard, tho', Fickett's not in London, gone off somewhere, and won't be back in time to speak up for you.'

'Piece of shit! Swore he'd be here to sort out the beak,' Loman groused.

'No need to get yer bowels in an uproar,' the turnkey told him. 'This gentl'man's willing to speak on your behalf… provided you answer one question.'

'Don't see how this potbelly c'n be of any use to me,' grumbled the prisoner. 'You buggers can't be trusted, so piss off and leave me be.'

'Your pigeon, but who knows what the beak will decide. Could hand you ten years' hard labour and by the looks of you, that ain't yer cuppa tea.'

The jibe hit its mark. A sullen Loman looked at Dunston. 'Who's this, then?'

'Mr Dunston Burnett, Inspector Fickett's colleague,' lied the jailer, the words sliding off a tongue apparently greased as liberally as his palm, 'and his voice'll carry a lot of weight with the magistrate. Anyways, what've you got to lose? One question, that's all.'

'S'ppose it can't do no harm and may do some good, tho' I got me doubts,' said the surly jailbird. 'But, so as we're clear, I want the same deal I had with Fickett. First an' foremost, no murder charge. I never killed no one. And no jail time for keeping a few girls for the pleasure of the city's gents. Agreed?'

'Agreed. Like Fickett said, no murder charge, no jail time,' replied the jailer glibly.

'Alright, get on with it, then,' Loman said to Dunston.

'Thank you… er… Mr Loman,' began Dunston uneasily. Then more forcefully, 'My question is this: Was the woman killed in Nightingale Lane

Mrs Henrietta Darwin?'

'Nah.'

And there it was. A single syllable and Loman had confirmed the pivotal point in Dunston's reconstruction of the crime. A good start. The straight-line set of Dunston's lips, though, made clear he was far from finished. Now, he wanted to know everything.

'Did you kidnap her?'

'One question, that's what you said,' sneered Loman with a careless shrug of the shoulders.

'Please, Mr Loman,' pleaded Dunston. 'Did you kidnap her?'

Loman took his time. 'Kidnap? Don't know what you're talking about. Don't know nothin' 'bout any kidnapping.'

Ha! The kidnapping was staged... Henrietta had walked out of Down house wearing man-size shoes to create the tracks reported by Grace, exactly as Dunston had seen in one of his 'how-it-was-done' images. Estelle, using her back-up brass figures, must have procured the backdoor key for her, and later replaced it. 'So what was your job?'

No response. Oh dear, this was like pulling teeth, one painfully slow verbal extraction after another. Dunston glanced at the jailer, silently imploring him to intervene.

The jailer, reading Dunston's look, said, 'Cat got your tongue? Listen, matey, none of my business, but if I was in your shoes, I'd be fallin' all over myself to tell this bloke everything he wants to know. Up to you, but...'

Loman stared at Dunston, seeming to weigh his options – satisfy this nosey barrel of lard, or be left to rot in Newgate. Decision made, he grudgingly began his story. 'Rum business and no mistake. Gent wanted—'

'Gent? What gent?' cut in Dunston. 'What was his name?' He was sure his suspicion about Slouch Hat was going to be confirmed, only to be disappointed by Loman's next words.

'Never said and I never asked,' answered the inmate. 'Short bloke, he was, always wearing this tatty slouch hat, cheek an' chin smooth as a baby's bottom, and not much of a toper neither, drank his ale like it was carbolic.'

Hmm, not Line-grade proof, but could be Henrietta. One way to be sure.

214

'Notice anything about this person's lips?' Dunston asked casually.

'Lips? Nah. Well… hang on, now that you mention it, they wasn't straight, slanted up on one side.'

'Which side?'

'Which side? What odds does it make?'

'I must know,' Dunston pressed.

'Alright, alright. Let me see. Right side, they slanted up to the right.' *Yes, exactly what Dunston had seen in her portrait.* 'Satisfied?'

Dunston was indeed satisfied. Mr Slouch Hat and Mrs Henrietta Darwin were one and the same. *What an extraordinary woman!*

'Lips, slanted or straight, didn't bother me tho' as long as he had plenty of clink,' Loman continued. 'Now here's the funny bit.'

Loman eyed his visitor, not sure he, or anyone else, would believe what was to come. 'Feller wanted a woman killed, not a *partic'lar* woman, mind you, but *any* woman, long as she was shortish, skinny, dark hair and mid-thirties. Piece of cake to find a woman fitting the bill, 'cept the silly bugger wasn't finished. She had to have a birthmark on her leg. Couldn't find no one who matched up to everything he wanted, until Martha, she runs my… my household, said that Mary Travers, one of my girls, had—'

'Scars on her left foot.' Dunston finished his sentence for him.

'Aye, two of them, one top, one bottom. Girl ran off when a young'un, and her old man, rotten bastard, took hammer an' nail to her. Nailed her foot to a floorboard and left her there all day. Mary never ran away again,' he said wryly.

'Penny short of a shillin', Mary was, did whatever we told her, so she gladly showed the bloke her foot and he took a long look at the scars. We was worried scars wouldn't serve, but he gave her a tanner and soon as he was outside he broke into a smile and said she'd do nicely.'

So it's Mary Travers lying beneath the tombstone bearing Henrietta's name, and Henrietta is out and about, alive and well. Good, puts the flesh of detail on another of yesterday's images.

Loman, fully into the oddest episode in his thirty-year criminal career, was already moving on with the story. 'He left saying he'd be back, and sure enough he showed up late one night, last week of January. Handed us a weddin' ring which we was to put on Mary's finger, and a gold locket to put in the pocket of her skirt. That wasn't all. He didn't want the silly cow just dead, he wanted us to larrup the livin' daylights out of her... 'cept for her feet. *'Cept for her feet?* Couldn't make head nor tail of this but, like I said, bags of blunt, so why should I care?

'Next bit bothered me, tho'. Wanted us to dish out the beating down by the waterfront but, and this was what raised me eyebrows, someone had to see Migston doing the business.'

'Ah, the witness,' said Dunston. Someone had to report the murder, he thought. Couldn't risk the body rotting away or being rolled into the Thames, the usual practice. Anything like that, and Estelle Moxley wouldn't have been able to make her false identification.

'Aye, a bleeding witness,' grumbled Loman. 'I was lookout at the top of Nightingale Lane and Migston was at the river end with Mary, dead as a doorknob. Soon as I saw this old fussock coming along, I gave Migston the signal and he set to. When the stupid slummock saw what was going on, she screamed her head off. Migston stopped, took the ring from Mary's finger but left the locket in the skirt pocket like the bloke told us, tho' why, I've no idea.'

Dunston knew: the ring taken to make it look as though the killer was trying to cover up the corpse's identity; the locket left in the skirt pocket as though by oversight for the exact opposite reason. This enterprise was thought through very, *very* carefully.

'Anyways,' said Loman, 'soon as we heard the night constable's whistle we scarpered, and that was the end of it.'

'But it wasn't, was it?' Dunston said.

'Nah.' Loman gave a shake of his head. 'It was quiet for a while, but then, after the inquest, the broadsheets came out with the murdered woman's name – *Henrietta!* C'n you believe it? How anyone could recognise the lump of mangled flesh Migston left behind is beyond me, and then to say she's called Henrietta when she's really daft Mary baffled us all to pieces.

'And this Henrietta's bleeding father-in-law is Charles Darwin. *Charles bloody Darwin!* Scared the shit out of us. Peelers would be all over the killin' of someone in the family of a bigwig like him and that'd spell trouble for us.'

Loman stopped, licking his lips nervously, a tell-tale sign of how troubled he'd been by the newspaper reports. His next words, though, revealed the man's mettle, the steel behind the mild looks.

'We needed to know what was going on,' he said, 'so Migston used a little friendly coaxing, if yer take my meanin', to get the Yard's desk officer – scab called Groggins – to keep us posted 'bout the crushers' doings. Then we got some good news. He told us the coppers had nabbed *Richard Darwin*. Why these Darwin people kept popping up flummoxed me, had no rhyme or reason 'sfar as I could see, but didn't matter 'cos this Richard bloke wasn't blabbing about Migston or me so the heat was off.'

'But then,' said Dunston, 'Groggins showed up with the telegram and Line's claim he could clear Richard. Must've given you a nasty jolt.'

'Course it did,' Loman snapped. 'If this Darwin was off the hook, scufters would start looking elsewhere, and we could end up right in the line of fire. When Migston showed the telegram to Slouch Hat, he was of like mind. Said Line had to be sorted out before he got to the Yard with his findings. Knew Line well, we did. Straight as a die, he was. Bribe wouldn't be no good with him, so Migston had to finish him off, and quick. Telegram said he was coming down from Carlisle that night so there we was waiting for him when he stepped outta the station next mornin'. Migston slit his throat, ear to ear.'

Sickened by Loman's casual account of his friend's death, Dunston turned to leave.

'Wait!' pleaded the prisoner. Obviously fearing his chance of freedom was disappearing with the departing Dunston, Loman played his one remaining card. 'There's more. Killin' ain't over.'

'What?'

'Slouch Hat, he's got another target in his sights. Wait, and I'll tell you… but you gotta swear to get me off.'

'Alright, I swear.' Dunston didn't really believe Loman had anything more to bargain with, but better safe than sorry. 'What's he planning?'

'Said he had another job for us, this time in some village in Kent, forget the name.'

'Down?' asked Dunston, alarmed.

'Aye, that's it,' said Loman evidently sensing he'd found his get-out-of-jail ticket. 'When I told him I didn't fancy doing a job in some back-of-beyond village, he had a fit, never seen anything like it. Started ranting an' raving 'bout some old woman. He was getting wilder an' wilder, screechin' like a banshee, working himself up, until he screamed, *A life for a life.*'

'The woman, did he mention her name?'

'Aye, he said *Emma has to pay*—'

'Emma!' Dunston's cry was an octave higher than usual. 'He wants you to… to kill someone called Emma?'

'Well, that was the only name he mentioned,' replied Loman readily, looking confident he'd hooked his fish. 'Said he'd give us the partic'lars in The George an' Vulture.'

'When?' demanded Dunston, his pitch back under control, his tone challenging, brooking no resistance.

'Yesterday, 'cos he wanted the job done on Thursday, and that's today. Hey, wait!'

Too late. Dunston rushed out of the cell like a man possessed. Emma Darwin was in danger and *he* was the only one who could save her.

Chapter Forty-Four: Panic

Dunston rushed out of Newgate Prison in high panic with only one thought in mind – get to Scotland Yard and convince the police to take all necessary precautions to safeguard Mrs Emma Darwin. The two miles to police headquarters took an eternity, but once there he darted in, launched himself at Officer Ruggles and loosed off a Gatling-gun volley of verbal bullets: *Slouch Hat – KILL – Mrs Emma Darwin – TODAY – Must act – AT ONCE*. Wailing and flailing like discordant, out-of-control bagpipes, the overwrought investigator didn't calm down until the policeman had said half a dozen times: 'Nobody's going to hurt Mrs Darwin.'

With Dunston finally listening, Ruggles said, 'Like as not, Loman was just feeding you a story to weasel his way out of jail. And anyway, even if he's right, Fickett killed Migston, so he can't go after Mrs Darwin, can he?' Dunston relaxed. He was being silly. Migston was dead and Loman locked up tight in Newgate. Henrietta's two hired killers were safely out of the picture, unable to do any damage to Mrs Darwin.

But there was still the arch-villain, Henrietta herself. 'What about Hen— I mean, what about Slouch Hat?' He wasn't about to waste time explaining that Henrietta was Slouch Hat. 'He may be willing to bloody his own hands.'

'No need to worry, sir,' soothed the young policeman. 'Got a tip yesterday morning that a lady with a withered arm and accompanied by a short gentleman wearing a slouch hat was sighted at Euston Station boarding the nine o'clock to Liverpool. Inspector Fickett rushed off after them. He wasn't going to let them take ship to America and get clean away. The next liner bound for New York is *The Lady Hobart*, set to sail at noon today, and the inspector will be right there, waiting to nab the pair when they embark.'

'Are you sure?' Dunston pressed, unconvinced.

'I am, sir,' said an adamant Ruggles. 'The ship's captain informed the inspector that passage was booked yesterday for a *Mr and Mrs Smith*. Mr and Mrs Smith, indeed. Can you believe that? Name's a dead giveaway. What a pair of amateurs. Inspector reckons they left Miss Moxley's house on Tuesday, shortly before he got there, and then travelled up to Liverpool on Wednesday. It all tallies. It's them alright,' he asserted confidently.

Dunston was almost there… but not quite. Noon! The vessel was due to depart at noon. A glance at the wall clock – a few minutes past eleven o'clock. 'The ship, it sails within the hour. Has Fickett seized them already?'

'No, no, too soon,' cautioned Ruggles. 'The suspects will wait until the last minute to sneak on board. Then the inspector will want to interrogate them, so not likely we'll hear anything 'till tomorrow.'

Tomorrow! Dunston sagged at what sounded like an age before he'd know whether the fleeing couple were in custody and Mrs Darwin safe. But then he bucked up when the police officer added that the inspector knew a career-boosting arrest when he saw one and nothing would thwart him. 'He'll get them, you can put your eggs an' bacon on that,' he said. Yes, he was right. Fickett would get them and that was all that mattered, thought Dunston, satisfied at last.

Satisfied maybe, but he still had a nagging feeling he should do more. If Archibald Line were still alive what would he do? He'd go the extra mile, hasten to Down House to make sure Mrs Darwin was indeed safe and sound. Well, Dunston would be as thorough as Line; he'd make certain his *client*, as he now thought of Mrs Darwin, was not in harm's way.

Chapter Forty-Five: Dunston's Eyes Are Opened

An hour after leaving Scotland Yard, Dunston was sitting back in a generously upholstered seat in the train's only first-class carriage on his way to Bromley South Station and Down House. The hypnotic clickety-clack of iron wheels on iron rails calmed his frazzled nerves, and for the first time since rising that morning Dunston unwound, tired but quietly pleased he'd exposed the heart of the mystery. At least as far as he'd understood it at the start of the day. But now, according to Loman, Henrietta had also targeted Emma Darwin. Why?

Her motive for entrapping Richard seemed clear – she found out about his affair with Lucy and wanted her pound of flesh. But she had no reason to harm her mother-in-law. He shook his head. Leave it to the police. They'll sort it all out when they capture Henrietta and her sister in Liverpool.

No sooner had he settled down than he bolted upright as though his cushioned seat had suddenly turned into the sharpened point of a Judas Cradle. Cutthroats were two a penny in London! Henrietta could have lined up replacements for Migston and Loman *before* fleeing to Liverpool. The new assassins could already be at Down House... Mrs Darwin struck down at any moment... pummelled like Mary Travers... or her throat slit like Line's.

Dunston bit his lip, chewed his thumb. What could he do? Damn, damn, damn! Line would have followed proper police procedure and sent instructions to the local constabulary to guard Mrs Darwin around the clock before setting off for Down House. Well, Dunston hadn't thought of asking the police to do that, and even had he done so, they wouldn't have listened. And now, here he was trapped on a train.

Without realising it, he felt for the silver medallion in his pocket, running his fingers over the letters – *R* for wife Rose, *M* for daughter May – and then, turning the keepsake sideways, the date when they died... and Line's world ended. The touch of the metal brought Line back to him, almost as though he was there in the flesh. Dunston felt his presence, and then heard his voice, challenging, insistent: *YOU, Dunston... YOU are the ONLY one who can SAVE her!*

If he wasn't frantic before, he was now. He *had* to get to Down House before it was too late. Pulse racing, blood pumping, he urged the train on but it continued at its own chugging, nerve-shredding pace until... it stopped. Three miles from Bromley South Station, the train shuddered to a halt and there it sat, steam-puffing its readiness but not moving an inch for a full hour. Dunston was beside himself, jumping up, looking out the window, collapsing back into his seat, the sequence repeated every few minutes until the train, with a blast of its whistle, slowly rumbled forward.

The powerful steam engine trundled along at half speed, or so it seemed to a worried sick Dunston, before finally pulling into Bromley South Station mid-afternoon. He donned his greatcoat and deerstalker as fast as he could, launched himself out of the railway carriage as soon as the train stopped and dashed along the platform towards the stationmaster. 'Excuse me, EXCUSE ME,' he shouted at the top of his lungs but to no effect.

In peaked cap and gold braided jacket, the stationmaster ignored Dunston until he'd waved his flag and watched the train leave the station. 'Now, sir, what's all this palaver?' he asked.

'I need a cab! At once!'

'Well, this ain't London, you know. Need your walking boots to get anywhere around here. Where you heading?' he asked.

'Down House.'

'Down House, you say. Good six miles, that is, but you may be in luck. Miss Lucy's here collecting some parcels. More of them scientific books for

Mr Darwin, I shouldn't wonder, has 'em sent down special from London. There she is now. Miss Lucy!' he yelled. 'Can you give this gentleman a ride to Down House?'

'Of course,' Lucy replied. She had on a slate-grey, hooded travelling cloak, and was sitting in a chaise, reins in her left hand, about to leave. She kept her right hand in her lap. It was no longer bandaged, but the purplish, swollen stump of an index finger signalled it was still too painful to be of much practical use. 'Why, it's Mr Burnett, isn't it?'

'Yes, yes.' He hurriedly clambered up, flopped down beside her, and grabbed her arm. 'Miss Lucy,' he recognised the young woman from the funeral, 'thank goodness you're here. I *must* get to Down House... as *quickly* as possible.'

'Yes, of course,' Lucy said. She was clearly taken aback by the urgency in Mr Burnett's voice... and his uncivil manner. She freed her arm, flicked the whip and set the over-the-hill horse ambling off.

'Miss Lucy, can't you make him go faster?'

'Any faster and old Toby will keel over and give up the ghost.' She eyed the obviously agitated man. 'Don't worry, we'll be there soon.'

Dunston glared at the animal.

Hurry on, horse!

'Mrs Darwin, is she... is she alright?' Dunston asked anxiously.

'I... believe so,' she replied warily.

That brought an end to the odd exchange and the journey continued in silence: Lucy frowning, keeping well to her side of the bench-seat; Dunston, jaw clenched, body straining as though trying to propel the conveyance forward; Toby, oblivious to the tension, plodding his way home.

A mile or so later, Lucy sneaked a quick glance at her grim-faced passenger and finally asked, 'Mr Burnett, whatever is the matter?'

'N-nothing, nothing at all,' he said brusquely. No point alarming her with what he feared he'd find at Down House. 'I'm just... eager to see Mrs Darwin, that's all.'

GET ON, you useless nag!

'Well, I'm sure she'll be pleased to see you,' she said, sounding more at ease. 'She was setting off on her weekly turn around the Sandwalk as I was leaving, but she should be back long before we get there.' Chatting, she'd clearly decided, was the best strategy for keeping her odd passenger's mind off whatever was troubling him.

'Um... the Sandwalk?' Dunston was barely listening, his thoughts leaping ahead to what might await them at Down House.

'It's a footpath, runs from the gate at the bottom of the garden,' she explained. 'Mr Darwin often strolls there when he's well, calls it his thinking path. He's not with Mrs Darwin today, he's poorly, but she has other company... *very special* company.'

Oh, no! Henrietta's assassins! Already there! I'm too late!

'Yes, her grandson, my Joey.' She smiled softly.

'Joey, you say. That's wonderful.' Thank goodness. I'm still in time.

'The Darwins desperately wanted a grandchild but it seemed as though destiny was against them. They were thrilled when Henrietta gave them a grandson, but sadly that didn't last long, only eighteen months. When the little boy died, something in them died as well, and the household was never the same after that.'

'Oh, dear. How distressing...' Dunston managed to say.

'Indeed it was. I remember every minute of that day like it was yesterday.'

She chanced another quick glance at Dunston. She could see the stress in his face, but her keep-talking strategy seemed to be working.

'Henrietta's little one,' she resumed, 'was crying and coughing, perhaps a bit more than usual, but nothing too serious. Mr Richard prepared a tonic for him and then went off to check on a patient. Henrietta had been up the previous three nights with the infant and was in desperate need of rest, so Mrs Darwin told her to go and lie down, promising to call her if the little lad took a turn for the worse. Barely an hour had gone by when the child passed away in his grandmother's arms. She was really shaken, sobbing her heart out and blaming herself.'

'An appalling loss,' Dunston heard himself saying.

'It wasn't her fault, of course,' Lucy continued, 'but Henrietta didn't see it that way. She came rushing down the stairs, grabbed the child from Mrs

Darwin and clutched him to her breast even though she knew he was gone. She was silent, unmoving for a minute, then she slowly raised her head and gave her mother-in-law a look so full of hatred I'm surprised Mrs Darwin wasn't struck dead on the spot. From that moment on, Henrietta loathed her, I'm sure of it, always polite to her but so cold and withdrawn, almost as though she was biding her time, waiting for something terrible to hurt Mrs Darwin just as she'd been hurt.'

Head thrust forward, eyes fixed on the road ahead, Dunston had barely heard half of what Lucy was saying but it was enough. *Revenge!* For letting her son die without calling her. *That's* why Henrietta wants Mrs Darwin dead. She wasn't *waiting* for something terrible to hurt her child's 'killer', she was *planning* every devilish detail of it. Same with Richard. She didn't target him for his affair with Lucy, but because he rushed off to assist some sick villager when his own child needed his care. Henrietta marked both of them for death; a double dose of revenge. That innocent child's passing unleashed a chain of events leading straight to Richard's execution and… and now to…

COME ON, you bag of bones, GIDDY UP!

'You know, the only good thing to come out of this sorry mess,' she said, 'is that Mr and Mrs Darwin have their grandchild – my Joey. Mrs Darwin is besotted with him. She takes him around the Sandwalk every Thursday afternoon, just as she used to with Henrietta's child. As I was leaving for the station, I saw her put a tiny woollen hat on him, wrap him in this beautiful, pale lavender blanket she'd crocheted herself, settle him in the baby carriage, and off they went along the footpath.'

The footpath! What if the killers were already on the footpath? Lying in wait for her!

Mrs Darwin... TURN AROUND... GO BACK!

Chewing his knuckle to the bone, Dunston struggled to contain the confusion of impatience, frustration and fear churning inside him through another ten minutes of one-sided chitchat before they finally passed through the gates of Down House and came to a stop at the entrance. He leaped out of the chaise, rushed to the door and hammered on it with both fists until it was opened by Parslow, the stand-in butler.

Dunston grabbed him by the lapels of his jacket. 'Mrs Darwin! Where is she?'

'Sir, really, sir...' An astonished Parslow politely eased Dunston's hands from his uniform. 'Madam is still enjoying her afternoon stroll on the Sandwalk. She hasn't come back yet—'

'What! We must find her! She's in terrible danger! Take me there... NOW!'

The three – Parslow confused, Lucy startled, Dunston driven – dashed through the hallway, out the backdoor, and across the lawn. Parslow, in the lead, suddenly stopped. 'There's a body. By the gate. It's... it's madam...'

Chapter Forty-Six: On the Sandwalk

Panicked by Parslow's words, Lucy raced to the garden gate. She arrived ahead of the two men, saw Mrs Darwin on the ground and knew at once she was dead – heart attack or stroke, but whatever it was, she was dead. She sank down on her knees beside the prone figure, only to jump back up screaming 'Joey! Where's Joey?' all concern for her benefactress thrust aside the instant she realised her baby was not with his grandmother.

Lucy pictured what had happened – Mrs Darwin taken ill; knows she must get help; leaves Joey in his baby carriage; hurries back to Down House; dies as she reaches the gate. It was the third image that gripped her – Joey, *her* Joey, left out there on the Sandwalk, alone in the falling darkness, crying for his mother. Her cloak flapping behind her, Lucy took off, disappearing down the Sandwalk before Parslow, the second to arrive, could stop her.

Dunston, third on the scene, hovered a good three yards from the body like a punch-drunk boxer unwilling to set foot in the ring. Parslow, who'd seen his fair share of corpses in his soldiering days, stepped forward and placed his fingers on Mrs Darwin's neck.

'No pulse, sir,' he said. 'Can't find a beat. She's gone.'

Dunston staggered back, his legs wobbly as a new-born foal's. Mrs Darwin dead. It was all his fault. If only he'd somehow made Officer Ruggles place a guard on Mrs Darwin. If only—

'Sir, you alright?'

Dunston steadied himself, summoned all of his two ounces of courage, and finally looked at Mrs Darwin's body. Nothing he could do for her now. But Lucy… and Joey… he'd have to go after them. 'Parslow,' he said surprisingly firmly, 'get help to move Mrs Darwin's body to the house. Quick as you can.' And without another glance at either corpse or butler, Dunston scurried off after Lucy.

The Sandwalk ran for a quarter of a mile between Great House Meadow and Great Pucklands Meadow before looping around a long narrow coppice of alder, birch and hornbeam. The halfway point was marked by a sturdy, wooden bench nicely positioned in an open space at the edge of now leafless shade trees. From there, the nature lover could enjoy the splendid view across the greenery all the way to the butterscotch walls of Down House.

Ten minutes of unaccustomed trotting and Dunston was winded. He stopped, hands on knees, heart thumping, lungs screaming in agony. When he straightened, Lucy was out of sight, and night was falling fast, the wintry sun dipping below the horizon and surrendering the heavens to darkness. He set off again, stopping and starting until he spied the coppice at the Sandwalk's turnaround point, and there on the ground, slumped against the garden seat, was Lucy.

He feared she was unconscious, but at his approach, she stirred and, without a word, feebly pointed to her left. Squinting into the deepening gloom in the direction of Lucy's outstretched arm, Dunston finally picked out something dangling from a bare branch in one of the bordering trees.

What was it? It looked like a bundle of rags tightly wrapped in a light-coloured fabric. He edged a few steps closer, peering through the twilight. Now, he could see that the mysterious package's outer layer was actually a rather fine, pale lavender coverlet, or shawl, hand-crocheted by the look of it.

Oh, NO! It couldn't be, could it? He spun around and quickly searched the baby carriage standing near the tree. Empty. He scanned the bench. Nothing. Then the surrounding ground. Bare. Unnerved, he turned back to the branch's disturbing burden. Held in place by a thin cord, it swung gently to and fro until the north wind, as if holding its breath for this particular moment, released a mournful sigh and the bundle turned half-circle.

Dunston recoiled in horror. Above the clearly visible bite of the cord, he saw what looked for all the world like the garishly painted face of a child's rag-doll below a new-born's woollen crib-cap. But that was *not* what it was, far from it.

Strangulation must have been slow and painful, gravity and the weight of the tiny body hardly enough to bring a swift end to the baby's life unless another's heft supplied the necessary downward pressure. Dunston didn't want to know how it was done; nor see the end result, but there it was, right in front of him – Joey, hanged by the neck just like his father.

Chapter Forty-Seven: Recovering the Dead

Parslow left Mrs Darwin where she lay and hurried to the house in search of help. Fortunately, the first person he encountered was Grace, Mrs Darwin's maid. As soon as he'd told her what had happened, she turned and without a word, hastened back to the garden gate, Parslow close behind.

Grace approached the still shape on the ground, steeled herself and then kneeled beside the corpse of her mistress. That was when she smelled it, a sweet odour, the same as she'd noticed in Henrietta's bedroom the morning after her disappearance. Chloroform! Mrs Darwin's been drugged. She might still be alive!

Grace felt her mistress's right wrist. No pulse. She tried the left. Same. Then, like Parslow, she tried her neck. Still nothing. She pressed more firmly, and, *yes*, this time she found the faintest of flickers, no more than the flutter of butterfly wings, but a beat nonetheless. 'Madam's alive,' she cried. 'Quick. We must get her to the house before she catches her death of cold.'

It was a struggle, but between them, they carried Mrs Darwin into the drawing room and laid her on the chaise longue. Grace removed Mrs Darwin's bonnet and undid the top two buttons of her coat. 'Mr Parslow, stay here with her,' instructed Grace, already on her way to the kitchen. She was soon back with two glasses, one of water, the other smelling strongly of brandy. Gently lifting Mrs Darwin's head, she dribbled a few droplets of water on to flaccid lips. Most of the liquid ran down her mistress's chin but the little that gained entry was enough to make her cough, and open her eyes.

'Help me to sit her up,' Grace urged.

Together, they carefully raised Mrs Darwin into a sitting position and Grace moved on from water to brandy. Same as before, most of the liquor missing its mark but some hitting home because Mrs Darwin coughed more earnestly this time, and put her hand to her mouth, her first movement. Once the spluttering fit had run its course, she looked around, bewildered, recognising neither her surroundings nor her attendants but clearly anxious to speak.

'J…Joey…Joey…' was all she managed before her eyes glazed over, her head flopped back and the weight of her upper body slumped against Parslow's arm.

Dunston stared at the obscenity defiling the tree for a long moment before crumpling to his knees, head in hands, shoulders heaving, openly bemoaning what he took to be the day's second death – first, the grandmother, then the grandson. Henrietta's assassins had more than earned their pay.

When at last he struggled back to his feet, darkness had fallen. He pushed his sorrow aside. The priority now – Dunston swallowed hard – was to free Joey's body from that damnable noose. A dozen forced steps and he was there, beside the dangling corpse, already wrapped, so it seemed, in its burial shroud.

He eyed the knot at the branch-end of the cord. Too high for five foot two Dunston to reach without climbing the tree, a feat well beyond someone as corpulent as he. It would have to be the eye-level one at the noose-end. Trying not to touch the still warm skin, he probed the tightly tied knot, feeling to his dismay, how it cut into Joey's baby-soft neck-flesh. To have any chance of loosening it, he'd have to slacken the tension. He lifted the bundle of death two or three inches with his left hand, and then, on tip toe, scrabbled at the knot with his right.

He tugged; he clawed. A nail ripped; then another. The knot held firm. Calf muscles straining, back arching painfully, Dunston stuck to his task as long as he could, but in the end he had to give up and let himself sink back to the ground.

He was not by any means ready to accept defeat but he was depressingly aware that his middle-aged body was not cut out for such an exhausting, above-the-head challenge. Nor his stumpy, pudgy fingers for unravelling a real-life Gordian knot. The task called for a younger person, someone with strong, slender fingers… and work-toughened nails. Lucy!

He hurried back to her. She was still lying against the bench, barely conscious, murmuring, 'Joey… Joey… Joey.' One glance and he knew she was in no state to help. Showing more resolve and purpose with each hurdle encountered, Dunston quickly made his decision. Joey would have to wait. He took Lucy's hands in his and pulled her upright. He draped her left arm around his shoulders, grasped her about the waist with his right, and stumbled off, trusting in his willpower to get them to Down House.

Chapter Forty-Eight: The Perfect Revenge

Grace was gently tucking a quilt around Mrs Darwin's legs when the drawing room door flew open and Dunston staggered in, half dragging a sobbing Lucy. Grace assisted her to a chair and turned to Dunston. The next few minutes were a babel of explanations – first Dunston's, interspersed with exclamations of horror and disbelief from Grace and Parslow; then Grace's, greeted with prayers of thanks from Dunston for Mrs Darwin's recovery.

'Should we go back for Joey's body?' Dunston asked.

'That will have to wait,' Grace said firmly. 'Our first job is to help the living. Mrs Darwin needs a doctor and so does Lucy. The closest is in Bromley. Mr Parslow, can you take the trap and fetch him here? And the police?' The butler nodded and set off.

Grace turned to Dunston. He looked every bit a man who'd be hopelessly lost dealing with females, especially semi-conscious, elderly ones. But as Grace's dad used to say, *A good workman makes do with the tools at hand*, and the only tool at hand was Mr Dunston Burnett.

'Mr Burnett, listen to me,' she began, her tone reassuring. 'I'm going to put Lucy to bed. You must stay here with madam.'

Seeing Dunston's uneasy look, she added, more confidently than perhaps she felt, 'No need to be alarmed. The drug – chloroform, if I'm not mistaken – will wear off soon and you must be here when she comes to. When she does, keep her calm, make sure she stays warm and give her water to sip.

That's all you have to do. I'll settle Lucy. Be back soon as I can. You'll be alright, won't you?'

Grace didn't wait for an answer. She helped Lucy to stand, and together they headed for the stairs, leaving Dunston to his watchman's duty. For the first five minutes, he stared at his unmoving charge, unsure whether he wanted her to remain unconscious until Grace returned, or wake up and show signs of recovery. In the end, he busied himself placing a pillow under her head, straightening the quilt, and making sure the glass of water was full to the brim. He eyed the brandy, sorely tempted to take a nip, definitely feeling the need for a little Dutch courage, but a clear head was called for and he wisely left it untouched.

It was as well the liquor stayed in the glass because Mrs Darwin was coming around for the second time. Her head shifted slightly on the pillow, a hand rose to her face, one eye opened then the other. Her eyes, still not fully focused, finally came to rest on him. 'Wh-what happened?' she asked.

'It's alright, Mrs Darwin. You're here in Down—'

'Joey!' she screamed, bolting upright, panicked eyes searching everywhere, hands fluttering like the wings of a dying moth. 'Where is he? Oh, God! No, NO, it can't be.' She sank back on the couch, exhausted by her outburst.

'P-please calm yourself, Mrs Darwin,' Dunston said, almost as agitated as she. 'You've been drugged,' he explained. 'Parslow is fetching the doctor.'

'No… no. It's… it's too late,' she moaned, straining to sit up, her head turning from side to side in torment. 'Can't… can't remember everything… but it's… it's too late.' She sagged back on to the chaise longue, struggling, Dunston guessed, to make sense of what had happened on the Sandwalk. And, evidently, what he'd told her, because she rallied slightly and murmured, 'Drugged?'

Then, more forcefully, 'Is that what you said?'

She grabbed his arm, bony fingers digging into his flesh, tight as a falcon's talons about its prey, pulling herself up. Where did that strength come from? he wondered.

'Well, yes, we believe so,' he answered, freeing himself from her grip.

'Then… then maybe what I saw was just some… some insane hallucination, a Devil-sent cruelty,' she said more to herself than to Dunston.

'Mrs Darwin, tell me what you remember, perhaps I can help,' he said softly. 'Think back. You were walking along the Sandwalk with Joey in the baby carriage. Then what happened?'

'It's all... all mixed up,' she said, frowning, 'but I remember a rag... or scarf over my mouth and an odd smell, sweet but somehow unpleasant.'

Yes, chloroform, Dunston thought.

'I... I must've passed out,' she continued, her brow still furrowed, 'because the next thing I recall is waking up... tied to the bench... the one on the Sandwalk. I looked around and saw a man wearing a slouch hat... standing by the trees, and... and a woman, familiar-looking, but her face was hidden by a heavy veil so I wasn't sure if I knew her.'

Good God! *Henrietta and Estelle!* Nowhere near Liverpool! They were right there, on the Sandwalk, waiting for Mrs Darwin. Fickett's been sent on a wild goose chase, the real goose and gander one step ahead of him all the time. Still struggling to come to grips with how thoroughly he and Fickett had been hoodwinked, he realised Mrs Darwin was continuing with her grim report.

'...had Joey in his hands. He lifted him up for me to see, like a savage showing off an enemy's severed head. When I tried to look away, the woman stepped behind me, clamped my head in the crook of her left arm and twisted it sideways, forcing me to face the... the horror. I closed my eyes, but Joey's crying was so unbearable I had to look... and I saw this... this *devil* shove my darling boy under his arm like a ragbag of dirty laundry and slip a looped rope over his head. I had no idea what was happening until... until I saw him throw the other end of the cord over a branch. Then I knew.'

The telling was taking a heavy toll on Mrs Darwin. She fell silent, her head drooping to her chest. Watchman Dunston should surely do something, but he had no idea what. Was she suffering an after-effect of the drug? Had she fainted from sheer exhaustion? Or had her mind shut down, desperate to block out whatever she thinks she saw? 'Mrs Darwin, are you alright?' was the best he could manage.

'Yes,' she said, raising her head, steadying herself before continuing her tale.

'I'm not sure what happened after that. There's a gap… maybe I blacked out, I don't know. All I remember is seeing Joey…' she began to wail, '…h-hanging from a tree…' She broke off, overcome with grief.

'I can see it now,' she resumed, once she'd recovered enough to speak. 'So clearly, as though it's been branded into my brain… the blanket I'd crocheted for him wrapped tight around him… the cord biting into his neck … the terror in his eyes… that little woollen hat still on his head…'

She broke off, trembling, wringing her hands as though trying to squeeze out the courage to move on with her ghastly tale. 'By… by then,' she finally said, 'his cries were desperate… and they went on and on. In the end, I was *begging* for his misery to be over. But he kept crying and crying. The man was watching me, smiling. When he thought I'd suffered enough, he walked up behind Joey, grabbed him and… and yanked down… not letting go until… until the crying stopped.'

Dunston felt as if he'd been struck by lightning, stunned not by Joey's brutal death – he'd already seen the evidence of that savagery – but by the sudden conviction that this… this *abomination* was *always* the plan. Make Mrs Darwin watch this grandson die, just as she'd watched while her first, Henrietta's little one, breathed his last. Mrs Darwin's punishment was not her own death, no, her punishment was to spend the rest of her days with the hideous vision of her one remaining grandchild swinging from a tree.

She was going to be spared, but only so her every waking minute would be lived in the cold loneliness of life without the joy of grandchildren, the one thing she desired most, forever weighed down by the harrowing loss of the only grandsons – first Henrietta's, now Lucy's – that God had seen fit to grant her. A Devilish plan, but for Henrietta… the *perfect* revenge.

'I can't believe it. It… it must've been a vision, some sort of mind's-eye trickery brought on by the drugs.' She looked imploringly at Dunston but he remained silent.

'Yes, that's it,' she rushed on, 'some sort of horrific nightmare, all in my silly head, because what I remember next *couldn't* have happened. The man, as though satisfied with his murderous work, turned to me, took off his hat and made a theatrical bow, stooping low to the ground. And when he looked up, he stared straight at me, but instead of a man, it was… *Henrietta!* He'd turned into Henrietta! I swear to God, what I saw was Henrietta. But she's dead and buried so… so none of it really happened, did it?'

What could he say? No, Mrs Darwin, none of it was real, it was all in your mind. And then what would happen when Joey's body was brought back from the Sandwalk?

When Dunston didn't answer, Mrs Darwin resumed her story, her voice barely audible. 'I think they drugged me again, because I felt the rag and smelled that sweet smell. When I came to, I was alone but so confused I barely knew what I was doing. I was no longer bound to the bench so I got up and stumbled off towards Down House. I… I didn't look back, *I couldn't,* to see if there really was… something… *something awful…* strung up in the tree. I just *couldn't.* If I didn't look, if I didn't see it, then perhaps… perhaps there was nothing awful to be seen.'

Mrs Darwin was spent. Dunston was sure that in her heart of hearts she knew her grandson was dead but a little part of her clung to the hope that it was all some dark and hateful trick of her drugged imagination. She looked once more at Dunston, a desperate appeal in her expression, before slumping back on the couch and closing her eyes, shutting out, at least for now, that *awful something.*

Chapter Forty-Nine: Sailing Away

'**B**uongiorno, signore. You like-a 'ot choc-a-letta?' inquired the steward. He'd been giving the two ladies a steady dose of his well-honed continental charm and exaggerated Italian accent ever since they'd boarded the *SS Santa Teresa* at Southampton. They looked like spinster sisters, ready to enjoy a harmless, sea-cruise flirtation and, if past experience was any guide, willing to tip well for some male attention. Each lady responded with a smile and a horribly mispronounced *Grazie mille*. With a flamboyant, nautical salute, the attendant, a grin on his lips and lira in his sights, disappeared towards the galley.

The women, wrapped in blankets, were reclining on deckchairs positioned on the ship's starboard side to catch the early-March warmth of the Mediterranean's morning sun. After leaving Southampton, their ship, bound for its home port of Genoa, had steamed south and then passed through the Strait of Gibraltar.

'He's an accommodating fellow,' remarked Estelle, 'though a bit of a simpleton. If he thinks a fancy uniform and a little flattery will earn him a fat gratuity, he's got another think coming.'

'Estelle, my dear, if life has taught me one thing it's that all men are fools,' her older sister said. 'Even the smart ones can be led by the nose because they're all so vain and ambitious. Take Inspector Fickett. Sharp fellow up to a point, but he swallowed that rubbish about *Aesculapius* as though it were the gospel truth. And why? Because he thought he was the *only* one clever enough to see the hidden clue, the only one to connect the dots from *Aesculapius* to the medical profession and then to Dr Richard Darwin.

Really!'

'What about the anonymous tip you had delivered to Scotland Yard?' asked Estelle. 'D'you suppose he fell for that as well and charged off to Liverpool?'

'Well, obviously I don't know for sure,' replied Henrietta, 'but he wasn't anywhere near Down House where he should have been, so my guess is he boarded *The Lady Hobart* and waited there like a good little boy for Mr and Mrs Smith to embark.'

Estelle laughed.

'The sad part, though,' Henrietta said, turning serious, 'is that men like Fickett run the entire country and indeed the whole empire, almost half the world. Government, military, police, clergy, lawyers, doctors... all men.'

'True, but that worked to our advantage,' Estelle pointed out.

'How d'you mean, sister?'

'Well, thanks to the *men* of Scotland Yard, the *all-male* jury, and that *old boy* in his ridiculous little black cap, Richard was arrested, convicted and condemned to death by his *fellows*. You pulled their strings and like puppets, they danced to your tune. As you say, all men are fools, yet your father-in-law, the illustrious Charles Darwin no less, had the nerve to claim in *The Descent of Man* – such a blatantly chauvinist title, by the way – that man's intelligence attains to a *higher eminence* than woman's. Can you believe that?'

'Bah, he may know something about *apes* but he knows nothing about *women*. Let him think we are inferior if he wants, but as Richard learned to his cost, we can be *fatally* inferior when it suits us,' replied Henrietta. Her quip was delivered in a light tone but her face was dark, the upward twist of her upper lip, usually so endearing, oddly sinister on this occasion.

'*Sono tonato...* I'm back,' cried the steward, arriving with a tray held head-high on one upturned hand. After setting down the two promised cups of hot chocolate and a plate of biscuits on a small table between their deckchairs, he gestured towards the delicate pastries and, with a broad wink, announced, '*Bellissime biscotti...* for... *bellissime signore!*'

Henrietta looked at Estelle. How many times has he used that line on how many lady passengers, the look said.

'Thank you, Fabio, you're too kind.' She waited for the man to leave before resuming. 'Anyway, I don't care what Charles thinks. All that matters is that Richard got what he deserved. And so did Emma.'

'Indeed, sister, but you took such a risk showing your face to Emma on the Sandwalk,' said Estelle, sounding like her childhood self, always the more cautious.

'Bah! And double bah!' Henrietta retorted, echoing the expression used so many times by yesteryear's Henrietta. 'It was worth it. Even though she was half drugged, she knew it was me. I saw the shock in her eyes when she realised who I was...' She paused for a moment, savouring again that final moment of the hated Emma's total destruction.

'But that's the point,' persisted the younger sister. 'She'll tell the police, and you'll be a *murder suspect.*'

'I doubt it. Anything Emma says will be dismissed as the ravings of a deranged old woman, traumatized by the loss of her grandson only ten days after the loss of her son. Who's going to believe her? Fickett? Not likely. That I'm alive is the last thing he wants to hear. He'll quash any suggestion that he's been made a fool of by a mere woman as surely as he'd crush a cockroach with a swift stamp of his boot. In his official report, he'll claim, and maybe even believe, that you and Slouch Hat escaped to America and that will be the end of it.'

'Yes, I suppose you're right. But still...'

Henrietta regarded her sister fondly. She loved her dearly, but Estelle was such a worrier and so dependent on her, always had been, always would be. Henrietta had no doubt she'd spend the rest of her days constantly reassuring her younger sister that they were completely in the clear, free as the birds in the sky. She didn't mind. Estelle was worth it. After all, she'd played a vital part in Henrietta's quest for vengeance. Estelle was the *only* person she trusted enough to involve in her revenge, and she'd carried out each of her assignments to perfection. Henrietta vowed to herself she would *always* be there for her sister, as her sister had been there for her.

'Estelle, stop worrying. Nobody will ever find out what we did. We covered our tracks too well. Migston's dead and Loman never penetrated my disguise so neither of them can connect us to the deaths of Line or that half-wit, Mary Travers. And as for Richard, he was arrested, tried and sentenced to hang, all legal and above board. Nobody even suspects we had anything to do with it. Nor can we be linked to Joey's death; no one saw you on the Sandwalk; and I'm dead and buried, and the deceased can't be accused of anything except taking up space in the cemetery. Stop worrying, and drink your chocolate before it gets cold.'

Henrietta followed her own advice and sipped the still-hot liquid, very satisfied with the cruise and with life in general. Death, she mused, smiling contentedly, can be very liberating. I feel free as a bird, ready to move on to other, more agreeable matters. First on the agenda, a charming, rich Italian husband for Estelle. And then, well, perhaps one for me.

Chapter Fifty: Next Steps

A week after the events on the Sandwalk, Dunston returned to Down house. He knew from Grace that Mrs Darwin was still recovering and under doctor's orders to rest, but Mr Darwin was well enough to receive him, and it was he Dunston wanted to see.

Late on the day Joey died, Parslow had returned from Bromley with the doctor and a pair of constables. The policemen cut down the body in the dark, but beyond that, there was not much they could do. There was no physical evidence at the scene of the crime, and the doctor would not allow Mrs Darwin, still delirious, to be questioned. Dunston, the only other possible source of information, had decided to keep to himself what Mrs Darwin had told him about seeing Henrietta, thinking this might be best for her sanity, at least for the time being. What ultimately he did or did not reveal was a decision for the Darwins to make. Hence his visit to Down House.

The butler showed Dunston into the study. 'Mr Burnett, sir.'

'Thank you, Parslow. Some tea for my guest would be in order, I think.'

'Of course, sir.'

Charles Darwin, in his dressing gown, was seated in his specially elongated writing chair. He rose and greeted Dunston as warmly as could be expected for a man grieving the loss of his son and grandchild. The strain on his face was clearly visible, his beard more unkempt than Dunston remembered from their encounter in London, the furrows in his brow deeper, his eyes sunk even further beneath his heavy forehead. Not surprising, thought Dunston. The poor man has had to deal with his own sorrow as well as console a distraught wife and a twice-bereaved Miss Lucy.

'Welcome to Down House, Mr Burnett.' He gestured towards the ladderback chair beside the specimen-strewn drum table, waited until Dunston had settled himself and then retook his own seat. 'Sadly, not the best of circumstances but I'm glad you are here. It gives me the opportunity to thank you for all you did for Mrs Darwin and Miss Lucy.'

'Only wish I could have done more, sir,' Dunston replied. 'My deepest sympathies on the loss of your grandchild. I cannot imagine how painful this must be for you and Mrs Darwin and of course Miss Lucy.'

'Thank you, Mr Burnett. We are all coping to a degree, each in their own way. For me, prior bereavements – three children and my first grandchild – have helped me cope with the horrors of the last few weeks. Nothing makes the heart immune, but losses can give you resilience, the strength to carry on. Life goes on, and I feel an obligation, a duty if you like, to soldier on for the sake of my other children and Mrs Darwin. She, I fear, is finding it more difficult, hasn't left her room once, not even for Joey's funeral.'

'And Miss Lucy?'

'A remarkable young woman. Marvellous spirit. Thankfully, she has the restorative power of youth on her side, and will, I believe, make a full recovery in time. I've suggested one way forward for her, and she has responded positively although she may simply be putting on a brave face for my and Mrs Darwin's sake. Ah, here she is now.'

'I've brought the tea,' she said, perhaps too brightly.

'Thank you, my dear.'

She laid the tray on the table and served both men. 'Popping in gives me a chance to express my thanks to Mr Burnett.' She smiled at him, but when the smile faded, Dunston saw a tell-tale flicker of sadness in her eyes. 'I am so grateful, sir, for all you did when you found me on the Sandwalk. I must have been a terrible burden to you, but you still managed to get me back to Down House.'

'It was a difficult day for all of us,' Dunston replied.

'My dear, have you thought more about my little proposition?' Darwin asked.

Lucy smiled again, her defences apparently back in place. 'I have. I can never bring Joey back but I can keep his memory alive and at the same time bring some joy to the world. Your proposal gives me a wonderful opportunity to do both. I saw how those near-dead mites in Mrs Sayter's Pig Pen suffered, and I want to do all I can to make sure other lost little ones do not suffer the same fate. So, yes, I am interested and have already thought of a name. If you agree, perhaps we could call it *The Joseph Darwin Home for Abandoned Children.*' As she said this, her mask slipped again and a tear trembled in the corner of her eye.

'A wonderful suggestion, my dear' said Darwin quickly. And then in a kindly tone, 'Perhaps, I could ask you to attend Mrs Darwin for a while? Please tell her I'll be along shortly. I need to speak to Mr Burnett.'

Lucy nodded and took her leave.

'Not there yet, but she's on her way,' Darwin said. 'Lucy is a fine young woman and will, I'm sure, attract the interest of many young gentlemen. Eventually the right one will come along and she will marry and have children of her own. They will not be Darwins by blood, but my wife and I will love them like they were our own.'

Darwin smiled sadly, lowered his head and sat in silence, evidently requiring a moment to recover himself. When he looked up, he ran his hand over his unkempt beard, deciding, or so it seemed to Dunston, what he wanted to say next. Then, he eyed his visitor, cleared his throat and said:

'Mr Burnett, I'm dealing with a very worrying situation and I thought perhaps you might be able to shed some light on it since you were there. It's Mrs Darwin. She's tormented day and night by what she claims she saw on the afternoon Joey died. It's the oddest thing, Mr Burnett, but she insists she saw Henrietta on the Sandwalk.'

Dunston was instantly on full alert, head up like a hound sniffing the wind for the first hint of a fox.

'Finding a way to help Lucy was easy,' Darwin continued. 'The idea of the orphanage came to me without any effort on my part. It was obvious. I'm stumped though when it comes to helping my own wife. I cannot find a way of consoling her. She knows we buried Henrietta and Richard two weeks ago, yet she still swears Henrietta was on the Sandwalk. My wife was drugged, as you know, so what she saw may have been an illusion, but she is so adamant that, well, frankly, she has finally convinced me. How can that be? I ask myself. There is only one answer. Someone else was buried next to Richard in St Mary's cemetery. *Henrietta is alive.'*

Dunston could not believe his ears. The great scientist had reached the same conclusion as Dunston, but in a much shorter time and without any of the information at Dunston's disposal. Dunston's mouth must have gaped wider than a pelican's open beak judging by Darwin's next words:

'I can see, Mr Burnett, you find my comment incredible, foolish even, and you are right. It is nothing but a wild conjecture on my part. What I need are *facts.'*

Ah, yes, the two sides of England's foremost biologist. First, a truly Darwinian leap, like his theory of survival of the fittest, so prized by Dunston, and then that unquenchable thirst for facts, that won Line's admiration.

'Mr Darwin, I do not think you foolish for even a second. In fact, I too believe Henrietta is alive. Not only believe, sir. I've heard compelling testimony that the body identified as Henrietta's by her sister, was actually that of a woman called Mary Travers.'

'Mary Travers? Who is Mary Travers?' Darwin raised his eyebrows questioningly, clearly not sure what to make of this wild-sounding claim.

'To answer your question it's probably best if I go through my findings from start to finish,' Dunston said carefully. 'In fact, that is why I came to see you today, to share with you what I have learned and decide what, if anything, should be done.'

It took Dunston half an hour to cover everything from his conversation with Mrs Smurkle, through his exchange with Inspector Fickett and his consultation with Dr Cullingworth, to his revealing interview of Loman in Newgate Prison. Darwin listened to Dunston's findings in stunned silence, uneasily stroking his straggly white beard after each of Dunston's shocking revelations, clearly staggered by every ugly detail of Henrietta's foul deceit.

At length, he swallowed, firmed his expression and said: 'Mr Burnett, your account of this... this vendetta is the most devastating, the most horrifying narrative I have ever heard. Henrietta has deceived us all... behaved most abominably. How could she be so revengeful, so evil, and so... so fiendishly cunning? And to think I was willing to sacrifice my entire life's work to secure her release from her kidnappers, only to learn now that she kidnapped herself. I have nothing but contempt and disgust for that woman and will do whatever I can to make sure she suffers the severest punishment under the law.'

'I agree wholeheartedly, Mr Darwin, but I'm not sure if my findings amount to what my late friend, Archibald Line, would call *hard* evidence. And there is also the question of how much of this you want to burden Mrs Darwin with, or reveal to the authorities for that matter. For these reasons, I've kept my own counsel, unsure what, if anything, should be done. Indeed, I feel that that decision is not mine to make. It rests, sir, with you.'

'That's very considerate of you, Mr Burnett. Perhaps, then we should go over your findings once more.'

Dunston again went through everything he'd discovered, step by step, but this time Darwin probed and analysed each point as might be expected of the country's leading scientist. Dunston's frequently interrupted recital took a full hour this time. The beard-stroking that followed its conclusion was not the grieving-grandfather stroking of earlier; it was deep-in-thought stroking.

Dunston waited patiently, his eyes tracking the slow downward movement of the scientist's hand and its more purposeful return to the top of the beard, the rotation repeated over and over again. And then, the hand stopped.

'Mr Burnett, if it is your wish that the decision on next steps be mine, then here's what we should do.'

Chapter Fifty-One: The Commissioner

It was ten days before Dunston received any further communication from Darwin.

'Parslow, butler at Down House, brought this, sir.' Nick handed his master a folded note.

Dunston wiped his mouth with his napkin. He was still in the middle of his breakfast but he quickly took the note from Nick and opened it, anxious to hear what progress Darwin had made. The first line told him all he needed to know: *Assignment completed satisfactorily.* Excellent, thought Dunston, exactly the news he'd been hoping for.

At the conclusion of their meeting at Down House, Darwin had set out tasks for each man. Dunston's was to turn two pieces of what up to that point were only third-party hearsay into Line-quality evidence. Darwin's to share Dunston's findings with his wife, matching how much he told her with how much he gauged she could handle. Only when they were satisfied on both fronts would they approach the authorities.

The next day at ten o'clock, the two men presented themselves at Scotland Yard, Darwin having secured a meeting with Sir Edmund Henderson, Commissioner of the Metropolitan Police.

Ruggles, still on desk duty, escorted the men into the commissioner's office. The two were oddly paired – one tall, dignified, white-bearded, smartly attired in a caped topcoat; the other squat, diffident, round-faced, lost inside his drab overcoat. Ruggles announced them to the commissioner:

'Mr Darwin, and Mr... Mr...'

'Burnett, Dunston Burnett,' Dunston supplied.

The commissioner, dressed in a dark brown day suit and sporting a regimental tie, rose to greet his visitors. 'Mr Darwin, great honour to welcome you to the Yard,' he said, courteously enough but with a guarded undertone. 'And a pleasure to meet you, Mr... Mr... Forgive me...'

'Dunston Burnett,' Dunston repeated.

The commissioner nodded but continued to eye Darwin warily, wondering, Dunston suspected, if he'd have to suffer through a tongue-lashing from the man whose son was executed thanks to the efforts of his chief of detectives.

'Please be seated.' He gestured to two straight-back, wooden chairs in front of his plain oak desk and took his seat in an equally uncomfortable-looking swivel chair on his side of the desk.

'Now what can I do for you, gentleman?'

As planned, Darwin wordlessly ceded the floor to Dunston, who passed to Sir Edmund two signed statements, one from Betsy Smurkle confirming that Henrietta's left foot was *unscarred*, the other from Dr Cullingworth attesting that the left foot of the corpse he'd examined in The Six Jolly Porters *was* scarred.

The commissioner examined the letters in silence for a few moments, his face darkening as his eyes moved from one to the other and then back. When he looked up, it was clear he'd grasped their significance – Henrietta Darwin was not dead, the trial should never have gone forward.

'Extraordinary! I knew it. Shouldn't have trusted the fellow. Out to make a name for himself. Came up with that ludicrous sleight-of-hand trick with the key just to get a conviction.' He looked at Darwin. 'Sir, this evidence totally undermines the case against your son. I... I don't know what to say. I am so... so sorry. I can't bring him back, but I *can* see to it that the verdict is overturned. And, by God,' right fist smacked into left palm, 'I'll have Fickett thrown off the force.'

Dunston could see that Sir Edmund was genuinely devastated by the travesty that had unfolded on his watch and was sure he'd carry out the commitments he'd made to the letter. In short order, Richard would be exonerated, and Fickett would be buried so deep he'd never see the light of day again. At least, not in the Metropolitan Police Force.

'My sincerest apologies, Mr Darwin. Terrible miscarriage of justice. Having your son's good name restored may, I hope, be of some consolation. And now that we know we are dealing with a missing person and not a dead body, we will be on the lookout for Henrietta Darwin, *and* of course Miss Estelle Moxley who clearly lied under oath. Let me thank you, gentlemen, for bringing this to my attention. Now, unless there is anything el—'

'Actually,' cut in Dunston firmly, 'there is.' Drawing on what he'd learned from Loman and Mrs Darwin, he quickly took the commissioner through Henrietta's diabolical incrimination of her husband, the death sentence she ruthlessly handed out to Line, and the foulest of her crimes, the hanging of baby Joey. 'I may not have hard evidence for everything this woman has done, but I *do* have someone who can corroborate my claim that Henrietta Darwin killed Mr and Mrs Charles Darwin's grandson. That witness is sitting outside in the carriage.'

Sir Edmund was clearly having difficulty coming to grips with the volleys of evidentiary bullets coming at him hard and fast, but he'd not been in the army for thirty years without learning how to regroup under fire. 'Ruggles, fetch the witness,' he ordered.

Five minutes later, a heavily veiled woman entered the office. At Darwin's insistence, she took his seat. The veil was removed, and Mrs Darwin's steely expression was revealed.

Sir Edmund listened, shock and disgust registering on his face as she went step by step through the horror of that dreadful afternoon on the Sandwalk.

'I realise,' she concluded, 'that my testimony may be challenged in a court of law given that I was heavily drugged at the time. But I've come today, sir, to implore you, to *beg* you, to do *everything* in your power to see that the full force of the law is brought down on that... that *woman.*'

'Mrs Darwin, let me assure you, I do not doubt your account for one moment, and believe me, you will make an extremely effective witness on the stand, especially when your testimony is bolstered by Mr Burnett's findings. Of course, one never knows with juries, but the evidence you have presented is more than sufficient for me to charge Henrietta with the murder of your grandson, and her sister with perjury at the very least. I'll make sure the pair are at the top of the Yard's wanted list. From what you've told me, the last sighting of them was in Kent over two weeks ago, so tracking them down may take time, but we'll get them in the end, trust me.'

'Sir,' Ruggles piped up. 'If I may?'

'What is it, Ruggles?'

'Well, sir, when Inspector Fickett came back from Liverpool empty-handed, he ordered us to check the other major ports for a bloke in a slouch hat and a lady with a withered arm. I was sent to Southampton. Didn't turn up anything about a pair like that, sir, but a lad at one of the shipping companies told me that two *women*, one with a withered arm—'

'Good Lord, it's them!' Dunston exclaimed.

'Well done, Ruggles,' the commissioner commended him. 'Anything else?'

'Yes, sir. The lad told me the ladies had arranged passage on an Italian ship bound for Genoa.'

For the first time, Mr Darwin spoke. 'Remarkably well observed, young man. And apparently you have an excellent memory to boot. May I inquire, then, if you know when the ship is scheduled to arrive in Genoa?'

'Indeed, I do, sir.' Ruggles was beaming with pride at being so richly praised by the world-famous Mr Darwin, even though his next words were not what the scientist wanted to hear. 'They should already be there, sir. Ship was due to dock six days ago.'

'Six days ago? I see. Commissioner?'

'We-ell, I can contact the Italian authorities, but based on past experience, I'm not sure that will do us much good. The Italian police, like the fellows I knew in their army, are a sorry lot, I'm afraid. And, anyway, our suspects have had six whole days to clear the port. They could be anywhere on the continent by now. I'll keep pressing, but I don't hold out much hope of us ever finding them.'

The meeting was over for all intents and purposes, but it sputtered on for another few minutes with promises from the commissioner to do everything possible, expressions of thanks from the Darwins for seeing them, and finally awkward farewells. The three visitors were then escorted out of the building.

'Can we offer you a ride anywhere?' Mr Darwin asked.

'Thank you, no. A walk will do me good,' Dunston replied.

He had much to think about. He was pleased that the good name of Mrs Darwin's favourite child would be restored. A small mercy perhaps, but it meant the world to her. And he was pleased that the men who'd murdered Archibald Line had been dealt with – Fingers Migston shot dead and Micus Loman strung up shortly after Fickett's return from Liverpool. They'd paid for their sins to be sure, but that still left Henrietta, the woman who'd cold-heartedly arranged his friend's killing. Now that she was beyond the reach of the English police, his vow to avenge Line would never be fulfilled.

Dunston sighed, massively disappointed in himself, and thoroughly depressed. He'd tried everything, and he'd still failed his friend. And now there was nothing else he could do. Best, perhaps, to put it all behind him, move on with his life. This train of thought, sensible though it might be, did nothing to lighten his mood or ease his mind, but he let it continue. Perhaps he should take some time away…

A week on The Isle of Wight was the only holiday he'd ever taken. The island's spas, coastal scenery, and mild climate were attractive enough, but the idea of a return visit did nothing to lift his spirits. As he walked, his hand instinctively sought and found Line's silver medallion. He'd no sooner grasped the coin than a vision of a vineyard-dotted landscape, somewhere he'd never been before, burst into life before his startled mind's eye, stopping him in his tracks. He shook his head, but the image remained adamantly in place and somehow or other he knew *exactly* where he should go.

Italy… *that* was it. *Yes,* he'd visit Italy. Starting in Genoa.

Chapter Fifty-Two: The Fool's Tower

'Are you there?'

'Hush, my dear, don't fret yourself. I'm right here.'

'You won't leave me, will you?'

'*Never.*'

The promise-maker watched, hardly daring to breathe, as the bedbound woman's face gradually relaxed. Her eyelids slowly drooped, and she slipped back into the silent world she had only just left.

They were in a small, windowless cell, its stone walls solid enough to insulate them from the tortured outpourings and wordless wailing of the institution's mentally deranged inmates. The silence inside their alcoved purgatory wrapped itself around the comatose woman, already lost in her own cocoon of madness. An occasional tremble of that oddly curled lip, a slight twitch of an eyelid, that was all.

The lady at her bedside reached out with her left hand, her right held close to her chest, arm awkwardly bent at the elbow. She stroked the inert woman's cheek, carefully removed a stray lock of bedraggled hair from her forehead and loosened the neck of her coarse cotton shift. No response.

She hadn't seen her sister for two weeks. Today, she had finally been allowed to visit her. The Fool's Tower, Vienna's asylum for the insane, was a fortress-like building that could hold over one hundred inmates in individual cells, all equipped with iron-barred doors, all furnished with reinforced chain-link restraints. It was in one of these cells that Estelle found her sister, or at least what remained of her. Cheeks hollowed, skin shrivelled, shoulders slumped, the withered creature on the bed was barely recognisable as the vibrant woman she'd known and loved all her life.

Estelle had only been granted half an hour and there was so much she needed to say. But their brief exchange, barely twenty words, was all that had transpired so far. She prayed Henrietta would open her eyes again and speak to her. But still no response. Not a sign of life until... until her head began to move from side to side, slowly at first, then faster and faster as though trying to ward off some terrifying vision or hateful memory. Estelle soothed her sister as best she could but nothing could repel whatever torment was invading Henrietta's mind.

Suddenly, Henrietta froze, and then with one violent shove, she pushed Estelle away and thrust herself upright in the bed. She glared, wild-eyed, at her sister, and words, not the ones Estelle wanted to hear, began to spit from her mouth. 'NOT – A – SOUL – KNEW!' The poor woman was reliving that horrific moment when her mind fragmented...

The sisters, in their Sunday-best dresses and bonnets, were in the Grand Hotel Wien's Rosengarten Lounge, an elegant restaurant with plush red chairs, similarly coloured drapes, magnificent faux marble pillars and a mahogany grand piano. They were enjoying afternoon tea and tartlets, the hotel's own delicious pastries, when the entrance of two uniformed members of the Austrian gendarmerie caused a stir among the otherwise sedate, tea-sipping clientele.

The officers were accompanied by an English policeman and that dumpy fellow they'd first seen in Florence six months ago, and then twice more after they'd arrived in Vienna. He looked like a middle-aged, English tourist taking in the sights of Europe on a limited budget. And here he was again, this time with the police.

The podgy tourist pointed at the two sisters. All eyes in the restaurant followed his finger. Henrietta glanced at her sister, her look saying clear as day, *What a rude man. Ignore him.* Estelle inclined her head in agreement. She, though, was a little more concerned than her sister about this turn in events.

The two Austrian officers approached the sisters. The taller one, apparently the leader, looked at Henrietta, then Estelle before settling on Henrietta.

She sipped her tea as though he wasn't there. Ditto Estelle, always willing to follow big sister's lead.

'Ahem,' he began nervously. No response from either sister. 'Frau Darwin…' Still no response. He tapped his chest. 'Polizei. Must send,' he gestured to both Henrietta and Estelle, 'England.'

At last, Henrietta turned to him, looked him up and down, and laughed scornfully at the man and his pitiful command of English. 'My good man,' she said, 'that's very kind of you, but we have no wish to go to England at present. Now, if you would be so good…' She obviously expected the man to cringe away, but instead he stood his ground and beckoned to the English officer.

The young policeman stepped forward and saluted. 'Officer Ruggles from Scotland Yard at your service.' He looked at Henrietta. 'Am I correct in assuming I am addressing Mrs Henrietta Darwin?' He didn't wait for an answer before turning to Estelle. 'And Miss Estelle Moxley?' Estelle nodded, beginning to feel frightened, only partly reassured by Henrietta's big-sister smile.

'I'm afraid, ladies, that Metropolitan Police Commissioner, Sir Edmund Henderson, has assigned me a very difficult duty. I have here,' he showed them an official looking document, 'orders for your arrest for the wilful murder of Joseph Richard Darwin.'

'Oh.' Estelle's hand flew to her mouth. Joey! They were here about Joey. Henrietta showed no outward emotion, obviously convinced that no one could ever fathom her intricate plan and trace their deadly deeds to either her or Estelle. Her plan was perfect, in conception and execution. They were safe.

Every eye in the room was fastened on the unfolding encounter. The watchers did not have to wait long for the next development. The policeman coughed apologetically and said, 'As my colleague was trying to explain, I am here to escort you back to England to stand trial.'

'Utter nonsense!' said Henrietta dismissively. 'You and your commissioner have no right to make such ridiculous accusations. English ladies do not expect to be treated in this atrocious manner. You, sir, may return to England, but not with me or my sister. And when you get to London, please inform this imbecile of a commissioner that there is nothing, not a shred of evidence that could possibly tie us to this crime, because, sir, we had nothing to do with it. Good day!'

Again, Henrietta expected her accusers to fade away. Again, they stood their ground. 'It might be better, ma'am,' Ruggles said, 'if we continued this discussion at police headquarters.' He deliberately glanced around the room apparently tying to draw Henrietta's attention to the many open mouths and shocked expressions.

'Quite unnecessary, young man. There is nothing to discuss. You don't know anything because there isn't anything to know.'

'Very well.' Ruggles motioned the fourth person in their party to step forward. He did so. 'Sir, please explain to Mrs Darwin what we already know.'

'Um… Mrs Darwin,' he began, 'I… er…'

Ruggles urged him on with his eyes. Dunston nodded and squared his shoulders. He'd been on the sisters' trail for ten long months. He was *not* going to falter at the finishing line. 'Yes, let me see…well, this is what we know,' he said firmly. 'We know that Mary Travers was the woman murdered in Nightingale Lane, not you; that Miss Moxley has a spare set of brass figures for your vanity; that Groggins intercepted a telegram, the contents of which led you to order Archibald Line's murder; that you put a rope around baby Joey's neck and then—'

'STOP!'

The room froze; waiters stopped waiting; drinkers stopped drinking; the policemen stood still as stone statues; the podgy little Englishman stayed quiet as a church mouse. Estelle was petrified. She could see what was happening. Her sister was going into one of her 'little fits', only ten times worse.

Henrietta was a ghastly white; spittle drooling from her open mouth; eyes bulging from their sockets; nostrils flaring. She leaned forward, body tensed, hands gripping the table so tightly every sinew and muscle in her arm strained with the effort. Her gaze zeroed in on the interfering little

Englishman, her look fiery enough to burn him to a crisp.

'Impossible,' she screamed. 'You can't know any of that! My plan was perfect. No one,' she wiped the slaver from her chin, 'no one, I say, can possibly know how it was done. Besides me, only one person—' Henrietta stopped. A slow, quarter-turn of the head, and her madwoman's glare fastened on Estelle, 'Only one person... TRAITOR!'

Henrietta lunged across the table, fine crockery and delicate pastries flying everywhere, and reached for Estelle. Her nails tore at the soft flesh on her sister's face until blood spurted from both cheeks. But that didn't satisfy. Far from it. The snarling tigress pushed herself forward until she was sprawled across the table, her face only inches from Estelle's. Like a vampire sinking its fangs into a helpless victim, she bit into the treacherous lips that had betrayed her.

The police finally managed to haul Henrietta off her sister and march her backwards towards the exit. She struggled every inch of the way. And she screamed. Lips curled back, bloodied teeth bared, she raged and raved at Estelle nonstop. Much of the stream of venom was too garbled to understand, but the last words Estelle heard, words she'll never forget, were hurled at her one at a time: 'NOT– A – SOUL – KNEW!'

In the two weeks since the attack, Estelle's wounds had almost healed, the scabs on cheek and lips largely gone. Henrietta had been carted off to the insane asylum, while Estelle had been cuffed, taken to the police station where she was formally charged and then to Vienna's city jail. Thrown in with the scum of the city's human refuge heap, Estelle suffered taunting, shoving even kicking from her fellow inmates, but that didn't bother her. What cut to the quick was that her sister believed her capable of such treachery. How could she even think I would stab her in the back?

Twenty minutes of her allotted half hour had already passed and she'd still not been able to get through to her sister that she had never betrayed her trust. She had to speak to her. But how could she reach her? The Henrietta of old was no more. The strong, stable, big-sister personality was gone, split in two, the separated parts drifting far away from what was once a solid core. In one half, the new Henrietta was a lost child, a needy follower, Estelle now the nurturing leader, a complete reversal of their lifelong roles; in the other, a screaming she-devil, convinced little sister was the treacherous snake who'd blabbed to the police.

'Fraulein.' The female attendant's rough voice broke in on Estelle's agonising. Dressed in the asylum's standard black uniform, the heavyset woman was standing at the entrance to the cell, Ruggles right behind her, ready to escort Estelle back to England. She jerked her head, indicating as plainly as any words, that it was time to leave.

'One minute please,' begged Estelle.

'Sorry, Miss Moxley,' Ruggles said. 'The carriage is waiting. We have to go.'

The attendant stepped forward, grabbed Estelle by the arm and dragged her out of the cell. At that moment, Henrietta stirred.

'Estelle? Sister? Is that you?'

'Yes, I'm here,' Estelle cried from the corridor

'Estelle, you will stay with me, won't you?'

'Alw—'

The cell door slammed shut.

A Note from the Author

If you have made it this far, you probably feel you've read all the words you want to read from my pen. My excuse for this extra page or two is this: whenever I read a novel involving historical figures and events, I always want to know which bits are real and which invented.Let me begin with what is not true in *Fatally Inferior*.

All the characters populating my story aside from Charles and Emma Darwin and George Mivart, are made up. The Darwins never had a son named Richard; his wife – Henrietta – never existed; Mrs Darwin never had a maid called Lucy Kinsley; Archibald Line and Dunston Burnett are figments of my imagination. The same holds for all the minor characters.

All the incidents driving the plot are also made up.Henrietta's scheming; Richard's unpleasant fate; Lucy's travails; the assault on Line; Dunston's investigatory efforts; all pure fiction. *Fatally Inferior* shifts the Darwin household onto an alternate timeline for the first three months of 1873 when the main events recounted in the novel are supposed to have taken place.

The above notwithstanding, this alternate history is firmly grounded in the life and times of Charles Darwin and his family. In particular, the two contextual circumstances that underpin the story – one to do with Darwin's professional activities, the other his family history – are true.

Regarding his professional activities, Darwin came under constant and often vicious attack for his theory of evolution from both the established scientific community and the upper echelon of the Church of England. The publication of *On The Origin of Species* on November 24, 1859 was greeted with an uproar rarely seen in Victorian England, with extreme reactions erupting on both sides of the argument.

On February 24, 1871, the year before the story begins, Darwin published *The Descent of Man,*in which he applied his theories of survival of the fittest and sexual selection more directly to the evolution of man, undercutting the Bible's version of man's creation even more squarely than in *On The Origin of Species.*Needless to say, this fanned the flames of fires already burning furiously in the breasts of men and women throughout England, and the vitriol moved to new heights. Darwin was bombarded with scathing reviews in academic journals, blistering editorials in the leading newspapers and crude cartoons in the cheaper broadsheets. He had many supporters as well, but it is this avalanche of disgust and hatred that prompted my inclusion of threats – the *Aesculapius* letter and Mivart's ransom demand – in *Fatally Inferior.*

George Mivart was a real person.A young, up-and-coming comparative anatomist, he wrote one of the most negative reviews of *The Descent of Man* and, as if that wasn't enough to upset Darwin, savaged a fairly innocuous article on divorce written by one of Darwin's (real) sons.Darwin's retaliation was swift and, frankly, petty. Sad to say for Mr Mivart, and contrary to what I assert in Chapter 6, the young man's application to the Athenaeum Club was rejected thanks to the efforts of Darwin and his allies. From that point on, the pair were sworn enemies. Mivart, to the best of my knowledge, never threatened to kill any member of Darwin's family but the acrimony between the two made him the obvious choice for my blackmailer.

The circumstance in Darwin's family life that provides both setting and inspiration for *Fatally Inferior* is his blood relationship with his wife, Emma – they really were first cousins, his maternal grandfather and her paternal grandfather being one and the same. In the nineteenth century, the offspring of marriages between such close relatives were thought to suffer from loss of vigour and even infertility.This brought to mind the image of a couple desperate for a grandchild but cruelly robbed by tragedy of any hope of a happy old age spent in the joyful company of their children's children.

Charles Darwin feared his kinship with his wife would have harmful effects on their progeny and, as alluded to in Chapter 8, devoted considerable time and effort to studying the effects of crossbreeding and inbreeding in plants, animals and humans. He even canvassed, albeit unsuccessfully, for a question about the number of children born to first-cousin parents to be included in the 1871 population census. As events turned out, his worry was unfounded – seven of his ten children with Emma reached maturity and three of those had offspring, ten in all – a far different outcome from the grandchild-less golden years portrayed in my story.

Most of the descriptive material surrounding the Darwins is also based in fact. Darwin's bouts of a never-fully-diagnosed, gastro-intestinal illness, for instance, plagued him throughout his adult life and often forced him to his bedroom, justifying his very limited presence in the pages of *Fatally Inferior*. His 'accursed stomach' as he called it, caused retching, flatulence, fatigue and vomiting to the point where he was obliged to keep a commode, hidden behind a partition, in his study.

Down House, too, is depicted as it was in 1872, the year of my story. The house, only an hour and a half's journey from Central London, is open to the public and well worth a visit. On a spring day, the visitor can enjoy the house, gardens and greenhouses, and follow the Sandwalk, the sand and stone path that figures prominently in my novel, all the way to its turning point, the perfect place for a quiet hanging. If that is not to your fancy, then you can stroll into the nearby village and down a glass of ale in the sixteenth-century Queen's Head, just as Nick and Gabby did.

If you wish to learn more about Darwin, including his five-year voyage on the HMS Beagle, his writings and experiments, and his family life, an excellent source is the two volume biography by Janet Browne, *Voyaging* and *The Power of Place*, published in the USA by Princeton University Press in 1995 and 2002 respectively. You'll find a more personal, fascinating and shorter account of his life in *The Autobiography of Charles Darwin*, first published by Collins (London) in 1958.

Acknowledgements

Writing a first novel is hard enough; the second turns out to be even harder. *Fatally Inferior,* Book Two in The Dunston Burnett Trilogy, would never have seen the light of day without the help, inspiration and constructive criticism of a coterie of professionals in the writing business as well as friends and family.

My literary agent, Jeff Schmidt, President, NY Creative Management Agency, was a constant source of support throughout the preparation and publication of *Immortalised to Death,* Book One of The Dunston Burnett Trilogy, and has proven even more valuable in seeing *Fatally Inferior* move from first inklings of a plot to a polished manuscript. Editors are worth their weight in gold. *Fatally Inferior* has benefitted enormously from the insights and critiques of some of the best: Herta Feely and Emily Williamson at Chrysalis Editorial, and Shawn Simmons and Deborah Well at Level Best Books. Promotion and publicity have been expertly handled by Corrine Pritchett and Layne Mandros at Books Forward. Their always positive, always purposeful advice and guidance has been a godsend, first with *Immortalised to Death* and now with *Fatally Inferior.*

Closer to home, George Alapas and Lisa Vohra, my test readers, did a super job. Their reactions and inputs helped put the manuscript on a firmer footing and improve its public appeal. And of course, my family, especially wife Jennifer to whom this book is dedicated, provided all the support and encouragement necessary to get it over the finishing line and into the hands of the reading public.

More Praise for Fatally Inferior

"If you're in the market for a good, old-fashioned mystery and you enjoy traveling to different places and different times, you won't do better than Lyn Squire's latest, *Fatally Inferior.* Squire has gifted us with a fast-paced, historical crime novel set in England smack in the middle of the Victorian Age... [He] draws us into a mystery filled with enough twists and turns that keeps us turning the pages."—Charles Salzberg, 3-time Shamus Award nominee and author of *Second Story Man* and *Man on the Run*

"*Fatally Inferior* is a richly layered novel set firmly in 19th Century England with complex and disparate characters that weave their way through a twisting plot of simmering angst, despair, and rage. Lyn Squire has the ability to bring the time, place, and people to life on the pages, creating a lush tapestry for the reader to tromp through as if they were perusing Theatreland of the West End of London... *Fatally Inferior* will leave you spent and exhausted and is not to be missed. Read the book."—Matt Cost, award winning author of sixteen histories and mysteries, including the Mainely Mysteries, the Clay Wolfe Trap Mysteries, and the Brooklyn 8 Ballo Mysteries

About the Author

LYN SQUIRE was born in Cardiff, South Wales. During a twenty-five-year career at the World Bank, he published over thirty articles and several books within his area of expertise, and was lead author for *World Development Report, 1990*, which introduced the metric – a dollar a day – that is still used to measure poverty worldwide. Lyn was also the founding president of the Global Development Network, an organization dedicated to supporting promising scholars from the developing world. He now devotes his time to writing. His debut novel, *Immortalised to Death*, published by Level Best Books in September 2023, introduced Dunston Burnett, a non-conventional amateur detective. It was a First Place Category Winner in the Mystery and Mayhem Division of the Chanticleer International Book Awards. Dunston's adventures continue in *Fatally Inferior* and *The Séance of Murder*, the second and third books in *The Dunston Burnett Trilogy*. Lyn lives in Virginia with his wife and two dogs.

AUTHOR WEBSITE:
  lynsquiremysteries.com

Also by Lyn Squire

Immortalised to Death, 2023